PRAISE FO

★ "Clever machines, well-drawn relationships of varying constellations, literal death traps, and world-threatening intrigue, headlined by an aspirational heroine, make this a winner."

—*Kirkus Reviews*, starred review, on *Shadow of the War Machine*

"Full of wonderful and deadly machines . . . this steampunk novel is replete with romance, suspense, and danger."

—*Booklist Online*, on *Shadow of the War Machine*

"A swashbuckling and clever heroine, a murderer intent on making her his next victim, fantastical beasts and devices, and a budding love affair that defies Victorian conventions only add tension, interest, and excitement to this first title in the Secret Order series."

—*Booklist*, on *Legacy of the Clockwork Key*

"Fans of the Infernal Devices series by Cassandra Clare will flock to this new series."

—*Library Media Connection*, on *Legacy of the Clockwork Key*

ALSO BY KRISTIN BAILEY

The Secret Order · Book One
Legacy of the Clockwork Key

The Secret Order · Book Two
Rise of the Arcane Fire

The Secret Order + Book Three

SHADOW
❖ of the ❖
WAR MACHINE

Kristin Bailey

Simon Pulse

New York London Toronto Sydney New Delhi

SIMON PULSE

An imprint of Simon & Schuster Children's Publishing Division

1230 Avenue of the Americas, New York, New York 10020

First Simon Pulse paperback edition February 2016

Text copyright © 2015 by Kristin Welker

Cover wolf sculpture and photograph copyright © 2015 by Matthew Lentini

Cover photograph of Paris copyright © 2015 by Thinkstock

Also available in a Simon Pulse hardcover edition.

All rights reserved, including the right of reproduction in whole or in part in any form.

SIMON PULSE and colophon are registered trademarks of Simon & Schuster, Inc.

For information about special discounts for bulk purchases, please contact Simon & Schuster Special Sales at 1-866-506-1949 or business@simonandschuster.com.

The Simon & Schuster Speakers Bureau can bring authors to your live event.

For more information or to book an event contact the Simon & Schuster Speakers Bureau at 1-866-248-3049 or visit our website at www.simonspeakers.com.

Series design by Angela Goddard

Cover designed by Regina Flath

The text of this book was set in Granjon LT Std.

Manufactured in the United States of America

10 9 8 7 6 5 4 3 2 1

The Library of Congress has cataloged the hardcover edition as follows:

Bailey, Kristin.

Shadow of the war machine / by Kristin Bailey. — Simon Pulse hardcover edition.

p. cm. — (The Secret Order ; book 3)

Summary: Meg has searched the globe for answers about why her parents were killed; where her grandfather disappeared to; and above all, the identity of the man with the clockwork mask behind all this treachery. At last, she has clues that will lead her to the shocking truth.

[1. Secret societies—Fiction. 2. Orphans—Fiction. 3. Love—Fiction. 4. London (England)—History—19th century—Fiction. 5. Great Britain—History—Victoria, 1837–1901—Fiction. 6. Science fiction.] I. Title.

PZ7.B15256Sh 2015   [Fic]—dc23   2014009547

ISBN 978-1-4424-6805-4 (hc)

ISBN 978-1-4424-6806-1 (pbk)

ISBN 978-1-4424-6807-8 (eBook)

To Angie, because I simply couldn't do this without you

SHADOW of the WAR MACHINE

CHAPTER ONE

"THIS PLAN IS ILL CONCEIVED." THE DARK STREETS OF London flew past the windows of the carriage, illuminated by the brief flashes of light given off by the streetlamps. I glanced at David. "And I wish you'd informed me of it at an earlier hour."

It was difficult to stay on the shallow seat as we bumped and jolted along. I didn't know why I had chosen to trust David. My reputation was at stake, and as we careened closer and closer to the docks, I feared my life was as well. There were too many risks.

"How else do you propose we discover the whereabouts of your grandfather?" David leaned back against the hard seat of a coach decidedly beneath his usual standard as an earl. In truth, I suspected David had bought a used cab off the street. I also questioned the sanity of his driver as the vehicle lurched over a cluster of broken stones in the worn streets.

As for his question, I had no answer, and that was the only reason he had convinced me to join him on this escapade. My grandfather had gone missing four years ago. Then my parents both died in a fire in our clock shop on Oxford Street. It was the greatest tragedy of my life. And later I learned it had been no accident.

Only then had I discovered that my entire family was part of a secret society of inventors, the Secret Order of Modern Amusementists. I had now joined their ranks as an apprentice. But being an apprentice didn't help my situation if it couldn't restore my grandfather to me.

I knew who was behind it all. He had nearly kidnapped me at the end of the summer but had escaped into the docks. With the help of David's men, we had tracked the ships he had used to escape.

Tonight we hunted the man in the clockwork mask.

"Both the ships are in dock?" I asked.

"Yes, and I've taken measures to ensure that the crews are distracted. We can search both ships if we're quick and careful." David's normally sly expression turned serious. The light from the lamp swung, making the shadows play across his face. His blue eyes seemed to catch the light and glow in the darkness.

There was an energy in him, and an excitement, and I worried he was caught in the thrill of the adventure and not nearly fearful enough of the consequences. At one time I had felt as he did, as if all of this were a daring challenge, like a game, or something from a storybook. However, I had learned that this story could cost my life, or worse, the life of someone I loved.

But David was an earl and unaccustomed to fear. His gilded life seldom handed him evidence that he was less than invincible, either in body or reputation. I, on the other hand . . .

I didn't need to be killed to have everything I cared for stripped away from me. All it would take would be a single person witnessing me in the company of the young earl, unescorted in the middle of the night in a part of town known for its seedy taverns and worse.

I had disguised myself as well as I could in a simple black servant's dress and wool cap with a thin petticoat that wouldn't impede my movement and a black shawl I could use to cover my head if I had to. I would be well concealed in the shadows and hopefully unnoticeable.

We rolled to a stop.

My innards dropped to my toes as David leapt out and offered me a hand. "My lady?"

I took his hand even as I admonished him. "I'm not a lady, David."

"Not yet," he murmured as my boots hit the uneven cobblestones. I really wished he wouldn't presume so much.

The coachman leapt down from his high seat, and I recognized his gangly limbs immediately.

"Michael! What are you doing here?" I rushed forward and took his hands. The ginger boy tipped his hat and smiled.

"Preserving your reputation. David didn't trust his driver not to talk. Couldn't have you expelled from the Academy for this—I fear my marks might suffer." His easygoing smile flashed in the dim light. No wonder the horses hadn't been handled properly. Michael was no coachman. He was a fellow apprentice and like a brother to me.

"You are intelligent enough without me," I said.

"That is up for debate," another voice called with a distinct Indian accent. I turned quickly to a trio of young men emerging from the shadows.

I recognized two more of my friends, Manoj and Noah, immediately, but the third surprised me. "Samuel?"

We hadn't exactly been cordial. Our relationship was fraught at best. He gave me a nod and gave another to David. "I've come to make amends. My family has much to repay, and if I can help restore your grandfather to the Order, I will."

Noah and Manoj looked at me as if they were uncertain whether or not they should trust him. Samuel's father had nearly ripped the Order in two. If he wished to restore his family's reputation, it was going to be a difficult road. But I knew what pressures he faced, and I felt for him in spite of how poorly he'd treated me. "Thank you for coming."

"So, where do we stand according to the plan?" David asked, naturally falling into his role as a born leader.

"The ships are deserted," Manoj informed us. "All the crews are taking advantage of the free-flowing gin across the way, thanks to the Strompton coffers."

"Samuel and I are taking the watch," Michael said. "If we stay on the corner here, and the one there, we can keep anyone from leaving the pubs or stealing the horses." He pulled up his sleeves, and I gave him a sidelong glance.

"Don't start any fights on my behalf," I said.

He gave me a wicked grin. "Don't worry, Meg. We'll be gentlemen."

"You'd better."

"Noah, you and Manoj have *The Triumphant*. Meg and I will search *Méduse*," David said. "We have only twenty minutes before we meet back here."

"Do we need to steal the proof?" Manoj asked.

"No, we only need a name. Search for passenger manifests or a ship's log. Note any passengers' names and the dates," David explained.

A shudder passed through me. "Remember that the man in the clockwork mask is an unrepentant murderer. Beware of anyone with a covered face. He may hide his mask in public. Take these." I handed my friends small brass globes. I had invented them as part of an alarm system at my shop after the man in the mask had planted a bomb in my home. "Turn the top half a quarter turn, then press both halves together. It will let out a loud wail."

"Good luck," Michael said as we dispersed from the alley.

David pulled me along by the hand as we snuck through the shadows toward a slippery gangplank. Though the stench of the river wasn't as fierce as it could be during the heat of summer, the sickly air hung around in the cold mist. We scuttled aboard the French trading ship like the rats scampering along the mooring lines.

"We should have told Oliver," I whispered. Oliver was older, and a mentor to me. I felt so exposed, and almost like I was betraying his trust by pursuing the man in the clockwork mask. But I was tired of hiding and waiting to be snatched away—or worse, killed. Sometimes in the moments just before I woke, I felt as if I were locked in a steamer trunk again, trapped and helpless. I couldn't live this way for the rest of my life. "Oliver knows what is at stake."

David glanced furtively right and left before ducking behind a stack of crates on the cluttered deck. "Oliver is headmaster of the Academy now. He's bound by certain constraints. It's not worth the risk. You're too valuable."

I let my tongue slip out to wet my lip. I wished I could trust that David only saw me as a friend. As it stood, I wondered at his words. Yes, I was the last of the Whitlocks, and our family name was now the most powerful in the Order, but my personal value within the Order was up for debate, unless one saw me in only a single light.

I was a valuable woman to marry so long as my name remained unsullied. Any man who did marry me would increase his standing among the Amusementists by an order of magnitude.

David put his finger to his lips and pulled me to the door of the cabin. He tried the latch. It was unlocked.

With caution we stole our way inside.

I nearly choked on the odor of mildew and stale rum. The cabin was a small affair, with a thick desk and some large cabinets and crates to one side. A weak lamp burned on the desk. I peeked through a shadowy doorway and into a dark bedroom.

"Meg, look here." David attempted to hold a ledger to the lamp. I skimmed the words running down the page. It was a shipping log.

According to the ledger, the ship was taking on cargo in New Orleans, then delivering it to Le Havre in France. After that it would make frequent stops in London, without accounts for any cargo. "This doesn't make any sense. What would they have to trade in London, and why isn't the inventory accounted for? They seem to be unloading all their cargo in France. Are they smuggling?"

"I'm not sure," David admitted.

I had a clever mind for numbers, and it didn't take me long to line up the calendar presented in the ledger with the known tragedies that had befallen me, including the day the man in the clockwork mask had escaped into the London docks. My throat felt dry. For every single date when I could confirm the presence of the man in London, this ship had been at the docks.

"This is the one." My voice cracked as I said it. "He's been traveling on this ship."

"We need to find the manifest." David and I were leafing through the papers on the desk when a loud snore broke the silence in the bedchamber behind us.

I froze. Then the slow heavy thumps of footsteps on the deck reverberated through the boards beneath my boots.

"Hide," I whispered.

David wedged himself behind the stack of crates, while I desperately opened the cabinets. One was filled with shoddily stacked linens. I shoved them aside and pushed into the small cramped space I had created. The door wouldn't fully shut, which terrified me. I could hear my heart pounding. It sounded as if it were echoing off the walls of the cabinet as a man in a dark coat passed in front of me.

"Clément! Wake up." He grabbed something heavy and threw it at the wall. The crash felt like a physical blow, and my legs tightened. My toes curled with cramping fear. I knew that voice. It was the man in the clockwork mask.

Whoever had been snoring choked on his own breath, then stumbled loudly into the room. "Oh, it's you," the captain moaned in French. "What is it you want? Did you finally acquire your precious package?"

The man in the clockwork mask shifted into my sight, though I could see only a narrow slice of the room through the gap. His entire face had been wrapped in a black cloth, save a slit for one good eye. I knew what lurked beneath the cloth. One side of the man's face looked like a machine embedded in his flesh. The one time I had even seen his full face, I had been terrified and shocked, both because of the mask and the fact that he looked so familiar to me.

The man in the mask squeezed his fist closed. "Unfortunately, no. My quarry continues to elude me. However, I have something I must deliver. We sail on the tide." The man rubbed the smallest finger on his right hand. The one I had broken during the summer. I felt suddenly as if I were in the box once more, trapped.

"If you have not forgotten, I am the captain here, and my crew is enjoying the night. We can sail tomorrow."

The man reached out and grabbed the captain by the throat, then pulled him over the desk.

"Drunk or not, we sail on the tide." He pushed the captain as he let go.

The captain wheezed and fell back. "Yes, monsieur."

The man in the mask swept from the room, the long tail of his coat brushing against my cabinet. The captain let out a string of vulgarity before he, too, gathered his coat and stumbled out the door.

I wanted to burst from the cabinet immediately. I couldn't breathe within it. I had to get out, escape. It was nearly impossible to wait. All my instincts screamed that I should leap out of the cabinet, but I didn't know if the captain would return. I didn't feel secure until we heard him shouting for his men from the docks. I opened the cabinet and spilled out onto the floor. David pushed out from behind the crates.

"We must leave here quickly. They'll return any moment." I grabbed my thin skirts and ran for the deck, with David close behind me.

CHAPTER TWO

WE HURRIED OUT ONTO THE DECK. DAVID SUDDENLY
grabbed me and threw me down behind a pile of canvas. I
gasped, but he put a hand over my mouth. I held deathly still
as he peeked over the canvas. "Stay down," he whispered.

I scowled. I was the one wearing a black wool cap over
my dark braids. His blond hair was far more conspicuous,
and my eyes worked every bit as well as his did. I didn't wish
to borrow trouble, but his insistence on watching the enemy
was placing us in greater danger.

"It's clear," he said, and pulled me up by the hand. Then
he ushered me behind him as we scrambled down the gangplank. I could see the man in the mask walking down the

street to my left. Secretly I prayed a thousand prayers that he would not turn and catch sight of us.

I outpaced David and reached the alley a couple of steps before he did.

"Where have you been?" Michael asked as Noah reined in his agitated horse in the dark alley. "We've been waiting here too long."

"We found him. The man in the clockwork mask is here. He's returning to sail on the tide. We'll meet at Pricket's Toys." David ushered me up into the cab and took a seat next to me.

The cab lurched, throwing us back against the seat as we hurried out of the docks and back toward the fairer side of town. "We must tell Oliver immediately," I insisted.

"There's no need. I'll send my men after the ship, and we'll have him arrested before morning. Your grandfather will be restored within the week." The lamp swung above David's head. He looked steadfastly forward, as if nothing could shake his certainty.

"Now is not the time for foolishness." I adjusted the shawl against the bitter wind. Light flakes of snow began to fall, appearing as ephemeral flashes of white in our small halo of lamplight. They flitted past as we sped through the slick streets.

"There's nothing Oliver can do for you that I cannot." David looked at me, his eyes turning as flinty and cool as the winter sky. "I am a wealthy earl with contacts and resources you cannot imagine."

And I was not a simpering girl who would fall at his feet for such things. "You are a boy among the peerage, and an apprentice in the Order. Oliver is a well-respected duke and the Headmaster. There are things he can do that you cannot." The cab splashed through an icy puddle, sending the spray from the wheel flying as the horse tossed his head.

"Why must you discount me at every turn?" David asked. "All I'm trying to do is give you what you need."

"I haven't asked for it!" I swore David had to be the most stubborn individual I'd ever met, and I knew a fair number of Scots.

"Only because you're befuddled by this romance you've invented." Now there was no hiding the bitterness in David's tone.

"This isn't about Will." The snowflakes grew thicker, catching on my cheeks and neck and stinging my skin with their sudden chill. I may have loved William MacDonald, but he was away in Scotland working at the Foundry that supplied the Amusementists with all the parts they needed to construct their amazing inventions. "Whatever I might feel for Will has nothing to do with you."

David's eyebrow lowered suspiciously. "Doesn't it?"

The cab rolled to a stop, and I felt comforted by the sight of Potter's bakery and Mrs. Wallace's bookshop. But something wasn't right. The lamps were blazing in my neighbors' shops so late at night.

A weak, high-pitched whistle cut through the otherwise still air.

My alarms.

I launched myself out of the cab, leapt to the ground, and ran toward Pricket's Toys and Amusements—my shop, my home.

"Meg, wait!" David called, but I didn't heed him. My heart was in my throat as I reached the windows at the front of the shop.

"Meg! Thank heaven you're alive," Mrs. Wallace exclaimed, gripping my arms. "We heard your whistles and found the window broken." Mrs. Wallace was a gentle and quiet woman with a thin face and blond hair tied back in a bun. She was not the first person I would have imagined to come to my defense, and yet here she was, unafraid. I glanced back at the boys. I couldn't let her discover me with them, or I'd be ruined.

"I'm fine, Mrs. Wallace. I've contacted the constable. Whoever it was wanted only money." I knew it was all a lie, but it didn't matter. I needed to get her back inside her own shop. I took her by the shoulder and led her back toward the bookshop, waving at the Potters in their window to let them know I was unharmed. "I'll silence the alarms, and the duke's men are coming to set things right. I'll be fine."

"You are so brave, dear. Are you sure you don't wish to stay with Kate and me? Robbing a toy shop at Christmas," she mumbled as she reached her door. "How heartless."

I took her hand. She was the most kindhearted person I had ever met. "There is much I still need to do tonight. I will be fine. Thank you for your generous offer."

I had a similar conversation with the Potters before they handed me a large round loaf of bread and retreated to their shop as well.

Only then was I able to face my home and this newest violation.

The glass in the window had cracked and was splintering through the lead holding the small panes together. I could feel the bile rising in my throat, my heart pounding as soundly as the hooves of the horses as my friends cantered up the street.

The door to the shop hung limply on the hinges, swinging open. The handle had been pulled loose. I reached out to open the door the rest of the way and stepped into the darkened shop.

It was almost Christmas. I had decorated the shop with evergreen boughs and bright holly berries. My toys had filled the shelves in cheerful profusion. Now the shelves had been spilled callously upon the floor, the boughs shredded, and the needles scattered amid the fallen tin soldiers. Expensive porcelain dolls had been trampled upon. Marionettes, pulled from their strings, lay lifelessly on the floor.

I felt the stinging in my nose as my eyes welled with tears.

An arm reached across my shoulder. I instinctively turned into the embrace, surprised to find it was Michael who stood next to me. Noah came up on the other side. He too was a shopkeeper, and seemed as horrified as I felt. "Oh, Meg. I'm so sorry."

"At least he didn't use a bomb," I said, and sighed. "This can still be set right, and no one was hurt." But that was a lie. I hurt. My heart was breaking, seeing all my hard work destroyed. The man in the clockwork mask had no cause to wreck the shop, other than to make it seem like a burglary. Or maybe it had been only for spite.

I used the edge of my shawl to dry my eyes, then pulled away from the comfort of my friends to cross the gallery and inspect my parlor.

I felt as if I were back in Rathford's house when I'd been a maid, delicately stepping around the broken shards of the vase at the bottom of the stairs. Rathford had never allowed anyone to touch the fractured pieces. Only, this time I stepped over the shattered remains of a pair of music boxes and the tangled ribbons from a puppet lying limp across the floor.

I didn't have to bend down to see the strongbox. It lay open on its side. To add insult to injury, he had taken my money.

Manoj approached. "Where is your housekeeper?" he asked as he made his way back toward the door that separated the shop from the parlor of my living space.

I sniffed. "Thankfully, she left to be with her sister in Dover for the holiday. There was no one here tonight."

If not for David's scheme, I would have been asleep in my bed, alone. I would surely now be in the clutches of a monster.

"That was very fortunate," Manoj said. "I'll inspect upstairs. If this is the man who planted the bomb last time, we should take caution."

David entered, but Samuel remained outside.

I reached up and twisted the top off the last alarm, which

was near the door and was still valiantly attempting to whistle for help. The sound died and left the shop in utter silence.

"Is there any wood we can use to board up the windows?" Noah asked.

I nodded. "In the mews out back." I picked up a doll. Her face was cracked, leaving a gaping hole where her eye should have been. She smiled sweetly at me as her head hung listlessly to the side. "There are tools there, a hammer, nails." I choked on the last word and the doll slipped from my hands, the remains of her face shattering against the unforgiving floor.

"David, take her away from here," Noah said. "Manoj and I will secure the shop."

"Thank you. I don't know what I would do without such friends," I said, then turned to Michael. "I need to see the headmaster. He must know about this."

He nodded. We exited the shop and climbed back into the cab. It was a short drive to the Chadwick home in St. James. The duke's coachmen met us at the gate and took the horses. I kept my eyes downcast and my shawl high around my neck to hide my face. I didn't want rumors among the servants, and most wouldn't notice me at all dressed as a housemaid.

Staying several steps behind Michael and David, I

followed the others up the stone steps. A footman quickly ushered us inside.

The interior of the luxurious townhome provided a stark contrast to my dark thoughts. The house was adorned with holiday cheer. Holly boughs trimmed with apples decorated the foyer. The scents of orange, exotic cinnamon, and cloves filled me with warmth, even though only a few candles lit the large halls at so late an hour.

"May I ask the purpose for your visit, my lord?" The footman addressed David, ignoring Michael and me completely, which was fine with me. I settled in next to Michael and attempted to remain invisible.

"I'm afraid it is an emergency. I must speak with His Grace immediately," David said.

"Of course. He's in the conservatory. Follow me."

At first I wondered what Oliver was doing in the conservatory this late at night, but once we reached it, the answer was clear.

Normally the conservatory was warm and inviting, a haven for prize fruit trees and plants that bloom through the winter. The conservatory should have been both humid and warm, capturing the weak winter sun during the day and trapping it within the glass walls. I was shocked when the footman opened the door and we were greeted with a blast of frost.

The entire room was filled with mounds of white fluffy snow.

The footman bowed as we entered, then shut the door quickly behind us, most likely to protect the main house from the sudden chill. Frost had painted itself over the glass walls and ceiling in delicate swirls of branching ice. All the trees had been moved. In their stead were several tables and chairs surrounding brass caldrons for fires.

As we turned a corner, I lost myself in awe.

Before us, taking up the center of the conservatory, was a glimmering carousel. Icicles draped along the canopy, and I marveled at the mounts. Each exquisite creature had been carved from ice, then saddled with thick velvet pads in deep blue and embroidered with silver thread. The shining poles pierced through the hearts of the creatures, holding the crystalline beasts in perfect form.

I had never seen anything so beautiful in my life.

Oliver, the Duke of Chadwick, poked his head out from behind a frosted mirror panel that obscured the view of the gears and mechanical structure that made the carousel turn.

His brown hair was as haphazard as I'd ever seen it, and

the gleam in his eyes as bright as ever. One eye did not open quite as wide as the other because of an injury he had sustained over the summer, but this gave him an air of curiosity and a certain roguishness.

"David?" Oliver straightened, removing thick gloves even as his heavy coat seemed to swallow him. "What on earth are you doing here? You're not supposed to see this before tomorrow night."

Oliver then noticed me and Michael. "Dear Lord, Meg? Why are you dressed like a housemaid?"

"There's been another attack on Meg's shop," David said.

Oliver came forward quickly, swinging himself between a glistening ice dragon and a delicate unicorn.

"Are you hurt?" Oliver took my hands and looked me over. I didn't know how to explain to him that I hadn't even been in the shop at the time it had been attacked.

"I'm quite all right, but the shop is in shambles." The thought made my stomach twist into dreadful knots, but I knew it could have been far worse. The first two times the man in the clockwork mask had broken into my home, he'd intended to kill. He'd started the fire that had taken my parents, and only last summer he'd tried to destroy the shop with a bomb.

Yet his intent now seemed fixed on kidnapping me. I had no doubt I was the "quarry" he had referred to on the ship. I just couldn't figure why his intent had changed. "The man in the clockwork mask has been sailing upon a French merchant vessel named *Méduse*. It's leaving for Le Havre tonight."

Oliver's normally bright hazel eyes narrowed. "And how do you know this?" He turned his scrutinizing gaze to David. "What have you done?"

"Well," Michael announced, swinging his hands and clapping them together. "It has been a lovely night, and your carousel is remarkable work, Headmaster, but it is really time for me to be going." He turned on his heel while tipping his cap, and with rushed steps walked back the way we'd come.

I reached out to stop him, but Oliver's voice sent a chill down my spine. "Let him go. You two, follow me."

David and I walked in step, like dutiful soldiers behind our commander. We followed Oliver up the stairs and into his large study. He took his place behind a desk that seemed fitting for a duke. However, he didn't kick his boots up onto it the way he normally would.

We were in severe trouble.

"Out with it." He wove his fingers together and awaited whatever explanation we were about to give.

"This was all my idea. Meg knew nothing about it before tonight, and she tried to warn me off the plan." David's words shocked me, and I looked at him as if he had suddenly sprouted a tail.

Oliver spared me a glance. "And yet I see she dressed appropriately for mischief."

I took a step forward. "We went to the docks to investigate the two possible ships the man in the clockwork mask might have used to escape after he attacked last summer. We were fruitful in that we discovered the man aboard the *Méduse*, and we were not caught."

David held his hand up. "I sent Samuel to fetch my men and have the fiend arrested tonight."

"What?" Oliver and I said in unison.

Oliver pushed to his feet and then called loudly for his footman. The footman entered with his hands folded elegantly behind his back. "Fetch Hawkins. I don't care about his state of dress. If he's in his nightshirt, so be it."

The footman exited with a bow.

Oliver then turned back to us. "If you were gallivanting around the docks at this late an hour without a chaperone, then what is this business about the shop?"

"While we were at the docks, the man in the clockwork

mask broke into the toy shop and ransacked it to look like a burglary. He had intended to kidnap me. He said as much when we spied on him at the docks. So you see, it was very fortunate I was not there," I explained in an attempt to defuse the situation. Still my stomach twisted a bit with nerves. What if I had been home? Even with my alarms, there would have been little to stop him from abducting me, save the pistol I kept close at hand at all times while alone in the shop.

Dear God, this night was a mess.

Suddenly the door opened and Oliver's valet, an older gentleman with close-set eyes and bushy eyebrows, entered in his dressing gown.

I looked down at the hem of my dress out of decency.

Oliver pulled out a small bit of paper and jotted down a note. "Hawkins, have this sent by swift bird to John Frank immediately. Then please rouse Mary and have her prepare the Rose Room for a guest. When it is ready, have her escort Miss Whitlock to her room. That is all."

The valet nodded, stepped forward and took the paper, and then bowed and left the room.

"Now, as for the two of you." Oliver planted his hands on his desk and leaned forward. "Meg, you are to stay here. So long as the man intent upon kidnapping you is in the city,

I want you under my roof. And you . . ." I'd never seen him look as serious as he did when he turned to David. "I'd like a word with you in private. Meg, would you please wait in the corridor for Mary to collect you."

"Yes, Your Grace," I said with a bow, knowing he hated it when I called him that. It was only a bit petulant, but he wasn't being himself at all. On more than one occasion he had personally put me in far worse danger than David had done.

"Meg," he said with a note of warning in his voice. He came around the desk and placed his hands on my shoulders. "Forgive me if I'm being overbearing, but I'm feeling protective lately. I know I am only a guardian in name, but I do feel responsible for your welfare, and I don't wish to see you come to a bad end. I have too many plans for you. If you feel the need to head out on an excursion to a shady part of town, do inform me first?"

I nodded. "I'll make an attempt."

He turned me toward the door. "Go with Mary. Rest well. You're safe here for the night."

I exited the study, then shut the door. There was no one in the dark hall, so I pressed my ear up against the wood, determined to hear what was in store for David.

CHAPTER THREE

"WHAT ARE YOU TRYING TO DO?" OLIVER SHOUTED. I heard him well enough through the door, though his voice was muffled. David's answer was harder to discern, if he answered at all. "If I didn't know any better, I'd think you were trying to compromise her on purpose."

I felt as if all the air had suddenly left my lungs. I had considered the dangers of having my reputation ruined, but I never would have thought that David would attempt to trap me in such a way.

Oliver said something, but I couldn't hear him, so I dropped down and pressed my cheek to the floor to better hear through the crack beneath the door.

"I'm being practical. Everyone can see how well matched we are. There is no other who can come close to being my equal. Our marriage was arranged from the time we were infants, so why shouldn't I pursue her? If she married another, it would be a waste of her potential." I couldn't see anything of the room, but David's words had me feeling both very hot and strangely chilled at the same time.

Oliver didn't respond at once. When he did, his voice sounded softer but held no less warning. "David, you are my brother by law, and believe it or not, I'm looking out for your best interest. You cannot trap her and expect to make her yours. If you wish to be a man, do what is right, not foolish."

"Excuse me, miss. Did you drop something?"

I scrambled up, hitting the back of my head on the door handle. Wincing, I rubbed it as I turned to the maid. "I lost a button. It slid under the door."

"I can fetch it for you," she said, reaching for the handle.

My arms felt shaky as I smoothed my skirt. "No need. Mary, is it? I'm quite tired. It's very late." I folded my hands in front of me and hoped the girl hadn't noticed we were wearing the exact same dress.

"Yes, miss. Follow me." She turned on her heel and then walked down the hall. I followed because I had little choice, but if I had had my druthers, I would have continued to listen to Oliver and David at the door. If that made me a horrible person, I'd have to live with my faults.

Mary turned up the lamps in the rose bedroom. The light seemed to bleed into the dusky pink silk adorning the walls and the rosewood furniture. The scent of dried rose petals was as overpowering as the luxury, and this was one of the more humble guest rooms.

I didn't belong here.

"Is there anything you might need, miss?" Mary asked.

"No. Thank you."

The maid left, and I perched on the corner of the bed. The feather mattress sank beneath me, but I couldn't let myself fall into it.

I had too much to think about.

What was I to do about David? I hated bearing the burden of having to discourage him. Unfortunately, it simply wasn't in his nature to give up the hunt. The trouble was, I admired David. I even enjoyed his company and his wit, but in his world I became a shadow or a prop for lovely dresses, someone who happened to be capable of hosting tea.

All my property, what little I had, would transfer to him. If I were a married woman, my husband would be in control of my life, my body—everything. I would have no recourse, and if I wished to pursue any of my own interests, it would have to be on his mercy until the day he died and I became a widow, and even then it would be my sons who could control my affairs. David would not allow me to continue running my shop, that much I knew for certain. It would be beneath my station as a countess.

Whomever I married, I had to trust that he would willingly give me my freedom when I asked, because by law and custom he would not be obligated to do so. I didn't believe I could trust David in that way. That was the problem.

I wasn't ready to marry. Not anyone, and if I weren't careful, that choice could be taken from me. I had to protect it.

I watched soft flakes of snow land against the cold glass of the window, where they hesitated before melting and dripping down the pane like tears. My heart was back in my lovely shop. I couldn't get the image of it wrecked from my mind. What was worse were the moments when the images of the shattered toys mixed with the memories I still carried of burned wood and shattered glass from the fire that had taken everything from me.

I hated living in the shadow of destruction.

It was exhausting.

But not exhausting enough to allow me to sleep.

The chill in the deep winter night seeped into my bones as I sat on the bed and waited for dawn to break.

It was only in the light of the new morning that I settled enough to finally sleep. I ended up dozing off in a large armchair fully dressed. The maids must have been under orders not to disturb me. When I finally did wake in the late afternoon, my lavish surroundings baffled me for several moments as I struggled to remember where I was.

Then Lady Briony, David's younger sister, burst through the door. "Meg! I heard you were here, but oh it is late, and you should be dressed. The other Amusementists are already gathering."

I stared blankly at the young girl with slightly garish ginger hair and the unfortunate freckles that covered every inch of her face and arms even in the dead of winter. She was dressed in a pale gray ball gown with her hair curled and done up in lavender ribbons. She hadn't been given the beauty of her sister, Lucinda, or the stature of her brother, David, but I liked her immensely. She reminded me of myself in a more innocent time.

Blinking, I rose from the chair, but I was stiff, and feared my foot had fallen asleep. "What is all this?"

"His Grace is demonstrating his latest Amusement tonight, and you're going to miss it." Lady Briony waved a rather intimidating platoon of maids into the room. "Lucinda sent me to make sure you were ready in time."

Lady Briony clapped her hands, and the maids set to work. I had learned very quickly that when Lucinda wanted something done, there was no fighting it. Now that she was a duchess, it had only gotten worse.

In no time at all I stood before a mirror, cleaned and dressed in a frosty pale blue dress with a soft matching wool cloak. Lady Briony took my hand and led me out of the rose bedroom and down the halls of the Chadwick townhome.

A crowd had gathered outside the doors of the conservatory. It was there that I caught sight of my very best friend.

Her Grace, the Duchess of Chadwick, should have looked resplendent in a snow-white gown with a matching cape. Instead Lucinda seemed faintly ill. With bright red-gold hair the color of dark honey, and vivid blue-green eyes, she was a breathtaking beauty. But at the moment, she seemed as if she hadn't slept in a month. Worry creased her brow.

As I drew closer, I noticed her eyes were rimmed with red, and she had a tight expression as if fighting to keep from becoming ill. I didn't like it one bit. "Are you well?" I asked in hushed tones.

"Oliver told me what happened at the shop. I'm terribly upset," she admitted. By all rights the shop was hers. She had inherited it from her first husband, Simon Pricket. I managed the shop in her stead. While Simon Pricket may not have been a duke, she had loved him deeply, and I knew she still mourned him even though she had found happiness with Oliver.

"I'm so sorry. I feel like I failed in my duty to you." I took her hand in mine.

"I was worried for *you*. I am so very glad you are unharmed." She drew me in to touch her cheek to mine the way a sister would.

"I might not be able to open the shop for Christmas," I confessed. "Our patrons will be terribly disappointed."

She sighed. "We will set it right once things return to the way they should be."

"Will they ever?" I asked, feeling the weight of the question on my shoulders as I thought about the man in the clockwork mask and his intent to hunt me down until he finally claimed his prize.

Lucinda pinched her lips together, but then brightened. "Darling! You're looking quite handsome this evening."

"And you are lovely, as always." I turned to see Oliver striding toward us dressed in his finest, though his hair could not be tamed. His wild brown locks defied constraint but suited the handsome young duke.

"You look quite fetching as well, Miss Whitlock." He leaned in toward my ear. "Might I have a word with you in private?" he whispered.

"Of course." A thread of fear wove through my heart. David had had quite a dressing down, and now it seemed it was my turn.

Oliver took Lucinda's hand and kissed her on the cheek. "I'll only be gone a moment. As soon as Victor opens the doors, sit close to the fires."

"Really, I'm well." She smiled sweetly at him. "Go. You have much to discuss."

"Follow me." Oliver's voice took on a stern tone as we slipped back down the hallway, unnoticed by the crowd near the doors to the conservatory.

Once again Oliver led me to his imposing study. Only, this time several papers had been scattered over his desk. On the corner of a table by the window, a small mechanical pigeon preened near a stuffed fox. The unfortunate canine wore a patch covering one eye like a pirate.

Oliver crossed his arms and leaned his hip on the desk. "You know what I'm going to say, don't you?"

"That I should guard my reputation more closely." I bowed my head, not in submission but because I felt the weight of my own thoughts.

"Do you wish to marry David? Is that why you were so reckless?" Oliver asked, reaching out and tipping up my chin. "I thought you wished to finish with the Academy."

"I do!" I took a step back but looked Oliver in the eye. "I thought my reputation would be safe with my friends."

"Your reputation is never safe with a man. Should something happen, it will always be your fault," he warned.

"It's not fair." I could never really be free. No woman could ever truly be free in such a world.

"No, it is not." Oliver placed a hand on my shoulder. "But until the world changes, it's the lot you've been given. I'll do what I can to protect you."

I looked down at my hands, not feeling very mollified. The world couldn't change quickly enough. "Thank you, Oliver."

He gave my shoulder a hearty pat. "When your grandfather returns, I hope to say I did my best for you."

Which brought us to the other pressing issue. "Did you

find the man in the clockwork mask?" I asked. "Please tell me he has been captured."

"Unfortunately, he managed to evade us once again." Oliver's expression turned grim. "However, I have made some inquiries around the docks. He has been making regular passages between London and the port at Le Havre, and even traveling up the river as far as Rouen. I had my men inquire in Rouen, but the French were much more tight-lipped, or less greedy for the sum I had offered to pay for information."

I sat down in a fine velvet chair near a large globe and felt as if I were still sinking. "So he's in France." I wondered if my grandfather was there as well, so close.

Oliver tilted his head. "Our trail grows cold in Rouen, though it would be a fair conjecture to consider Paris, with the link to the Seine."

I nodded. My hands trembled ever so slightly. I folded them neatly to still them. "Is there any connection to the Haddock family in Paris?"

The bomb the man had planted in the shop last summer had borne the mark of a man named Richard Haddock. There had to be a connection. While at the Academy, I had discovered what I could about Haddock. He had been given the Black Mark by the Order and had paid with his life.

Haddock had a clear reason for waging a vendetta against my family for our part in his downfall, and he was at the top of my list of suspects. There was only one problem. According to all accounts he was well and truly dead and had no heir to carry out his revenge.

Oliver twirled a small gear over the backs of his fingers. "Haddock's only connection to France is his grave."

It wasn't enough. There was no certain place to begin, or a clear path to follow. "I'm afraid this isn't very much to go on," I muttered.

The gear paused its motion. His brow furrowed as Oliver shifted the gear back and forth with an imperceptible flex of his fingers.

"What is it?" I asked, needing to know what he was holding back.

He considered his next words carefully. "It appears our time is also running out."

"What are you saying?" I leaned forward, away from the plush softness of the chair.

"The *Méduse* is due to sail back to New Orleans on the New Year," he said. "And he knows we are watching him now."

The New Year was only weeks away. If the *Méduse* sailed

clear across the Atlantic, the only clue I had would grow cold. Gracious. I wanted to help my grandfather desperately, but now I found myself with little time, and even fewer resources.

Should the man in the mask slip our grasp, I'd have to wait for another attempt on my life before I could find his trail again, especially if he learned of Oliver's bribes for information about the ship. Oliver's attempts at espionage wouldn't remain secret for long, knowing the loose tongues of the dockworkers.

I refused to live like a terrified rabbit in a warren, wondering if the hawk perched in the tree nearby had finally given up the hunt. This man had already killed my parents, nearly killed me, and he had callously drugged me and locked me in a trunk. He had proven he could break into my home. What if his next attack against me was the one that hit the mark?

Even with that horrifying thought, I didn't wish to pursue a murderer, but I couldn't leave my grandfather to the fiend's cruel machinations either.

Oliver placed the gear down on the table. "Meg, I don't want you chasing after a madman."

"Then what am I supposed to do? Should I wait for the strike that finally kills me? Perhaps I should hand over my grandfather's key next time I see him. I'll wrap it up with a neat little bow. At least then he can spare my windows." I let out a hard breath. "No one in the Order, aside from you, cares about the fate of my grandfather. He's the next in line to become head of the Order, and so long as he is missing, everyone else's prospects at advancement seem brighter."

"That's not true," Oliver said, but the defensive timbre in his voice proclaimed otherwise. "There isn't a single member of the Order who would wish harm upon Henry so that he might increase his standing."

I lifted one eyebrow and didn't say a word. After all, Lord Strompton had murdered several members of the Order to increase his family's standing and had hidden his evil plot by framing another. It was a circumstance Oliver had unintentionally benefited from once he'd married Strompton's daughter.

Oliver held up a hand. "Don't even say it."

Clearly he understood me quite well. "You know I would never speak of it."

He let out a heavy breath and leaned against the desk, then folded his arms. "What do you wish to do about all this?"

"Will you help me? The man in the mask won't suspect you to follow him to Paris." My cards were on the table. In the last year Oliver and I had demanded much of one another. I could tell by the conflict written on his face, this request was simply too much to ask.

"I am needed here in London at the present until things are less—unsettled." Rising up straighter, he tugged his fine waistcoat down. "I'm sorry."

"Don't be. This isn't your battle."

"Well, it's not as if you should travel either," Oliver said. "And I'm not saying that solely because I don't wish for you to confront a murderer on your own. The oath will be given at the next Gathering of the Order on New Year's Eve. It is mandatory, a worldwide call to assemble. If you are not back in time to take your vow, your place as an apprentice will be forfeit. You will never be welcome within the Order again."

"I am aware of the situation." I looked down at a callus on the heel of my palm. "You needn't lecture."

The fight drained out of him, and he ran a hand through his unruly hair as he often did when stymied. "Listen. I'll write to my friend Gustave and send it through the Order's urgent channels. He's in Paris right now. Perhaps he can help discover more about this mystery."

I needed more certain information and greater resources with which to confront this danger. As a nobleman Oliver had those resources. As a shopkeeper and an unmarried woman, I did not. But I had grown to learn that I needed to rely on myself. Oliver had done enough, and I now had more information than I'd had before. "I appreciate your offer. Thank you."

Oliver came closer and gave me his hand. He folded my palm in his and looked into my eyes with the most earnest expression I had ever seen. "Don't think I don't want to see Henry return," he said, using my grandfather's name. "Don't ever think that I would wish for any of your family's misfortune. I want to see his return. It's only that we have so little information with none of it confirmed, and the dangers are so great."

"I understand," I said. "Truly. I have never had cause to doubt your intentions. Thank you for all you have done for me thus far. It is more than I could do on my own." He led us back out to the hall and toward the conservatory. I only wished there were something more that could be done.

My grandfather was the only tie to my family I had left, and I felt the thread of that tie slipping through my fingers.

CHAPTER FOUR

OLIVER TOOK MY ARM AND ESCORTED ME INTO THE conservatory. The frigid air washed over us, even as the bright fires burned merrily in the large freestanding braziers. The crowds had gathered around them. Most members of the houses of both Chadwick and Strompton had assembled. While I was familiar with the other Amusementists and Society members, I felt distinctly out of place.

This was an event for the gentry.

Oliver left me at a table, then wandered around greeting the various people seated around the fires.

"Fancy meeting you here," David said too close to my ear. I spun around.

His eyes met mine, and his lips tipped up to the right in his usual uneven grin. Blessed with a golden hue to his fine hair and handsome features, tonight he was the epitome of a proper noble gentleman. "You look lovely this evening. What did Oliver have to say?"

"Must every conversation we have begin this way?" I asked.

"In what way?" He smiled a too knowing smile.

"You know in what way." He was handsome, of that there was no doubt. He was elegant, wealthy, titled, intelligent, and I felt the allure of him. But beneath it all something was missing, something solid and real, like the feel of the ground beneath my feet.

Still, I'd been born an Englishwoman, and he was an earl. I had to be gracious. Yet every time I tried to be kind to him, I felt I was giving him encouragement when I shouldn't.

It didn't help matters that I honestly wished I could have the same relationship with him that I had with my other good friends. I wished I could trust him in the same way I trusted Manoj, Noah, Michael, and Peter.

He touched a curl of hair at my cheek. "You're bothered by something. What did Oliver discover about the man in the mask?"

"Nothing of significance." If I told David anything, he'd come up with a new plan, and I couldn't be certain he fully had my best interest at heart. Not after what he had said to Oliver.

"Tell me," he insisted.

"David, really. You've done enough."

If David knew of my troubles, he would help, but that aid would turn into a debt I couldn't repay.

"You can depend on me, you know. I can provide anything you desire, no matter the cost." His voice dropped low for a moment.

"I know you would." It would be wonderful to run to France without thought or consequence. I wanted my grandfather to come home. The problem was, in a short year's time I had learned much about the dangers of acting rashly. I was determined to rise above my more foolhardy nature. "I would question the price."

At that moment Oliver took his place at a lectern carved from ice and addressed the crowd.

"My dear friends and family," he said with a sweeping smile. "At our last Gathering my honorable friend Albrecht had the audacity to imply that my efforts on the last Amusement lacked *finesse*."

David's old Prussian uncle stood. "Your dancers for the Amusementist ball shook more than I do." The other Amusementists in the room let out low and hearty laughs. The mischievous old inventor crossed his arms and returned to his chair.

"Perhaps they had succumbed to their nerves. Falling in love is a terribly risky affair, after all," Oliver countered. Again the crowd responded to the jab with laughter.

David glanced at me out of the corner of his eye, but I kept my attention fixed on Oliver.

"In defense of my reputation as an Amusementist, allow me to present this. A carousel of the most delicate nature." Oliver reached out a hand, and Lucinda rose like a queen. "My darling love, will you be the first to ride?"

Lucinda smiled and stepped toward the carousel.

It looked even more breathtaking than it had the evening before. The light from the fires caught in the facets of the ice and made it seem as if a million tiny fires had been trapped within the glittering ice and cool silver. I had seen many beautiful things in my time with the Amusementists, but this was by far the most remarkable.

Lucinda stepped up onto the platform, and a dark figure rose out of the crowd. "Oh no, dear. That isn't good at all for someone in your condition," Lucinda's mother proclaimed from underneath her heavy mourning veil.

I sat straighter, as everyone's eyes turned to Lucinda.

What condition?

I hated to think that Lucinda was ill with some horrible affliction, but she really didn't look well.

Oliver tucked his wife close to his side as the crowd murmured in low, hushed tones. "Since Lady Strompton has already caused some undue speculation, I'd like to announce my great joy. I'm proud to welcome the forthcoming Chadwick heir, or the daughter I shall dote on like no other." The rumbling murmurs turned into a surprised gasp of collective delight. The people at the tables burst into rounds of congratulations.

It took a moment for it all to sink in. Lucinda was increasing with child! That was why she was looking so ill. She must still be early on and not feeling right. It was no wonder Oliver didn't wish to leave her to travel to Paris. She had lost one child from her first marriage, and she had to be terrified.

"Perhaps it is best for my lovely wife to remain on firm ground. So who will be the first to ride? Apprentice Margaret?" Oliver swept his hand toward the carousel, and I rose. My mind was full with thoughts about the coming baby, but I couldn't miss an opportunity to ride the beautiful machine before me.

I was first to reach the carousel, but others had followed. I climbed atop a beautiful shimmering griffin and sat side-saddle on the dark blue velvet pad that insulated me from the cold chill of the ice. I admired the artistry in the lion's claws, and the chiseled feathers of the creature's head.

Albrecht waved to me from the twisting coils of the drag-on's back, and I was surprised to see Oliver's grandmother perch regally upon the Pegasus in front of him. The flying horse tossed its head high, with its translucent mane sweep-ing through the air as if the creature were frozen in flight. As the light shifted within the ice, the animals seemed to come alive, flexing and straining to run as the carousel began to turn. Uncle Albrecht tipped his hat to the dowager duchess, and I thought I saw her blush.

I laughed before I could help it. I held on to the silver pole with my gloved hands when the carousel began to move more quickly, and I gasped in delight as it swirled around and around to the beautiful music pouring from the machine.

I hadn't felt so free or so joyful in such a long time.

Every other concern melted away as the wintry conserva-tory swirled around in a blur of frosty white.

I knew how desperately Lucinda wished for a child after the untimely loss of her first husband and the child she had carried from that marriage. I was so grateful she had been given a second chance to be a mother. She would be a wonderful one.

Already in my mind I was sorting through my inventory at the toy shop and wondering which of the delights I should give to the baby, or if anything suitable had survived at all. I could invent something new entirely. Oh, the thought had merit. It would be such fun.

Dizzy and elated, I didn't want the carousel to stop, but it slowed its wonderful spin. I stepped off the turning platform and fell into the nearest chair.

That was when I noticed David next to Oliver by the lectern.

Then the unnatural silence.

And the stares of everyone in the room had fixed on me.

Perplexed, I turned my gaze to Oliver. His mouth was set in a hard line, and his bright hazel eyes seemed to catch the light of the hot fire of the braziers within them. He looked as if he were about to cuff David over the back of the head.

David gave me a victorious smile as he lifted a glass of Eiswein and took a sip. His expression reminded me of a hunter striding through a pack of dogs, knowing he had a fox in his snare.

I felt the flush on my neck as the room became very hot and crowded all at once, in spite of the glass walls and piles of snow.

"What has happened?" I whispered to the kindly old woman to my right. She reached over and patted my hand. She shook with palsy even as she gave me a crinkled smile. "The earl just asked His Grace for your hand, dear."

The significance of the moment was so far beyond me that the first thought to cross my mind was, *He needs my hand for what?*

But then her words settled and my mouth went suddenly dry.

He asked Oliver for my hand in marriage?

Oh, dear Lord.

David turned to me.

It took every ounce of strength I had to stand. I could feel my hands shaking. I tried to hold my head high.

"Miss Whitlock." David smiled, so sure of himself as he strode forward between two of the blazing fires. "What do you say to becoming my wife?"

Everyone in the conservatory was grinning at me with

gleeful expectations. I could feel the pressure like a physical thing pressing down on me even as I felt as if I were about to explode. "May I have a word with you in private?" I managed to force out.

David lifted his glass to the others. "Whatever you have to say to me, you can say to us all. They will be family soon."

There were times when David's confidence was a terrible, terrible thing. I had no choice but to give my answer. "My lord," I said with as much force as I could muster. "I must refuse."

The horrified gasp that resounded through the conservatory matched the sound my own heart was making perfectly. Determined not to lose my composure, I backed away.

"My apologies, Your Grace," I said, nodding to Oliver. "But I should be leaving now."

As I gathered my skirts, someone announced, "She's daft" in an overly loud voice.

I turned my back to them all and walked out of the conservatory.

The sudden heat from the house felt oppressive. As soon as I passed into the hall, I broke into a hasty run. I needed to escape the house. I wanted to be home in my own workshop with my own things, free of the pressure of expectation.

The sound of my soles striking the hard marble echoed off the walls as I reached the front doors. I didn't wait for a footman to open them for me. Instead I reached for the doors and flung them wide, letting the wind and snow pour into the warm house.

At the shock of cold air, I let out a gasp.

I had just been humiliated in front of several members of the Order. At least three served in the House of Lords. In the end it would be my reputation that suffered for it, not David's. I would become the irrational shrew in their eyes, not a girl who had been carefully manipulated.

A familiar coachman approached, his brow creased with confusion as he looked at me standing in the winter chill. "Is there a problem, Miss Whitlock?" he asked.

"Yes. I need you to take me home at once."

"As you say." He nodded and returned to the carriage house.

My heart pounded as I waited for him to hitch the horses. I didn't have time to linger. For a moment I considered walking back to my shop, but decided against it. The streets weren't safe for a young woman, even in Mayfair, and I wasn't dressed for a jaunt about town alone in the dark.

I took a step down onto the icy stone hoping to be closer to the carriage house the moment the coachman reappeared, but a strong hand grasped me by the arm.

I turned, wrenching my arm free at the same time, only to come face-to-face with David.

CHAPTER FIVE

"MEG, STOP," DAVID SAID WITH A NOTE OF HURT IN HIS voice. "I know that the proposal was sudden, but you didn't have to humiliate me like that."

Humiliate him? He'd humiliated me. "I asked to speak with you alone. You would have none of it," I said, unable to contain my disbelief. "What in the name of the dear Lord were you thinking?"

David pulled on his collar in frustration. "I was thinking we are well matched. I have no desire to parade my title, my Amusementist lineage, and money around the Society while hungry mothers shove their witless daughters under my nose. I'd rather avoid the entire ordeal. Your name within the

Order is as powerful as mine. If the rumors about the hidden Whitlock fortune are true, your wealth is as great." He lowered his head a fraction, one of the few times I'd ever seen him do so. "You are the only woman I have ever met who could *almost* best my intelligence."

I closed my eyes for the briefest moment, gathering my patience. "That was hardly intelligent, what you did in there. Did you think you could force my hand by making a spectacle? Or do you intend to force my hand in some other way?" A cold gust of wind cut through my cape and dress. People certainly married for all those reasons, but that didn't give David cause to assume that the answer he wanted was the only one I could give.

David looked incredulous as he motioned back toward the open door. "I only thought that I would make you a good husband. Think of it. As a countess you would be able to do whatever you pleased. I could give you all of this and more." He motioned toward the grand house. His voice softened. "Don't act as if there is nothing between us. We shared a kiss."

"You stole that kiss moments before we were flung into an icy lake. I chose to ignore your indiscretion, considering we nearly died." I took a step away from him, fearing he might take liberties again.

As soon as I retreated, he pulled me into his body and whispered against my ear, "And what of the dance?"

For a moment I remembered what it had felt like to be in his arms. I could feel the rush and tingle of excitement and the confident strength of his arms holding mine.

No. It wasn't right. I pushed him hard and nearly toppled myself over with the force of it. "You're an earl. You are the product of more than seventeen generations of fine breeding, wealth, and refinement. You were *born* to be attractive. If I feel it, it means nothing more than that I am English and a woman. That is not love. At one time I may have mistaken such yearnings for love, but not anymore."

David paced a tight, frustrated circle. "I know you fancy yourself in love with that Foundry worker, but truly, Meg— where is the future in it? Marriage is best served with practicality. Love can grow with time."

"Will has nothing to do with this." Will had been a loyal friend and ally to me in the darkest of times. My feelings for him ran deep. But even without Will, I couldn't have accepted David's proposal. There were things David said, and small actions that I couldn't ignore.

"Do you think I'm a fool?" David asked.

"No, I have never thought that, never for a moment," I

replied. "But you are misguided. I was born above a shop, and I keep one now. These hands have bled while I've spent hours on my knees blackening grates day after day as a housemaid. You imagine some fortune that should be mine, but I still must work to earn my bread. I am not whatever it is you have constructed me to be in your mind. You treat me like some fantastical beast at a circus, one you can keep in a cage to show to your many admirers." I held out my arm with bravado. "Look here! It's the amazing woman inventor. The rarest of breeds, she can perform sums as well as a man."

David took me by the arms and held me out, forcing me to be still. "You have a gift, Meg. You *are* rare. Think of the minds our sons could be gifted with. Think of all that we could give them." He lifted his proud chin, and I saw in him a brief flash of the raw ambition that had ruined his father.

I hadn't even thought of children. Certainly he hadn't thought of how bearing those children before I became a full member of the Order would ruin any future I had as an Amusementist. It wasn't as if I could attend my lectures and nurse my babes at the same time. Children wouldn't inconvenience him. And I knew for certain that denying him his conjugal rights as a husband would.

"I will not marry you."

"You're being ridiculous." He took a step toward the door. "Come back inside. It's cold out here."

"No." The cold was reaching deep inside me, and I had to clench my teeth to keep them from chattering. "I've said my piece." I knew he wanted to abide by the will of his late father. Lord Strompton had handpicked me for David's bride when I'd been little more than an infant. I couldn't ignore the political implications of a union between us either. But as I looked at David now, it was raw jealousy that tortured him.

He slashed a hand through the air, then fisted it so tightly, his knuckles turned white. "You can't know what I feel," he shouted.

His words twisted through me, and the sharp sting of them bit more fiercely than the cold. I took a step back, afraid of him. What he felt for me was not a burden I should have to bear. I hadn't asked for his affections. I hadn't tried to break his heart, and I did know how he felt. "I'm sorry, David," I said gently. "I never meant to hurt you."

The sound of hooves clattered against the flagstones, and a pair of fine grays emerged from the carriage house, pulling the duke's coach.

I gathered my skirts and turned back to him.

"Will asked me to marry him once, and I refused him as well," I said.

David watched me with a guarded look. "You take too much for granted. Don't be surprised when you turn around and it is gone."

My ears burned as I took the hand that the coachman offered and stepped inside. Within the security of the coach, I sank against the back of the seat. The first thing I lost control of was my breath. I had to hold it to fight the panicked gasps struggling to claim my lungs. I closed my eyes and tried to block out the ringing in my ears and the pressure I felt in my heart and in my head. It took all my strength to gather my composure.

"Take me home," I said softly to the coachman before he shut the door, enveloping me in the darkness.

I looked back and watched as Oliver joined David at the stairs. The duke wrapped an arm around him and led him back inside.

The fine home disappeared in the dark winter evening, and as it did, I felt all connections to the home fading. Oliver and Lucinda were moving on to a new phase in their lives. I was being left behind. I knew in my heart that, as much as I loved them, they couldn't be the same friends they had been just a year before. As for David, he might have made my search for my grandfather easier, but it would have come with a heavy cost indeed.

As the lonely carriage rumbled through the streets of London toward my broken and ruined home, I realized I'd have to find the strength to help my grandfather myself.

There had to be a way, and I needed to find it quickly.

We finally reached the toy shop. The snow softly fell as I looked at the dark shop with the windows boarded up. My friends had nailed my closed sign to the board on the front window. The coachman helped me down, and I walked to the broken window and touched the rough wood covering it.

I looked down at my elegant dress, and a heaviness settled in my heart as I opened my door.

"Will you be a'right, miss?" the coachman asked.

"I'll be fine," I said as I slipped through the door.

A chill ran down my spine as I found myself alone in the dark. The shop was so silent. I could hear carolers on a distant corner. I lit a lamp, and saw the breath drifting around my face. Fear became a palpable thing as I lifted the small lamp and carried it through the ruined gallery to my parlor beyond. I hadn't made it this far the other night.

As I opened the door, my breath pushed from my lungs and wouldn't return.

Papers littered the parlor, scattered over the disturbed furniture and the broken tea service. A single red ribbon rested at my feet like a trail of blood across the floor.

The papers were my letters from Will.

I always kept them in a neat bundle by the fire. I dropped to my knees, my skirts pooling around me as I gathered as many letters as I could. Some were rumpled and had even been trod upon.

> *Dear Meg,*
>
> *I have finished reading* Oliver Twist *and find I enjoyed it much better than* David Copperfield. *I am very glad you recommended it to me. Perhaps another day, I will make a second attempt to read the latter, but I have been busy with my work here and find I have little time for leisure.*

A tear slipped over my cheek and fell onto the paper. It touched the precise block-looking letters that must have taken Will ages to write, and the ink blurred out into the damp.

I gathered another.

> *My dearest Meg,*
>
> *It is beautiful here, possibly more beautiful than any*

other place I have known. It is hard for me to remember
my childhood, but I think I have memories of the skies over
the open roads. I used to walk beside our wagon and watch
the clouds. London never had skies like this. Sometimes it
was difficult to see anything but walls and stone. I wish
you could see it too. I'm certain you would find some magic
within the clouds that I don't have the power to see. Or
share a story of what it is like to touch them.

I hastily wiped my eyes with the backs of my wrists and gathered as many letters as I could reach, and returned them once more to a careful stack. We had fallen into the habit of writing every day at least. The record of quiet moments that I'd shared with Will through the letters had been disregarded and thrown about carelessly, instead of treasured.

Dear Meg,
   The cabbage soup at the inn is awful. I'm a little
baffled by how this could be. Though my knowledge of
cooking is somewhat limited, boiling cabbage in water
doesn't seem too difficult a task. Perhaps I am missing
something.

I am missing something.

I'm missing you.

I let out a sniff and then a chuckle. He hadn't yet tried my cabbage soup. I was willing to place a wager that the soup at the inn at Inverness was by far the superior.

Looking down at the smudged and torn pages, I wondered if he had kept the ones I had sent in return. I had written stacks and stacks of letters filled with all the little things that I needed to share. I didn't know if the day would come when I would run out of words and we could sit silently side by side knowing all there was to know about one another. I didn't imagine such a thing was possible.

It seemed such a luxury. I let out a deep sigh. I wasn't sure if we would ever find a way to be together so often that we ran out of words. We had very different goals. I only hoped whatever it was that linked the two of us was strong enough to keep us anchored.

Without Will, I felt adrift, but with every day that went by, my own life continued on. I wished that we could be together, but wishes and dreams make poor bricks for building. I wondered if time would eventually draw us completely apart.

A knock sounded at the shop door.

I clutched the letters to my chest as my blood rushed in my ears. I was alone. The lock was damaged and my alarms disabled.

The knock fell harder, beating against the wood with a grim insistence. The person knocking wanted in, and badly.

The pistol Will had given to me for protection lay uselessly within my workshop. If I retrieved it, I would have to pass into the gallery of the toy shop and closer to danger.

The iron poker lay against the fireplace. I grasped it, plotting where I should strike, the head or knee.

Knock, knock, knock.

I fervently prayed for the knocks to fall silent as I clasped the poker so tightly, my fingers felt numb.

"Meg! For the love of Pete, are you in there?" a voice called with a distinct Scottish brogue.

"Oh my goodness." I dropped the poker to the floor and ran into the gallery as fast as I could. I couldn't open the door fast enough. My fingers were shaking.

As I flung open the door, swirls of snowflakes danced about and landed on a familiar black tam. There at the threshold, in the swirling snow, a young man stood in a thick black coat. He seemed larger and stronger than the last time

I had seen him. His work gave him a hale glow and, even in winter, a swarthy look to his tanned skin. The snow clung to the dark hair curling behind his ears, as if it wished to whisper to him a secret.

"Will!" I held on to the door, barely containing the urge to throw myself into his arms. "Whatever are you doing here? And at this time of night?"

"I'm standing at your door freezing."

I opened the door slightly wider, then hesitated. I looked behind me. The house was empty. I didn't have a chaperone. If we were caught together, we'd be forced to marry, and either Will would have to give up his position at the Foundry or I would have to give up my apprenticeship. "Come in quickly. Before you are seen."

I grabbed him by his coat and pulled him inside. He slammed the door and pulled me against him into his warm embrace.

Finally in that moment, like the greatest of Christmas miracles, all the fear and darkness fell away and for that moment in his arms, I felt safe.

He held me tight, cradling my head against his warm chest. The velvet of his doublet felt soft on my cheek. "Why did you leave Oliver's?" he asked. "You aren't safe here alone."

"How did you come to be here?" He was still wearing the uniform of the Foundry. Dressed all in black, from the tam at his head to his high stockings, the only color in his otherwise traditional Scottish attire was his MacDonald plaid kilt. He must have come straight from the ship, but I hadn't realized it had arrived already. The Foundry workers weren't due in London until the oath.

"I had some time and took the train. Oliver wanted me here for the reveal of his latest Amusement and asked Gordon to release me early. Lucinda wrote that David had volunteered to collect me, but when I arrived at the station, no one was there." Will looked around the shop and scowled at the mess. He bent and lifted a tin soldier from the floor.

I had always assumed that "seeing red" was nothing more than a turn of phrase, until that very moment. "David was supposed to collect you?"

That bastard!

"When I realized no one was coming for me, I took a cab. But when I arrived at the town house, Lady Briony informed me that you had left for here. What happened?" He looked around the ravaged gallery.

"David proposed," I confessed, though a second later I realized he was probably asking what had happened to the shop.

Will straightened, and I felt the chill of the air on the back of my neck. "Should I be offering my felicitations?" His voice was cautious, but more reasoned than I had ever heard him when it came to David.

"Only to Lucinda and Oliver. They are expecting a child. I turned David down." I twisted my fingers. "It was quite humiliating, actually."

His shoulders softened. He looked at me. I couldn't read his expression. I knew he had to be pleased that I had refused David, but that wasn't what I saw when I looked at him. There was something much starker, much more serious in his face.

"I hope that you didn't refuse him for me," he said. "I adore you, Meg, but if you have any affection for him at all, he is clearly the better match for you. He can give you things I simply cannot."

"Stop this." My voice sounded sharp even to my own ears. My heart was too raw. "I cannot bear when you attempt to convince me of your terrible little worth. For your information I would not marry David, even if I had never met you, especially not after what he did tonight. And I would not marry him if he were as rich as Midas."

"He's richer," Will mumbled.

I reached out and touched Will's cheek, turning his face to mine. "And he can be as foolish. He believes me to be something I'm not, and I refuse to conform myself to his ideal. I couldn't live with myself if I did." I took a deep breath. "I have my own means, and I'm quite content with them."

I leaned in toward him and brushed my own kiss across his warm lips. "I am content," I whispered.

Will reached out and cupped my cheek, then leaned in and brushed the softest kiss across my forehead. I felt myself melting as surely as the snow clinging to his hair.

"Your means are in a disturbing state of disrepair," he commented. "What happened *here?*"

"The man in the clockwork mask paid a visit. I wasn't at home at the time. He left his calling card." I sighed as I looked at the ruins. "At least he didn't burn the place down."

"I'm glad you're safe," Will whispered with a strain in his voice.

"I'm not safe. That is the problem." I pulled away from him and gathered the matches so I could light the rest of the lamps. At least we didn't have to remain in the cold and the dark. "I won't ever be safe so long as I'm hunted."

Will let his gaze drop to the floor, then looked up with

the steady resolve I had always admired in him. "I'll start a fire, and we can set the shop right."

"Thank you for your help," I said, hoping he could feel the depth of my sincerity.

"I'm very glad to give it." We both set to work. I took a lamp upstairs and changed back into a simple dress I could work in. By the time I came down the stairs, Will had a cheerful fire roaring in the fireplace, with a kettle of tea on the cast-iron stove in the kitchen.

He had gathered up the letters and was leafing through them.

"You kept these?" His deep brown eyes looked up at me in both confusion and wonder. "They say nothing of importance."

"I disagree." I took the stack of letters and crossed the room to where the ribbon still lay on the floor. I tied the bundle and returned it to its place on the small table near the fire.

The corners of Will's lips tipped up in a slight smile. He rolled up his sleeves as we entered the gallery.

We set to work. It took us most of the night, but as we restored things to order, I told about finding the *Méduse*. He listened intently as I recounted everything I had seen in the ledger and the possibility that the man in the mask would be traveling across the Atlantic in a matter of weeks. I confessed that my lack of resources disheartened me, but there really wasn't much evidence that could prove my grandfather was in France.

He could still be anywhere. We only knew that the man in the mask frequently traveled to France, but I couldn't tell if he was traveling beyond to the rest of Europe.

"I don't know what I should do," I said as I set the remainder of the cloth dolls on their shelf.

Will looked up from repairing one of my alarm balls. "You're right. We need to know more."

"We?"

He tossed the ball to me, and I caught it and put it into my pocket. "You pulled me into this entire mess nearly a year ago. You think I don't wish to see the end of it?" he asked.

"I thought you were more clever than that."

"Not nearly clever enough, it seems."

I shook my head in bemusement. "I'm not willing to take a risk on so little information," I said, looking around at the clean and restored gallery. "It would be foolish."

"Then we need more information." He bent over and inspected the lock on the door, then searched through my box of tools. "This all started when you found a letter from your grandfather in Rathford's workshop."

I felt a chill run down my neck. "Yes, what of it?"

He looked up at me, and the light caught in his dark eyes. "Perhaps it is time for us to return."

CHAPTER SIX

"DEAR LORD, WHY DIDN'T I THINK OF THAT?" I ASKED.

"Because I'm the clever one." Will flipped a hammer into the air and caught it again by the handle. "You're good friends with Rathford's heir, aren't you?"

Lord Rathford had been our former employer and an Amusementist. He had surreptitiously invented a powerful and extremely dangerous invention, and then manipulated both Will and me into opening the locks that my grandfather had used to keep him from finishing his abomination and destroying the fabric of time itself. Rathford had been the last person to contact my grandfather. Rathford must have known something.

After Lord Rathford's death, his estate had been inherited by one of my fellow apprentices.

"I can write Peter a letter. He wouldn't have any objections to our searching the workshop." It felt as if a heavy weight had been suddenly lifted from my chest.

"No, Peter would not." Will's expression took on a roguish quality, which was accentuated by the ruggedness that suited him so well in Scotland. I felt the tremor of excitement deep in my middle. He was a very attractive man, and I was completely alone with him. I had to remember to keep a wary eye on my baser nature. I now knew how impetuous it could be.

Will hammered at the door, realigning the broken latch. Then he set to work on the frame. "Peter's mother might have some objections to your spending time in a secret workshop alone with an unmarried Scot and her son."

"That's a very good point. We can't do much confined to the parlor while under the eye of a chaperone." Peter's family was forced to endure a lot of scrutiny from the Order and needed to maintain the strictest propriety to avoid scandal. "I'll still write him. He'll know the best way around his mother. Would you deliver the letter to him on your way to Oliver's town house?"

"Of course."

I took a sheet of paper out of my counting desk and penned a quick letter explaining the situation to Peter, then sealed it and handed it to Will. He tucked it into his sporran.

I stood before Will, unsure of what to do with myself. Now that the house was in order, the impropriety of being alone with him had suddenly come into stark relief.

"You should be going," I mumbled. The wind outside made the house creak. I didn't want him to go, but he had already stayed most of the night, and if anyone saw him leave the shop in the morning, I would be ruined.

Instead he took my hand and led me back to the restored parlor, where hot tea waited on the table.

"We've been working all night. Let's just take a moment," he murmured as he took a seat.

I found myself watching his lips. I'd be too tempted.

Far too tempted.

He reached out and touched my arm above the elbow. His fingers slid down the length of my forearm until they wrapped gently around my hand. He drew me in, and I was helpless to resist.

"You can trust me, you know." He curled his warm fingers under my tender palm and placed a chivalrous kiss on the back of my hand.

"I fear I can't trust myself," I whispered. "I'm not ready for this."

Will's gaze turned up beneath the dark fringe of his thick lashes. We seemed to breathe as one being, slow heavy breaths that carried the weight of the longing between us. "I understand."

He pulled me forward and onto the seat. I curled my body into his and rested my head over the beating of his heart. He held me and stroked my arm as we watched the fire dance in the hearth.

If only we could stay this way forever. I had never felt so filled with contentment. Will began humming a tune. The sound resonated through his body as I kept my head close to his heart. Eventually he sang. It was the same melancholy tune he had sung to the horses when I'd entered the carriage house a year ago.

I wanted to marry this man. I wanted a million nights like this without having to push him away, but it wasn't our time. Not yet. Four long years where I served as an apprentice stood between us, and I wasn't so naïve to think our lives couldn't change in that time. As I listened to him sing, four years seemed such a terrible long time to wait.

I didn't know at what point I succumbed to my exhaustion and lost myself in restless dreams of heather and mountains, fire and the forge. They were misty images, fleeting through my mind. Men's good-natured laughter, dizzying folds of plaid.

When I finally regained a sense of my own body, I found myself lost in a heavy fog. The metallic clang of gears turning surrounded me. A man strode toward me through the mist.

At first I didn't know who it was, but he had a regal presence and proud, wide shoulders. He wore a naval captain's coat that reminded me of the one I had taken from an automaton on a clockwork ship. As he emerged from the haze, I recognized him at once.

"Papa!" I called into the darkness, and ran to him. His eyes were hidden behind dark goggles. He embraced me without saying a word. "Where were you?" I asked. He didn't answer, his expression stony. I had to see him, to know it was really him. I lifted the goggles from his face.

His eyes had been sewn shut like a corpse's.

I stumbled backward and fell into a deep dark hole. A lid closed over me with a loud boom. I pounded against the lid, kicking against the dark box, a coffin. Heavy thumps banged against the coffin from falling shovelfuls of dirt. I knew I would die, buried alive.

I screamed as I woke, feeling confined and restricted. Suddenly I tumbled, and hit the floor hard. I was in the parlor, though the fire had gone cold in the grate. I was still dressed, and tangled in a thick blanket.

"Goodness, Miss Whitlock. Have you hurt yourself?" Mrs. Brindle's granddaughter, Molly, came in from the front of the shop.

"Molly, what are you doing here? I . . . I don't know what happened," I stammered. I looked back up on the seat for Will, then glanced in a panic around the room, but he was nowhere in sight. A dried thistle rested near my stack of letters. Thank heaven. Suddenly the image from my dream tormented me, and I wished he were there.

It was irrational, I knew, but I wasn't fully awake and was still shaken.

"Lucinda sent for me. She said there was some trouble, that someone had tried to break in. She thought you might need help setting things right, but I see you've already done it." Molly reached down and helped me up. "Goodness, did you work all night? No wonder you're so exhausted. I rekindled the fire in the stove. There's boiled eggs with toast and tea in the kitchen."

"Thank you, Molly. I'll be ready in a moment." I took

several deep breaths and tried to slow my racing heart. It took me most of the morning before I felt I had regained my composure.

With the shop restored I was able to open to patrons in spite of the broken window. Having the shop full of customers kept me distracted until tea. Molly and I took tea in the narrow kitchen. I was too exhausted to insist on anything formal. Toast, cheese, and jam at the worn table in the corner was enough.

"This note came for you," Molly announced as she placed it on the table. I recognized the badger's head of Peter's seal at once. I quickly ripped the note open and read.

Meet at midnight at the Lion's Gate.

Excellent. Hopefully I would find the answers I was searching for.

It wasn't until I had shut down the shop and Molly had returned home that I realized I had no way of getting to Peter's house. It was very late and bitterly cold outside. I didn't trust hailing a cab at so late an hour, not on my own. It simply wasn't safe.

I had to reach Peter's house somehow. I didn't have time

to waste. My grandfather was out there, and Rathford had probably known where he was. I buttoned my heavy coat and secured my bonnet, then wrapped a thick shawl around myself. I wished I could hide my silhouette to avoid attention from men in the street, but I couldn't dress myself as a man, so I had to hope that the dark and cold would keep most people off the streets between the toy shop and St. James.

I decided to take a chance.

With my keys in hand I pushed through the door and turned to lock it. A hand grasped my shoulder.

I spun and screamed at the man behind me.

"Easy, Meg. It's me." Will stood there, though he looked much less Scottish without his kilt. Instead he wore simple dark trousers and a heavy coat.

"Oh, thank heaven." I embraced him, then quickly locked the door. "Scare me like that again, and—"

"And you'll what?" Will smiled, full of mischief.

"Never you mind. Trust that my revenge would be swift and horrible." I cuffed him on the shoulder. "Did Peter send you a note as well?"

"Of course," Will said as we started off down the street. During the day the wide avenues and shop fronts had been bustling with people and the spirit of holiday cheer. Now that the deep part of the long winter night had settled over Mayfair, the cheer was gone, and a sense of desolation and cold misery set in that the holidays could not quell. Will stepped closer to my side. "I had intended to visit the shop so we could make a plan, but Lucinda mentioned she had sent Molly to help you, and I didn't want to rouse any suspicion."

I let out a breath that turned to mist and curled around my face. "I'm glad you're here now," I said as I wove his fingers with mine.

A bony old horse with a low-hanging neck and a deeply swayed back pulled a knacker cart. The driver looked equally bent as he listlessly snapped the reins and the horse plodded forward with weary steps that rang against the street. The image from my dream still haunted me. Over the course of the last year, I'd found myself in danger more times than I could count. Will had almost lost his life on several occasions, and the thought had the power to stop my heart cold. A year ago I hadn't thought of the consequences. Now they invaded my mind even in sleep.

And in spite of all that, I was still glad he was with me.

As we entered St. James, we walked beneath the tall London plane trees, with their branches dusted in a fine white snow. Occasionally the muddled conversation of a holiday party would escape the confines of the elegant homes with their high garden walls, and reach the street.

Finally we arrived at a large townhome surrounded by a thick stone wall. On either side of the gate stood bronze lions with glistening black eyes. One lion peered at the street, the other watched the courtyard. I knew of the device within Rathford's workshop that allowed him to see through the eyes of the lions. Perhaps Peter was watching for us. I waved at the statue facing the street, but the house remained quiet and still. Peter had told me he had intended to tinker with the lions to increase their function as a security device. Perhaps he could hear us now.

"Peter?" I called. "Are you there?"

The lions remained motionless.

"Now what?" Will asked, gazing in through the wrought iron gate.

"We could always scale the wall," I suggested, even though it would be nearly impossible for me in my dress.

"And contend with those spikes? We're not desperate yet."

And so we waited, and we waited, but time kept slipping by, leaving us shivering in the cold, and there was no sign of Peter. "What time is it?" I asked Will through clenched teeth to keep them from chattering.

He glanced at a pocket watch. "A quarter past one. Something must have happened."

"Well, I refuse to stand out here like a frozen ninny any longer." I inspected the gate. It was locked. We'd have to climb. "Give me a lift up." I found purchase on the foot of a lion, then climbed up onto his knee and found a handhold on a curl of mane behind his ear. If I went over the masonry of the wall closest to his shoulders, I could avoid the black iron spikes along the top of the stone. I didn't wish to get a hem of my skirts caught on one of them.

I turned back toward Will, keeping hold on the frozen bronze. My hands were numb with cold in spite of my gloves. "Are you going to help me or not?"

"I'd call you mad if it weren't a foregone conclusion. We're resorting to burglary?" He folded his hands together even as he said it, and allowed me to place my foot in his palms.

"It's not burglary if we don't intend to do any burgling. This is merely a social call at a very inconvenient hour." I looked back up at the head of the lion as Will lifted his hands, launching me up onto the lion's neck. I folded over the top of it and struggled to gain a hold before sliding my body around over the mane, and scrabbling for a foothold on the other side.

I lost grip on the lion's ear and slid down over the curved

back of the beast. I hit my chin and pushed off from the statue out of some sense of self-preservation, the way one throws oneself from a dangerous horse. Though I tried to catch myself, I landed hard, and my momentum carried me backward until I rested on my bum in a pile of snow.

Will clambered over the lion and jumped effortlessly down on the other side. He offered me a hand.

Boys.

"Let's hope no one notices that dainty impression," he said to me, chuckling as I took his hand and he lifted me to my feet.

"That's not amusing," I said, brushing the snow from my backside. I removed my bonnet so I could shake it out, and I tucked it into the pocket of my coat. While functional, I didn't like how the brim limited the range of what I could see. "Now how will we get into the house?"

"Do you know how to pick a lock?"

I stared at him. "Do you?"

He shrugged. "Let's test the doors. We're going to have to be careful not to wake anyone."

I looked around the familiar courtyard. It seemed like only yesterday that I had stood here on a snowy night much like this one and found the courage to enter the carriage house. It rose above us like a quiet sentinel, with icicles dripping from the roof and the dormant ivy.

Wait, that was it. "We don't have to go into the house at all."

"What are you talking about?" Will said as he rubbed his own arms for warmth.

"There's an entrance to Rathford's workshop in the carriage house." I immediately headed toward the tall stone building, but Will clasped my hand and held me back.

"No, there isn't. I lived in that carriage house, remember?"

"Neither of us could have imagined a secret society just beneath our feet. Of course you wouldn't have noticed a hidden entrance. It would be well concealed.

"When I first discovered Rathford's workshop, I had to walk down a spiral stair, then through a long narrow passage. That passage must have connected to the foundations of the carriage house. Rathford had pieces of machinery that could never have fit down that stair. There has to be another way in, and I believe we'll find it in there." I pointed at the large door.

Will hesitated, unwilling to yield. If I hadn't known any better, I would have thought he was afraid.

That was when I realized what was wrong. "You're not

trapped there anymore," I said gently as I stepped closer to his side and squeezed his hand. "You have a new life now."

He looked down at me, then lifted our hands to his lips and placed a sweet kiss to the back of my gloved hand. "Thanks to you. We'd better go through the back door. The hinge isn't as loud."

We crossed the snowy courtyard, staying in the mush of the paths that had been well trod through the winter. We reached the back door, and Will tested it. It opened easily, and we quietly slipped inside the stable area of the carriage house.

Everything within the stable was completely still and shadowed with silvery shards of moonlight slicing through the narrow windows.

Warmth enveloped me, washing the cold out of the layers of my clothing and waking my frozen hands and feet. I immediately ran toward the old stove in the corner and held my hands as close as I dared to the fat iron belly. They stung as they came awake.

A piercing neigh broke the silence, and I let out a squeak as I jumped back. Old Nick, the sweet brown gelding that Will used to care for, stretched his neck over the door of his box, reaching out for his former groom.

Will crossed to the horse in a flash and enveloped the

horse's large face in a loving embrace against his chest. "Quiet, boy. There's nothing to fuss about," he whispered to the horse as he scratched Old Nick's ears and rubbed his face. The horse nickered in loving greeting and let out a heavy sigh.

The second horse, Little Nancy, had woken and was reaching her head around for affection as well. She squealed in indignation, then tried to nip at Will's sleeve.

Something thumped directly above me. The timbers of the ceiling groaned as footsteps from the small groom's quarters in the loft made their way toward the old wooden stairs to our right.

"Will, hurry," I whispered. He backed into me, and together we turned the corner into the large room that had held Lord Rathford's old landau coach. A more practical calash was standing beside it, but the large landau was still there, only it had been covered with a set of large white sheets that hung nearly to the floor. The horses cried in protest as we left, their voices ringing off the stone with such a sharp pitch, it hurt my ears.

"Under there." I ran to the coach and Will scrambled under the cover. I dove down to join him, but my skirts made crawling impossible. Will grabbed my hands and pulled me to him.

We lay flat on our stomachs beneath the coach, trying to make our bodies as still and small as possible. I didn't dare move as the heat from Will's breath curled over my ear and the side of my neck. There was still a gap of a foot between the sheet and the floor. If we weren't careful, we could be seen.

"Easy, easy," a deep rumbling voice called over the cries of the horses. "What has gotten into the two a you? Wakin' the dead at this hour."

The cries of the horses settled somewhat. Meanwhile our hiding place seemed tenuous at best.

A flare of light stretched over the floor and illuminated the sheet. I froze as the swinging glow from a lantern slowly patrolled between the two carriages. "Something spooked you good," the groom mumbled half to himself as I watched his thick boots pass by the spokes of one of the wheels.

He rattled the latch of the large door at the front of the carriage house. Satisfied it was secure, he turned back toward us.

I felt a tap on my shoulder. Shifting as silently as I could, I perched up on my elbows and glanced at Will. He had placed a finger to his lips, and now pointed to one of the stones only a foot or two in front of us.

Amid the rectangular stones that paved the floor of the

carriage house was one singular round stone, not much wider than the width of Will's palm. Three holes had been bored into it. Will placed his fingers in them and lifted up. The stone gave way. It was only perhaps an inch thick. Will placed it to the side without a sound.

I craned my neck forward as far as I could.

The light from the lantern shifted, illuminating the shallow round pit.

The dim light revealed the seal of the Amusementists.

CHAPTER SEVEN

I PLACED MY HAND OVER THE SEAL SO I WOULD BE ABLE to find it in the dark. Will put an arm over my back and scooted closer as the light from the groom's lantern disappeared around the corner. We heard him tromp back up the stairs, and then everything went still.

We waited, motionless for what felt like forever. I could only hope that the groom had returned to his bed and that he was a heavy sleeper.

The last thing we needed was the housekeeper, Mrs. Pratt, catching me and Will and accusing us of impropriety, again. Only, this time we shouldn't even have been in the carriage house at all. It would defy explanation, if the old woman's heart didn't collapse before we could give one.

We couldn't lie under the coach forever. I turned my head to look at Will. I could barely see him in the dim light.

"What if this wakes the groom again?" I asked.

"Well, we did have an invitation."

I let out a chuckle, and a little rebellion took hold. I felt the medallion, then took my grandfather's master key from around my neck and fitted it into the lock. The key was all I had left of my grandfather, and it had the power to unlock any Amusement, so long as one knew the song it played and could complete the musical phrase the key started.

I listened to the song coming from the key, but I already knew Rathford's musical code by heart. I turned the thin dial around the edge of the seal, playing the notes to release the lock.

Immediately the floor beneath us shuddered with a low rumble. Then it dropped with a sudden lurch. I clung to Will's forearm as the noise reverberated through the carriage house. I could feel the shaking in my bones. We sank deeper and deeper into a pit, taking the large coach with us.

Once we had lowered at least ten feet, we heard another piercing neigh, then a shout. I rolled to the edge of the sheet and peeked up from beneath it. We were now at least twenty feet beneath the ground, and sinking ever faster. The groom stood at the edge of the pit with his mouth agape and his lantern swinging helplessly in his hand.

"Oi, oi!" he shouted, turning this way and that, as if he didn't know where to look for help. A grinding noise of old gears coming to life filled the pit. I had to cover my ears as the hole closed above me. Two dark panels slid together, reforming the floor of the stable and plunging us into darkness.

I felt Will's body crawl next to mine as we continued our descent in pitch black. Then I heard a familiar whirring.

Spinning wheels with flint edges rubbed against strikers, showering sparks in the darkness. It was an eerie sight, like fountains of raining stars.

Braziers beneath the flint wheels caught fire and lit a large chamber deep beneath the carriage house. We were in a room cluttered with the remains of half-formed inventions and large mechanical parts. One of Rathford's mechanical lions lay on his side with a panel in his chest open and parts spilling out. Though I knew in my head it was only a machine, I couldn't shake the feeling I was staring at a dead beast, some poor creature brought low on a safari to prove the manhood of a stuffy blue blood paying to feel the thrill of adventure.

Dust and cobwebs had settled on everything, giving the room a ghostly quality. The platform we were on lowered five more feet, until it became a seamless part of the floor.

As soon as it settled, I scrambled out from beneath the coach, with Will close behind. Looking around, I quickly examined the structure of the gears and rails set into the walls on either side of the platform that we had descended upon.

"It's going to be difficult to explain away a disappearing coach," I said.

"If we put it back, maybe they won't notice it was missing. It's the same mechanism as the lift in the Foundry," Will said, stepping quickly to our left.

"I think it will be difficult to forget watching it sink through the floor. There!" Just beyond him was a large lever. He grabbed it, and I helped him pull. The lever was stiff from lack of use, but together we managed to break it loose.

The floor rose once more. Will and I watched the covered coach ascend the shaft, disappearing into the ceiling. It continued its upward progress until the gears in the lift stopped turning and fell silent.

"Perhaps he'll think this was all a dream?" Will offered.

"I sincerely doubt that." My heart was pounding, and the bubble of laughter began deep in my chest. It felt so naughty to be sneaking around this way, and in this house. I placed my hands over my mouth, trying to hold back my mirth as Will's eyes crinkled in the corners. Then he too joined me in conspiratorial laughter.

I tried to take a few deep breaths to compose myself, but it was no use. "That poor man. He must be certain he's lost his mind."

Will shook with his own forbidden laughter. "Good, he'll fit in with the rest of the servants, then."

That did me in. To keep my balance I had to place my hand against a large gear wheel protruding from a half-constructed engine. "Can you imagine the look on Mrs. Pratt's face when he tells her the coach is gone?"

"It won't be half as good as her reaction when she comes to the carriage house and sees the coach right there." Will took a deep breath and wiped the corners of his eyes. "I don't envy that poor groom."

I did my best impression of the stiff-lipped old house-keeper. "My dear man, do you expect me to believe that a coach could sink through the floor? It's preposterous. Now get back to your bed."

"Uncanny. That's exactly what she said."

I jumped at the third voice in the room and spun on my

heel. Peter stood in the gap of a large sliding partition.

"Peter!" He was still in a nightshirt and dressing gown. His round and youthful face smiled back at me even though his expression was a mix of relief and exasperation.

"I'm glad you both think this is humorous," he said. "It's going to be nearly impossible to get you out of here without suspicion." He crossed the room to Will and offered his hand. "MacDonald, good to see you again."

"I'm sure between the three of us, we'll think of something," Will said. They shook hands, and Will patted Peter on the back. "What took you so long?"

"I swear Mrs. Pratt never sleeps. It's unnerving. She found me sneaking out to meet you," Peter said as he walked back to the partition. We joined him and passed through into the part of the workshop I had explored once before.

"What did you tell her?" Peter wasn't a very good liar. When he was caught in a lie, it showed all over his face.

"I didn't say anything. I started flushing, and Mrs. Pratt thought I was coming down with a fever. She fussed over me for an hour at least. I couldn't get away. She was brewing me some sort of curative when the groom burst into the kitchen in a panic. That's how I knew you were down here." Peter brushed away a veil of hanging webs.

The workshop looked as if no one had set foot in it since the day I had, a year before. The same mechanical clutter filled the shelves behind a large worktable. And the haunting empty bassinet still sat next to the faded armchair in the corner by the tall bookshelves. Spiderwebs had created a new blanket of chilling lace across the top of the small bed.

The thin coat of dust from before had turned to a thick gray blanket coating everything. The smudge from where I had accidentally placed my hand remained on the table next to the machine Rathford had used to spy on everyone in his house. The letter from my grandfather that Rathford had left out for me to read was now missing.

It was disturbing. In some respects Rathford's workshop seemed as if it had frozen in time exactly as he had wished. In other respects, time had eaten away at the space.

"Have you been down here at all since you inherited?" I asked Peter.

"Only once," he admitted. "To be honest, this place unsettles me."

"You should straighten it up and make it yours," Will suggested.

"I would, but the only servant I have who is sworn to the Guild is Tibbs, and he doesn't have the strength left for this kind of work. I couldn't ask it of him," Peter said, drawing his finger through the thick dust on the table. "I wouldn't wish this on anyone."

"If you need help, let me know. If the ship is down from the Foundry, I can get some of the men together. We can take most of this mess back to the storage vaults under the Academy." Will fiddled with a knob on the spying machine.

"I'd appreciate that." Peter leafed through a pile of drawings and diagrams that had been left on the table. "Now, what are we looking for?"

"Rathford left a letter for me to find here on this table. It was from my grandfather and it said something about Rathford being the only one who knew my grandfather was alive. There must have been more correspondence between the two of them. Perhaps another letter has a clue to where my grandfather might have gone." I knew it was foolish, but I continued to search around the spying machine in the hopes that the letter was still near it, even though logically I knew it was no use to search there. Rathford would have collected it and placed it back where it belonged.

Peter nodded thoughtfully, then used a candle to light another lamp before fixing the candle in a holder and turning toward the shelves. "Our task is simple enough, then.

I'll search through these papers here. Meg, you have a very discerning mechanical eye. Why don't you look for hidden compartments where Rathford might have tucked something away, and, Will, you can take the bookshelves."

While Peter and Will both jumped immediately to their tasks, I needed a moment to think. From what I knew of Rathford, he was the kind of man who'd kept everything locked away. Yes, this workshop was hidden, but nearly all the Amusementists had secret workshops that weren't really secret at all.

Rathford didn't trust easily. If I were him, where would I hide things?

I inspected the partition we had come through into the main room of the workshop. I hadn't even noticed it the first time I'd been in this room. It created the illusion of a solid wall.

The backs of my ears tingled. That was it.

I leaned through the partition and gazed into the room beyond, then back into the main workshop. The two rooms together were at a right angle to one another, forming a sharp corner. We were beneath the carriage house. One would expect the rooms below to follow the footprint of the building above, which was a stout rectangle.

There had to be a third hidden room.

"Boys," I said, taking several quick steps over to the wall and pressing my bare hand to it. "Look at this. There's another secret room here." The wall had been covered with wood paneling in a pattern of squares carved with intricate molding. I leaned my weight against the table, pushing it back from the wall.

The others joined me and helped to clear away the cobwebs and pieces of machinery leaning up against the wall.

"Do you see anything that could mark a covering for one of the locks?" Will asked.

I scanned the wall, but there wasn't a single round thing in it. The surface almost looked like a woven basket. This was quite a puzzle.

The answer came to me slowly even as my eyes settled on one thin sliver of molding missing from the edge of a panel low on the wall and to the right.

"It's a puzzle." I stepped toward that small missing sliver. If I hadn't been staring so intently, I never would have noticed the slight hitch in the pattern. I ran my fingers over it, inspecting the square panel. Acting on a hunch, I placed my fingers on the edge of the part of the molding that was like all the rest and pulled it toward the nearly imperceptible gap.

It slid and clicked into place, revealing a new gap in the panel with a groove carved into the wood.

"Look here! It's like one of those Russian puzzle boxes." I looked up at Peter, who crouched down next to me and began to feel the wall. "If we find the right method of sliding the panels, it should unlock."

"Now, that is brilliant." Peter slid a piece of the molding from the square above down into the new gap.

This was it. Whatever Rathford was hiding, we would find it here.

Together we worked, testing each piece of wood, finding the places with give and trying new combinations as larger and larger gaps opened up. On three different occasions Will saved us from folly by noticing the pattern of grooves and stopping us from moving a piece of molding or a panel too far, which would have prevented us from moving the next piece.

It was a pattern of careful mind traps. Our movements became a dance, holding the shifting panels of the wall as we slid them around, shifting what was before us, turning something solid into something mutable. It was the sort of task that lit a fire in my mind, a challenge of wit. With patience and observation we defeated every trap, and the puzzle unfolded in our hands.

Dear God, I loved being an Amusementist.

Finally we slid a flat square of a panel over to reveal a hidden latch.

Peter opened the latch, and together we pushed the entire wall of panels to the left.

Will lifted one of the lamps and carried it through the narrow opening.

I followed him into a third room, expecting a cluttered study with mountains of papers lying around, but the room was stark and nearly empty. A single machine took up the majority of the center of the room. A large cut crystal had been set within a framework of smaller crystals and gears. It reminded me of the center framework of Rathford's infamous time machine.

Around the walls, nothing. No bookshelves, no desks with letters, no indication of any correspondence of any kind that would lead us in the right direction. The only furniture at all was a small table in the corner with a rack filled with dozens of crystal tubes.

"This is useless," I muttered, prepared to go back to the main room of the workshop. I'd turn everything in it over until I found what I was looking for. "Come on. Let's search the other room."

"Are you daft? Look at this thing!" Peter exclaimed, standing in front of the massive structure. "It's glorious. I wonder what it does." He held his arms out, then leaned over, closely scrutinizing the various lenses in the framework.

"Who cares what it does? It isn't what we're looking for, and our time is limited." I couldn't hide my exasperation, but Peter ignored it completely. "Will? Are you coming with me?" I asked, but even as I said it, I turned to see him twisting his back and neck for a better view of the innards of the machine.

"What was that?" he said, but didn't bother to extract himself from his contorted position. "Fascinating. There's a very powerful lantern at the heart of this. I wonder how the light from it would project through these lenses."

"Let's light it and find out," Peter proclaimed, grabbing the candle. "Is there oil?"

"Will you two stop this at once?" I shouted. "We don't have time to tinker with this nonsense. We have to find a letter. You can play with this contraption to your heart's content tomorrow."

Will grasped a lever. "This is the winding mechanism here. I don't see a lock." He pumped the lever several times.

Then Peter reached up and touched a flame to the core of the machine.

It began to hum and whirr. A large gear at the base spun as a wispy smoke emerged, filling the room with a sweet-smelling white mist.

"What did you two do?" We were going to burn down the entire carriage house, with us in it.

The flame at the center of the machine grew hot, then turned to bright white light as it flared through the various lenses in a web of bright beams.

I gasped in awe and horror as the ghostly image of Rathford appeared fully formed in front of the machine. He looked so young and haunting as he turned directly to me and smiled. He reached out. Then a voice came from the machine, distant and tinny but distinctly his own and matching the movement of his translucent lips.

"My dear, it's so wonderful to see you."

CHAPTER EIGHT

A SEARING LIGHT BLINDED ME FOR A MOMENT. I COULD feel the heat of it on my face, and I instinctively ducked and turned my back to the machine. Rubbing my eyes, I blinked through the flashes of color floating through my vision. As my sight returned, I nearly screamed in my shock and horror as I watched a very real ghost walk toward me.

She was the perfect likeness of the portrait that hung in Rathford's study. Beautiful and delicate with dark eyes and hair, the deceased baroness floated through the fog. Her translucent hands caressed her swollen belly. She must have been only days from delivering her child.

I watched her, mute and transfixed, as she continued

toward me with a soft and welcoming smile on her full lips. Except for the lack of color in her face, she seemed so real, I expected her to step around me as a normal person would. Instead Rathford's wife continued forward. I took a step back and gasped as the woman made of nothing but smoke and light walked right through me.

I bent over, holding my arms over my middle just to feel I was real. Then I spun quickly, not wanting to miss a single moment of what transpired.

"If I didn't come down here, I would never see you at all," she said. Like Rathford, her voice sounded distant, as if she were speaking from within a glass bottle. "Do you finally have it working?" She kissed Rathford's cheek. He stood and embraced her for a long time.

"This is so strange," Peter commented, stepping closer to the couple as the machine behind us shifted the lenses and made a whirring noise. He waved his hand in front of Rathford's face. The smoke curled in the breeze, making the image waver like a reflection in a pond. "It's as if they are alive, but not."

"I've seen some of the old plans for moving-picture machines, but this is beyond words," Will said even as my eyes began to water. The smoke stung them, or perhaps it was the lingering effects of the bright light.

Rathford leaned back, his gaze taking in his wife's translucent face. The wisps of smoke curled away from her, and her body faded for a moment. The lights flickered, and yet Rathford noticed none of it. "My love, you shouldn't have come down those stairs at all. Are you still feeling faint?" Rathford laid a reverent hand against his wife's belly.

"I'm fine. Whatever came over me passed yesterday. Does your invention function as you had hoped?" She turned and looked up at the machine. "Can it really capture a moment in time?"

"We shall see. I'm testing it now." Rathford placed his hands on his wife's delicate shoulders and gazed up at his creation. I knew the look I saw in his eyes. I knew the hope and the feeling of fullness in his heart that I could so plainly see on his face. It was part of the power of invention, the intoxicating allure of creation. Rathford had been a brilliant man, but the dark temptation of that talent had corrupted him.

"I cannot wait to see what you have done." She turned to face him. "I am so proud of you."

He kissed her hand. "Go upstairs and have your tea. Promise me if you feel weak or faint at all, you will go straight to bed."

"Straight to bed, I promise."

The lights flickered and died, and the ghosts faded into the curling smoke. I felt a heaviness deep in my chest. Rathford had been obsessed with the moment of his wife's death. She had fallen down the stairs after she had spilled her tea in the sitting room. Dear Lord, we had just witnessed their final moment together.

"Well," Peter interjected with an overly cheery voice. "That wasn't disturbing at all, what?"

Will shuddered next to me even as I tried to shake off my lingering horror. That was when it dawned on me. "The other crystal tubes over there on the table, they must be for the machine." Will and Peter met me at the table. We inspected each of the large murky crystals. They were shaped a bit like hexagonal prisms. I held one up to the light shining through the crack in the panel door. Within the crystal were thousands of tiny images, miniature shadows trapped in the glass.

For the life of me, I could not figure how Rathford had printed them within the clear confines of the prism. As I turned the crystal between my fingers, the tiny images shifted like the falling pieces within a kaleidoscope. I turned the prism in the light, and my fingertip brushed against a roughened etching on the flat end of one side. I peered at it more closely. It was a set of faint initials scratched into the surface.

After placing the crystal carefully on the table, I inspected the others. Peter and Will were still marveling at the ones they had chosen, holding them to the light. While they peered into their prizes like fortune-tellers with oddly shaped crystal balls, I felt the ends for etchings. Finally I found one marked with my grandfather's initials. "It's this one."

It took a moment, but Peter discovered the small chamber in the machine meant to hold each crystal in place. It was difficult to work the crystal through the various brass arms. Perhaps there was a section we could open, but we hadn't figured out the mechanism to release it. With the dexterity that had always served him well at the Academy, Peter removed the crystal that showed Rathford and his wife, and replaced it with the one I had selected. Will pulled the lever to wind the machine again.

Fog spilled out from the base of the machine. First it curled over the floor the way mists do in a deadly bog. Then it reached higher, seeking to drown us.

The light flared.

The apparition of Rathford appeared once more, this time bent over the collection of crystals at the table. Peter, Will, and I backed toward the wall to stay out of the way of the haunting projection. Rathford looked much older than he had in the first turn of the machine, his face creased with a heavy sadness that settled in his drooping eyes. He caressed a crystal lovingly and waited, glancing at the sliding door every couple of seconds. He was expecting someone.

A second apparition appeared. My breath left me and refused to return. Like the captain of a valiant sea vessel, my grandfather marched into the room with his head held high and an austere air of command. His chiseled features and smooth bald head gave the impression of a great bird of prey. His winged eyebrows and the piercing intelligence in his silver-gray eyes only added to the effect. He wore charisma like a mantle upon his shoulders. He wasn't the sweet and loving Papa I knew. This was another man entirely.

"Haven't you done enough?" Rathford spat the words. His hunched manner reminded me of a growling dog with his hackles raised. "I'll find the pieces of the plate lock. You can't keep me from what is mine."

"Ulysses. It's over," my grandfather said. I felt a tingling deep in my body at the sound of his resonant voice. Rathford must have made improvements on the crystals, because the voices didn't sound as hollow. "We are not the enemy," my grandfather continued. "We are trying to help you see reason."

"I can have her back." Rathford stood, clenching the crystal in his hand. "I can reach her. I know I can. If I had only been there to lead her up the stair to the bedroom."

"She's gone."

"She will never be gone so long as I live."

"I know how you must feel." Grandfather attempted to place a hand on Rathford's shoulder, but he shrugged away from the touch.

Rathford let out a derisive snort. "Do you? Tell me how you would feel if you were responsible for the deaths of everyone you loved. George. Elsa. What of your precious granddaughter?"

Grandfather grabbed the ghostly Rathford by the throat, and I leapt back, slamming myself against the wall. Will took my hand and squeezed it. This wasn't real. It wasn't happening in the moment. It was all smoke and mirrors. I had to remember that.

My grandfather's gaze turned icy. "Charles told me how you tried to bribe him to return the plates we stole from your lock. Now he is dead. Edgar is as well."

Edgar and Charles had been Amusementists and had helped my grandfather in his endeavors. Their murders almost tore the Order apart.

"I didn't kill them. I swear it," Rathford choked out.

Grandfather released him with a hard shake. For a moment the memory of the way the man in the mask had grabbed the captain on the *Méduse* came to the fore of my mind. "If you ever threaten my family again, the Black Mark would be a blessing," Papa said.

Rathford rubbed his neck. "It wasn't a threat. You claim to have come to help me see reason. Consider it my attempt to enlighten you. I told you before. I don't know who killed either Charles or Edgar. For all I know, it could have been you. You cannot deny that the political winds within the Order are shifting as a result of their demise."

Whatever Rathford was attempting to do, it didn't rattle my grandfather's steely composure. "Murder for the sake of ambition is unthinkable. It goes against everything the Order stands for, and the benefactor's motives would be too transparent. Such a man would be discovered."

"Would he?" Rathford cocked his head. "Or would he need a convenient scapegoat?"

With that, the first flicker of doubt crossed my grandfather's face. "Know this. If an attempt is made on my life, I will disappear and I will do everything within my power to stop this madness."

"You think Pensée will hide you?"

Papa seemed startled at Rathford's observation. I came away from the wall. *Pensée*. It was the clue I was looking for. French. A flower. A pansy.

My papa cleared his throat. "Please, Ulysses. Your obsession will consume you until the day it takes your life."

"So be it," Rathford proclaimed.

Papa's striking silver eyes narrowed as they swept up and down the ruined shell of the other man in the room. "I refuse to believe it is too late for you." Without saying another word, Papa walked back out through the door, and the apparitions faded away.

I continued to watch the smoky room, waiting for the men to reappear and tell me more. Secretly I wished for another glimpse of my grandfather, but the light within the machine died as the cogs and wheels wound to a stop.

"That was certainly more dramatic than a letter," Peter said as he covered a cough.

"This is no time to jest," I scolded. "Pensée. Do you know what he was referring to?"

"Haven't the slightest." Peter waved his hand in front of his face, then slid the door open wider and motioned us to go through. We closed the door to smother the last of the smoke, and I found myself staring with new and tragic understanding at the bassinet tucked against the arm of Rathford's old chair. I had to let it go. I only hoped that Rathford had finally found peace and a way back to the love he had lost.

"We need to find the first letter, the one that Rathford left out for me," I said. I had to be sure. It had been a long time since I'd read it.

"Is this the one?" Peter said, pulling a letter from the pile of papers he had been searching before we'd discovered the secret room.

I skimmed over the words again and again, to be certain I hadn't missed anything. It was horrifyingly vague. The only bit that pertained to my grandfather's disappearance said very little at all. I read it aloud for the sake of the others.

"It says here, 'I shall disappear in earnest. I find being dead has certain uses. As you are the only one who knows I am indeed alive, if anyone searches for me, I shall know you are the one who betrayed us. The matter of the traitor will be settled.'"

"That gives us very little to go on," Will said. "Your grandfather didn't confirm that he was indeed going to this Pensée."

"Yes, but *'pensée'* is French," I said. "If my grandfather

did travel to France, he may have met with an old enemy while he was there." When the man in the clockwork mask had captured me, there'd been no mistaking the hatred burning in his one human eye. Whatever grudge he held against my family, it was deeply personal.

"The man in the clockwork mask has been traveling to and from France. It is enough of a connection to make it worth investigating." I took another glance at the letter, as if something invisible might appear between the neatly written lines to show me the right path. "I can search through the historical records in my workshop easily enough and see if I can discover what this Pensée is."

I glanced at Will, and he took my hand. "It's near dawn. We must be going," he said.

I nodded. This place held too many ghosts.

"One thing, Meg," Will added.

"What is it?"

Will's brow knit into a starkly serious expression. "Should we find your grandfather, remind me to never make him cross."

CHAPTER NINE

WILL AND I NEEDED TO HURRY. IT WAS DANGEROUSLY near morning, and Mrs. Pratt was known to be an early riser. Her constant scrutiny had been difficult enough when I had worked as a housemaid. I didn't wish to face her wrath now, or worse, her disappointment in my moral character. The last thing we needed was for her to raise some sort of alarm with Peter's parents. Then Oliver would have to step in to save my reputation, but by that point it would be well past repair.

Peter braved the cold in his dressing gown. "Take care, both of you. Let me know what you discover." He opened the gate even as he looked back over his shoulder toward the house.

"We will," I promised as Will slipped through the iron bars. I followed after him. At last we were free from the shadow of Rathford's house.

Will and I maintained a brutal pace back to the toy shop. In spite of all I wished to say to Will about what we had discovered, I found I could barely speak, simply because I had no wind to do so. Instead I concentrated on placing one foot before the other as fast as I could bear.

At the threshold Will gave me a quick kiss to the cheek with the promise to return, then ushered me into the shop and continued on his way as quickly as we had come.

I took a minute to catch my breath, placing my palm on my counting desk to steady myself. If I weren't careful, I'd faint dead to rights. Finally my exertion waned, leaving me with the lingering excitement from sneaking in and out of the Rathford house without getting caught.

Simon Pricket's journals were waiting for me in my workshop, and I knew without a doubt they would hold the answer I was searching for. I reached for the hidden latch on the shelves.

"Oh, good morning, miss," Molly's cheerful voice greeted me as she came in through the door that led to the sitting room. "I see you are up bright and early, which is good because the glaziers will be here first thing to repair the window. Then we have to open." She gave me a bright and far too eager smile.

I was so thankful that Molly hadn't come in a minute sooner to discover Will at the door. I paused.

"I beg your pardon?" I had no intention of opening the shop, even though it had finally been set right. The window was still boarded up. Once the glaziers fixed the window, things would be normal but I was too exhausted to open.

"Today is Christmas Eve." Molly's tone implied my sanity had cracked. "We can't disappoint the children."

I had never felt such an urge to be completely blasphemous. *Dear Lord, why did you choose this night of all nights for your birth?* It would be the busiest day for the shop all year, and I didn't feel prepared. My mind was on too many other things.

"Yes, of course." I'd have to make do as best I could.

The day passed by in a torturous blur. All I wanted was to slip through the secret door hidden behind the shelves. Instead I had to straighten the items on the shelves over and over as anxious customers accosted my merchandise, panicked that they would not find a suitable gift for their child.

If that weren't horrible enough, I was so tired, my hands

kept trembling, and I nearly fell asleep in the middle of calculating a man's order. I couldn't concentrate on the numbers. Figures that should have been second nature to me were a struggle against my lack of sleep.

And the noise—oh, heavens, the noise.

By the time I finally ushered the last of the customers from the shop, my ears were ringing, my patience spent, my eyes burning, and my wits completely gone.

I told Molly that she could have Christmas Day off, and then promptly closed and locked the heavy doors and set the alarms. I looked with longing toward my workshop, but I could barely stand.

I needed to heed my limitations.

And so I let Pensée wait until morning.

As I fell into bed, the soft feather mattress embraced me, sinking me deep into the warmth and comfort of my small but cheerful room. Sleep like death took me, and I didn't wake until I heard the church bells pealing.

I sat straight up, then fell back into my bed. Strands of my hair fell against my cheeks and eyes.

Christmas Day.

The old urge to leap from bed and run down the stair stirred deep within me. It was as if I couldn't escape the ephemeral joy that had marked my childhood—the gifts, the food, the songs I'd played on the pianoforte with awkward learning fingers alongside my mother's. Her hands used to dance across the keys with merriment, deftly covering my enthusiastic mistakes.

And the scent of such a morning! Succulent roasting bird, breads, puddings, crumbling biscuits, and spiced cider; sometimes I felt I could sustain myself for a year on the smell alone.

My papa and my father would both be dressed perfectly for church, and I would come down in my finest with my hair done up, and they would treat me as if the young queen had entered the room.

As I rested my head on my pillow, the air around me smelled cool and vaguely like the dust and dying smoke that still clung to my hair. No laughter drifted up from the house below, only the distant ringing of bells calling London to rejoice and sing.

With a sigh I sat up once more, and washed in the cold water left in the basin from the night before. It didn't matter. I had a task to do. I had to find Pensée.

I was running out of time. I only had six days left before the start of the New Year, when the man in the clockwork mask sailed beyond my grasp.

My hair was still damp as I finished tying it into a braid while descending the stair. The hearth would be cold, and I needed my tea. I had not yet shaken my sluggishness from not sleeping at all the previous night.

I had my head tucked as I entered the sitting room, so I could tie my braids into a knot and pin them at the base of my neck.

"Merry Christmas, Meg." Will's clear voice greeted me.

My heart leapt into my throat as I looked up. The fire burned cheerfully in the hearth, and a steaming pot of tea sat like a fat partridge beside sliced apple cake and fresh cream.

I brought my hand to my chest, for I felt my heart would either stop or burst. I wasn't sure which.

"I made the cake myself, so it might be a bit dry." Will looked up at me from under his heavy lashes as he twisted his cap in his hands.

"Oh, Will." My heart fluttered. It truly did. I had always assumed that was only a turn of phrase. "This is the best present anyone has ever given me," I whispered.

He held my hand as we sat and enjoyed the tea and cake. We were taking terrible risks. He was visiting the shop far too freely, and . . . "How did you get in here?"

Will had the decency to look sheepish. "Lucinda was

worried about your being alone, so she sent me to watch over the house. She lent me a key."

I furrowed my brow at him, and he held up his hands. "It was not my idea. I was following orders."

"Lucinda should know better," I said. Oliver suspected David was plotting to ruin me. His wife would actually manage the task one of these days if I weren't careful.

"Lucinda has always done things in her own fashion." Will smiled at me, a wicked grin.

"She also tends to act from her heart and not her head." My position demanded more temperance. Will didn't respond to the slight rebuke toward my dearest friend.

"What have you discovered of Pensée?" he asked.

"Nothing yet. We can look in the workshop." I opened the secret panel, and we went inside. Will lit the lamps as I pulled down several of the journals I had neatly organized on three tall bookshelves. The books I had chosen had been written by Simon Pricket when he had been in training to maintain the archives for the Amusementists. His personal writings were often both thorough and enlightening when it came to the history of the Order.

Will sat in the chair at the desk, leaving the softer armchair in the corner by the bookshelves for me. I was able to skim most of the pages. I had read them all at various points during my lessons over the summer, and Simon Pricket's handwriting was as familiar to me as my own.

Will's pages turned much more slowly as his brow crinkled in concentration. Simon's tight and slanted hand must have been difficult for him to read, but he kept on diligently.

"You have learned so much in such a short time," I commented as I closed the book I was currently looking over.

"All thanks to you. If you hadn't come to the carriage house, I would still be there, serving Peter as his groom now, and I wouldn't be able to read this at all." His gaze locked to mine, as serious as the hand of death. "I can never repay you for that."

"If you hadn't helped me that day, I would still be there trapped as a housemaid," I said. "You had your own part to play in all of this." I didn't know if Will really understood what he had done for me. If I were ever brave or bold, it was only my attempt to live up to his regard.

Will shook his head as he turned another page and inspected the writing there. "That's not true. You came to that house like a firebrand. It wouldn't have taken long, but you would have opened the key yourself. You discovered

Rathford's letter on your own, and you would have found a way with or without me. No cage can ever hold you."

I could feel the heat in my face as his words worked their way into my heart. "And I would have died five times over in the attempt." I stood and returned my book to the shelf, then joined him at the desk. I placed my hand on his forearm, drawing his attention back to me. "I still owe you my life."

He covered my hand with his and gave it a squeeze. "You owe me nothing. It seems you have quite the pedigree," he commented. I looked down at the page he had been inspecting. It was a list of members of the Order alongside the personal marks they used in correspondence and as a stamp on the Amusements they'd had a hand in creating.

I recognized many more names from the list than I had the first time I'd looked at it, but it was still out of date. When I became a full member of the Order, I'd have my own mark, a design of my own creation. I didn't know what it should be.

My eye was drawn to the inked-out smudge at the bottom of the list. I suspected the name Richard Haddock lurked beneath it.

The spiral motif that served as Haddock's mark lingered next to the blacked-out name on the page. I had seen

Haddock's mark once, on the bomb the man in the mask had left for me.

I still did not know the full extent to which my grandfather was involved with the Haddock scandal or how the man in the clockwork mask may have been involved.

The black mark on the page filled me with frustration and I turned back to my chair in the corner.

Will continued to peer at the page, then leaned in as his eyes pinched with focus. "Does *pensée* mean anything in French?" Will asked.

"It means 'thought,'" I answered automatically. "Or it could mean 'pansy.'"

"Are pansies the little flowers with the dark masks in the center?" Will asked, lifting the book from the desk and holding it in his hands. I joined him at his side.

There, deep in the list of marks, was a clear and unmistakable pansy. I took the book from Will's hands and drew my trembling finger across to the name that accompanied the mark.

Maurice Durant.

"Durant. I haven't heard of this name in the Order, have you?" I handed the book back to Will. He shook his head.

"No. His name comes well before the names of either of

your grandfathers. He must be from the generation before theirs. Did Simon Pricket do any genealogy?"

"He did." I turned back to the bookshelves and found the correct journals on the bottom shelf. "He spent some time tracing family connections and how they affected the political power structure in the Order. I suspect it was part of the reason Strompton murdered him. I think Simon may have discovered that Strompton had been playing Macbeth."

"What does clan Macbeth have to do with this?" Will looked at me, baffled.

"Never mind. It's a play. The answer to your question is, yes. Pricket has some elaborate family trees. . . . Here."

I pulled the books out onto the floor, and Will joined me there. We opened the journals containing pages and pages of branching family trees.

"If Rathford believed your grandfather would seek out Durant, they had to be connected somehow. Check your own family tree," Will said.

I found it and traced the branching roots up through the family I had known. It was sad to me that so few births had left me the last lingering twig on the dying tree. However, as I traced it up past my grandfather, I found the name I was looking for.

"Maurice Durant was my grandfather's mother's cousin." I felt the swell of hope.

"If he's not already dead, he must be ancient," Will said as he stacked up some of the books.

"During the argument, Rathford didn't sound as if he were talking about a person. It sounded as if he were talking about a place." It still wasn't making sense.

"Could it be a family home?" Will ran his finger over the spines of the other journals on the shelf.

"Yes, Pensée could be the name of an estate. But how are we going to find a single house that could be anywhere in France?" Or Belgium for that matter, or parts of Switzerland. Dear Lord.

"If Pensée is an Amusementist estate from an old family, then chances are likely it has some sort of Amusement on the grounds like so many of the estates here. If we can find any mention of Durant in Simon Pricket's histories, perhaps there will be a clue to where he lived." Will selected one of the journals and pulled it down into his lap. He opened it to a sketch of the inner workings of the clockwork Minotaur we'd discovered on the abandoned Tavingshall estate.

"Will, you're brilliant." I pulled more and more books down into the pile between us, and we set to work.

As the hours wore on, Will brought the tea in and we snacked on the apple cake as we continued with our task. Right about noon I discovered what we were looking for.

"Here it is!" I inched over next to Will so he could see it too. It was the only mention of the name Durant we could find. "He created a large observatory in his home." I skimmed over the description of the lenses until I came across the single sentence that confirmed everything.

I sent a quick prayer of thanks to the ghost of Simon Pricket for his unceasing attention to detail. I pointed to the words as Will studied them.

While Calais proved easily accessible to the Foundry ships, the real challenge for moving the lenses became the journey to Ardres and the final installation at Pensée.

CHAPTER TEN

"CALAIS IT IS, THEN," WILL SAID AS HE GATHERED THE books and placed them indiscriminately on the shelves. "We can take the train to Dover, and then cross the channel from there."

I stopped him by placing a hand on his forearm. "It isn't so simple. It's Christmas. Passage across the channel will be hopelessly booked with people traveling to Paris for the New Year, and the weather is unpredictable. We can't take the risk of being caught in Dover for a week. We only have six days before we must return for the oath." The tides felt like they were turning against me, and the ship I was on could only struggle uselessly against them.

On the one hand, this was the link I'd been hoping for, a clue that might lead me to my grandfather. On the other, years had passed since my grandfather had left for Calais. Maurice Durant could be alive, but it was quite possible he was deceased. We might travel to Calais only to find ghosts.

Even so, time was running out. If I didn't discover where the man in the clockwork mask was hiding before the *Méduse* crossed the Atlantic, the consequences would be dire.

But there were consequences either way. We'd never make it back to London to take the oath.

What was my apprenticeship worth to me? Acceptance at the Academy was something I had never expected. It had taught me things about myself I would have never learned, about strength, tenacity, and courage.

I didn't want to give that up, but when I closed my eyes, all I could think about was the quiet moments when I'd rested my head against my grandfather's chest as a little girl and listened to the rumble of his voice as he'd hummed. It was home.

Not walls, not clocks or wealth, or the trappings of middle-class convenience. My family was my home.

I had to find my grandfather. If it had been me captured and held against my will, he would have stopped at nothing to find me. I would do the same. It was what I had set out to do, and I would see it through to the end. Any strengths or talents I had would come with me, and if there were prices to pay, they would never equal my grandfather's life. He was worth more to me, always. "So be it," I said to myself, certain of my course.

"I'm going to find him," I whispered. I had no other option.

"We'll do our best." Will gathered a new set of books and shelved them.

His words reached my heart even as it felt as if it had fallen to the floor. "Will, you shouldn't come with me."

"Of course I'm coming with you." He rose and offered me a hand. I took it and let him pull me toward him. "Are you still worried about your reputation?"

"I'm worried for my reputation only so much as any scandal would be an excuse to remove me from the Academy. If we aren't successful, then that becomes irrelevant, since we won't be able to take the Oath. Beyond that, I'm quickly coming to the conclusion that I don't care what people think of my moral standing any longer. They will assume the worst anyway." I let out a deep breath. Saying that thought aloud was freeing. "They don't know me, and they don't know the truth."

"I do," Will said with conviction. "Don't tarnish yourself with such talk."

"Do you believe it tarnishes me?" I asked. I felt a sharp jab deep in my heart.

"No," Will said. "Not in my eyes. But living with scorn is difficult. Trust me. I should know."

Will had paid the price for his gypsy blood in terrible ways. Now that he had reclaimed his life, I didn't wish to take that from him.

"You must be here for the oath. If I lose my position as an apprentice, that is a sacrifice I must make for the sake of my grandfather. You have no such duty to loyalty." I placed my other palm over his heart, holding a slight distance between us, even as I reveled in the connection of our hands. "I can't let you sacrifice all you have gained."

He drew both my hands together over his heart and pressed his warm palms protectively over mine. I stared at our fingers intertwined.

"I do have a duty to loyalty," he said. "I'm not going to let you face a murderer on your own. We started this together, and we'll finish it together."

"I've read your letters. I know your desires plainly—a home, a family, safety. That's what the Foundry is for you. It's what you've always wanted." I couldn't bear to look him in the eye. I feared it would break my heart. He reached up and tucked a lock of hair behind my ear.

"I wanted to be able to make a future for us. I know now that we can, with or without the Order." His fingertips brushed the shell of my ear. "I'm no longer a stable boy who can barely read a sign in the road, and you are so much more than the penniless girl who first came through Rathford's gate."

"I'm still penniless," I argued. The man in the clockwork mask had made certain of that. As for the alleged Whitlock fortune, I had yet to see any evidence that it was real.

"You're a fine shopkeeper, and I would make a decent blacksmith." He gave me a soft smile. "Between the two of us we will make our way as best we can, if the future is kind."

I remembered making a similar argument to him on a distant moor. It seemed so long ago, when I had been swept away by adventures and drunk on all the feelings I had believed were love.

Now I knew so much more. I looked at Will, and my heart was breaking, not for me but for him. "I can't ask this of you. I won't." For the first time, I knew that what we felt for each other was something so much more than selfish and childish infatuation. I could not ruin what he had built. He meant everything to me.

"This is my choice," he said. "I'm with you to the end. Always."

"Oh, Will." I leaned into him. He held me, and my words were lost. My heart was lost. His embrace was tender, but I felt safe and cherished in his arms. He pressed his forehead to mine, and we held one another in the quiet seclusion of my workshop.

"Two tickets for Dover, then?" he asked.

I shook my head. "If only there were a faster way to France. What I wouldn't give for Albrecht's airship."

"It's a pity you crashed it into the lake," Will said.

"That wasn't my fault!" I protested. "Still, we'd have much better chances of making it to Calais and back before the Oath if we had our own means of transportation across the channel. We could be in Calais by nightfall."

Will's eyebrows crinkled together as a thoughtful scowl crossed his features. He glanced at the door. "There might be a way, but we need to go to the docks."

"Do you know of a ship that can make the crossing?" My heart surged with hope. We could go to Pensée and be back before the New Year.

"Not a ship, no," Will answered. "But if rumors are true, there might be something better."

Together we hastily packed some supplies and made our way across London to the docks near the old monastery that served as the Academy and central meeting place for the Amusementists. In spite of the cold, Mayfair was alive with Christmas cheer. Fine women and men bundled in fur-lined cloaks and neatly brushed top hats strolled the streets, bearing gifts and greeting friends and strangers alike with laughter. They hung holly boughs and wreaths on the doors as they invited one another in to share in their good cheer.

A small gathering of people sang carols in front of a bookshop while a young boy sold mistletoe to a cluster of young girls. The air was heavy with the combined scents of rich feasts from every hearth, as the smoke curled up into the brisk air.

I felt so awful that my own shop, the one that should have been bright and alive, had become so dreary. It was closed and shuttered on this, the happiest of nights.

As we traveled deeper into the city, those with less kept their revelry hidden within narrow doors and dark streets, if they had anything with which to celebrate at all.

A tiny girl in rags sold matches on the corner, huddled

under a shawl that had been worn through. I stopped our cab, and though the driver looked at me as if I had lost my mind, I gave the girl my heavy shawl and what was left of the apple cake that I had bundled into our pack.

Will smiled but didn't say a word. I returned to the cab and leaned against him for warmth.

On the docks the ships rose and fell with the lazy swells of the river. Icicles clung to mooring ropes. I watched a pair of men hunched under thick coats rhythmically knock ice off the bow of a ship. Will kept his head down and led me along. Desperate people with hungry, suspicious gazes watched me from dark corners as we reached an empty dock. Will glanced over his shoulder, checking to see if anyone was following us, before grabbing me and tucking me next to a large crate covered with netting.

"What are you doing?" I asked. I couldn't help feeling unsettled. The last time I'd been here, I had nearly been caught by the man with the mask.

"Hush," Will whispered. Then he clanged a bell attached to a large wooden post.

I tugged my coat more tightly closed across my chest and we waited. The cool stench permeating the air felt as if it were clinging to my skin.

"I hope he's here." Will gazed expectantly at a large iron cleat. Next to it a ginger striped cat slept in a coil of rope. I wondered if the poor creature was dead. The snow had settled on its fur and hadn't melted.

To my surprise the cat suddenly stood with a rigid, almost mechanical motion, then blinked open black marble eyes and meowed.

Will stooped to the cat and said, "It's about time. We're freezing out here. Let us in, will you?"

The cat stretched its neck up, and I noticed the gear wheels turning beneath its worn fur. One ear twitched unnaturally. The cat howled out another cry that sounded suspiciously like "Word now?"

"Lake fire," Will answered automatically.

The cat settled back into his original position in the coil of rope. Meanwhile the front of the crate creaked open. Will opened the crate farther and motioned me in. "Quickly."

We ducked inside, and Will shut the crate. He held my arms, and the crate shook. I clutched Will's coat as the floor sank, and we disappeared into the dark.

The platform we crouched on stopped suddenly, and a door opened into a small room. Along most of the walls were intricate controls with large levers and gauges. They made the room look like the inside of a clockwork engine. I recognized one of Rathford's spying machines near the corner, but not the man standing near it.

He had the darkest brown skin I had ever seen and a flashing smile framed by two large muttonchops. A faded red knit cap flopped at an angle across his smooth high forehead.

"William MacDonald, come to bring me a Christmas present?" the man teased as he shook Will's hand. I didn't know what to say. He turned his warm gaze to me. "Cat got her tongue? I suppose she's never seen an Irishman," he said, then burst into deep belly laughter.

"Meg, I'd like you to meet John Frank. He's one of the most trusted members of the Guild, and in charge of operating the lock systems that help the Foundry steamships dock at the Academy."

I knew a couple of Guild members. Like the Foundry workers, they were essential to the functioning of the Order. Most Guild Members were essential servants of the Amusementists who had also sworn to the Order's secrecy. I had always been curious who was responsible for the water chamber lock that allowed the steamship from the Foundry to sink beneath the Thames and hide deep in the catacombs under the Academy.

John Frank reached a hand out. He'd cut the fingertips off his gloves. "So this is the infamous Miss Whitlock. Pleasure to meet you."

I took his hand and shook it. "I'm infamous? Whatever could I have done to earn such a reputation?"

"From what I hear, love, you've done quite a lot. You destroyed a castle, broke several casks of wine in the cellars, crashed an airship—"

"None of which was my fault!"

He held up one long finger to silence me. "You also saved the Foundry, and several of my close friends." He smiled again. "Now, what brings you to my humble control room?"

"We need your help," Will said. "Some time ago I heard a rumor in the Foundry about a tunnel. Some of the men still talk about the challenges of the construction. From what I heard, it sounded as if the tunnel went beneath the channel. I figured if anyone knew anything about it, you would."

"Thinking of sneaking off to France?" he asked. "It would be less trouble to take the train back to Inverness if you want to elope, though I admit France is probably more romantic."

"We are searching for my grandfather," I said with a fair

amount of impatience. "There may be information about his whereabouts in Calais."

"I knew Henry well. He always treated the Guild members with respect, not as though he were above us at all. He knew there weren't nothing that happened within the Order without the Guild and the Foundry making it so. He was a good man." There was an earnest quality in his expression. "You believe he's alive?" John asked.

"I do, but we don't have much time." I deeply hoped he could help.

"Come, come. Sit. We'll talk." John ushered us through a narrow door into a small room with a table and a bed, and a cheerful fire burning in a small hearth. He pulled out a chair for me like a gentleman. Will took a seat beside me.

"There *is* a tunnel. It was many years in the making, started during the wars with France. The Amusementists wanted a secret way to bring people from the Continent to London and back. But it was too dangerous. Early on there were collapses during the digs. Several good men lost their lives.

"When Edgar took over the project, the tunnel was finally finished, and even the track were laid. But with Edgar's murder during those dark times, everyone went into hiding and the tunnel was never revealed."

"But it was completed?" I asked. "There's a way through?"

"Oh, the tunnel went through all right. Unfortunately, it's been, what? Five years now? No one knows the condition of the tunnel or the tracks. I was given the task of inspecting them come springtime, but they are likely in a sad state of repair."

"Is there any other way we could get to France?" Will asked.

John let out a heavy sigh. "Not if you need to get there quickly."

"We only have until the New Year to discover what happened to my grandfather." I needed some other way to convince him. "If we find him, he will become head of the Order when Octavian steps down. If we don't find him, chances are likely the Earl of Strompton will take his place."

John's entire demeanor changed. "That pup knows nothing. His arrogance is as bad as his father's was. He won't heed the concerns of the Guild. He treats us all as if we were his personal footmen." John watched the fire a moment, then turned and considered me. "If Henry is not found, the next head of the Order might be you."

"I sincerely doubt the others would allow that. But if it should happen, wouldn't it be lovely to have me in your eternal debt?" I gave him my most winning smile. "And should we find my grandfather, wouldn't it be even more lovely to have him owe you a favor?"

John chuckled, then spoke to Will. "Be careful with this one. She's dangerous." He rose and dumped a kettle of water over the fire. The flames hissed as they died in a plume of curling smoke. "Very well. I like to get ahead on large projects. We can inspect the track together. I'll take you as far as I can, but I can't guarantee we'll make it through."

I rose with Will, my excitement carrying me forward. I almost didn't hear John whisper as he lit a lamp, "That is, if we even survive."

CHAPTER ELEVEN

WE FOLLOWED JOHN INTO A NARROW PASSAGE AND THEN down a long spiraling stair. It ended at the large dock chamber deep beneath the ground in the catacombs.

I had been here before when the steamship from the Foundry had docked to make deliveries to the Academy, but I had never seen the chamber so dark. The light from John's lantern seemed lost in the enormity of the room. The hull of the steamship rose out of the darkness like a mountain above a black fog.

Faint memories of being attacked in this place came back to me, and suddenly I felt wary. I curled my hand into a tight fist to soothe the memory of the injury I had sustained in my attempt to escape.

Will moved closer to me but stayed a step behind, so I could walk between both men. It was such a small gesture, but it meant I didn't need to worry about being grabbed from behind.

To one side of the massive lock was a canal with a gondola floating on the black water. A man in a long dark cloak stooped in the back of the narrow vessel. The light from the swinging lantern flashed over his face, and I saw clockwork gears embedded in his cheek.

I screamed.

Will immediately pulled a knife and put an arm in front of me.

"Hey, now. No need for that," John said, jumping into the boat. "Charon isn't going to hurt you. He only looks like death." John reached over and knocked on the cloaked figure's face. I heard the distinctive *ting, ting, ting* of metal beneath the hood of the black cloak. The cloaked figure didn't move.

Oh, thank goodness. It was an automaton.

Once the panic receded, I realized the mechanical ferryman was leaning on a large oar. The passageway was arched overhead, but the ceiling felt so low, I ducked as I took John's hand and he helped me into the boat.

"This tunnel used to be used for overflow from the

lock," he said. "When the Amusementists rebuilt the catacombs, I suggested they extend the tunnel so the Guild could use it."

Will took the seat beside me as John climbed out, untied the moorings, and then turned a large wheel next to the dock. He pulled hard on a lever, then jumped back into the boat.

It tipped, and I held on to both rails to steady myself as the boat rocked back and forth, then lurched forward. The swell of water from the bow slapped against the stone docks in waves. The ferryman behind us silently pushed the boat through the canal with his long oar. I could feel the ominous machine hovering over my shoulders, and it kept me ill at ease.

I had known too many automatons, and the ones based on Greek mythology tended to be dangerous. Despite my reservations, the ferryman of the dead managed to behave himself.

The boat came to a stop, drifting up against a second dock. It hadn't been a long trip, only long enough perhaps to cross beneath the Thames. I liked to think we hadn't crossed the Styx.

Will helped me out of the boat, and we found ourselves at a large door that was covered over with heavy steel bars, gears, and metal plates. I peeked back over my shoulder, and Charon lifted his hand in a slow wave.

I didn't wish to linger another moment.

John turned a second wheel at the dock and switched the lever, sending Charon and the boat back the way it had come.

John pressed his hands to certain square plates on the door and slid them along the face, winding and turning the gears as the plates passed in a deliberate pattern. He brought each plate to the center and locked them together like puzzle pieces until the entire door seemed as if it were whirring and spinning.

Once the plates had come together, large bracing bars retracted from the wall and the door swung open under its own power. "This way," John said, lifting his lantern and swinging it as he stepped through the doorway. As I passed through, I glanced over and noticed that the door itself had to be at least a foot thick.

As soon as we were through, it swung closed behind us, sealing us in a long tunnel with only John's swinging lantern to guide us. I could hear the rats screeching in the dark, darting into holes in the mortar as soon as the light reached them, only to scuttle out again once we had passed.

The tunnel itself desperately needed repair. It reeked of mold, and shattered bricks that had fallen from the wall or the ceiling littered the floor. Our footsteps echoed in the endless dark.

"I asked Octavian if we could install braziers down this corridor, but he said there was no need. Hardly anyone uses it," John said, his deep voice filling the darkness and briefly silencing the rats. Perhaps it was best if we continued to talk.

"Where does it lead?" Will asked, taking a chunk of brick from the ground and throwing it as hard as he could down the passage in front of us. It clattered in the darkness, scattering the rats. He squeezed my hand, then threw a chunk of brick again. He knew I hated rats.

"We used this tunnel to help smuggle some of the membership into the Academy during conflicts between England and their homelands. Before we built the canal, we had to climb a stair and then ferry members across the river. It was risky. No one wanted to be caught in the company of a foreigner in a time of war. Being convicted of espionage and consorting with the enemy would mean the hangman's noose. Keep up. We've a long way yet." John marched along, though I hadn't the slightest idea how he could figure how far we had walked.

I didn't wish to linger on discussions of treason to the Crown for being a part of the Order, so I changed the subject. "You said you knew my grandfather."

John didn't take his eyes off the unchanging dark before us, but he answered. "Well enough. He was always involved when land for various projects was being prepared for a build. That's part of why . . ." He looked at me then, the whites of his dark eyes catching the light of the lantern.

"What?" I asked.

"I can't say." He returned his attention to the tunnel again as if he had never said a word to begin with.

"You were about to say it was part of why he worked on the machine his mentor built." I didn't want to say Richard Haddock's name. He had the Black Mark. Breaking the rules of the Order in front of an important Guild member didn't seem wise. "From what I read, my grandfather's mentor tried to defend himself by saying the machine was intended to clear land. Do you know anything more about it?"

"I know we're not supposed to speak of it, not even here in a tunnel where no one could possibly overhear us. Do you understand?" It was a clear warning, and I heeded it.

"Did Henry Whitlock have anyone else who might have been considered an enemy?" Will asked. His question surprised me only for a moment. He was as determined to get to the bottom of the mystery as I was.

"Henry burned a lot of bridges." John glanced at me

again, considered what he wished to say, then spoke. "A lot of beautiful bridges."

I felt heat rise to my cheeks. This was not the first time I had heard of my grandfather's dalliances in his youth. This was not proper discussion when a lady was present.

"Would any of those bridges have resulted in a duel?" Will asked.

"The only man who had enough reason to draw pistols at dawn met his end before he could." John didn't seem concerned. "Once your grandfather married, he behaved as an honorable husband should."

"Well, that is wonderful to hear," I mumbled. "Is there any other reason someone might wish him captured?"

"Captured, no," John said. "It's possible someone might wish him dead because of his position within the Order, but there would be no point in capturing him and keeping him alive."

I felt as if John had dropped a brick into my innards. The man in the clockwork mask had implied that my grandfather was still alive. He acted as if he needed my grandfather for some task. It was my only hope.

Clinging to that hope, I walked faster. It was difficult work keeping pace with the men. They had much longer legs and weren't wearing skirts that weighed nearly forty stone.

We had been walking for a dreadfully long time. It felt as if we could have been halfway to Dover by now. We had to have traveled a couple of miles at least.

"Could someone have taken Henry because they needed his knowledge as an Amusementist? Perhaps they needed him to unlock something," Will said.

"That is a possibility." John lifted his lantern and squinted his eyes. "The Amusementists have many things stored away and hidden, even from each other, but we don't make a habit of locking the Amusements that have been retired, in case someone wishes to borrow parts or study them."

The darkness opened up to an enormous cavern that devoured the light from the lantern. In the deep shadows I could see corroded forms in metal. They waited quietly in the dark: great, terrible beasts and monsters silently watching in the shadows. John lifted the lantern higher. "Take your pick of any of these, for example."

"What is this place?" I asked, stepping out toward the enormous cavern. John grabbed my arm and pulled me back.

"It's an elephant graveyard." He pointed the lantern toward a new tunnel passage ahead of us. "Where old Amusements go to die. Most of the ones you can see are from the old World's Fair competitions."

The darkness made a cruel game of my curiosity. It tempted me with glimpses of finely crafted metal, the occasional stare of a polished eye. It wasn't nearly enough. Exploring machines with my own hands was far more enlightening than studying drawings of them, and this was a treasure trove of inspiration. "Where are we exactly?" I asked, hoping perhaps I could find a way to sneak back in with my grandfather's key at a later date.

"Beneath the Royal Observatory," John answered even as we entered the new tunnel.

Of course. There was a large hill in Greenwich Park. The observatory perched on top of it. It had access to the river and yet was far enough from the center of London to keep from prying eyes. It was the perfect place to hide things.

We entered the new tunnel and made a gradual turn to the right. This tunnel was much wider than the first, and taller. It must have been an access tunnel to the chamber, large enough to move the Amusements to their resting place.

"And here we are," John announced. He placed the lantern on the ground and rubbed his hands together. "Will, if you would, the flint wheel lever is right over there."

Will grasped the lever and pulled it. The raspy whirring

from the wheels filled the silence even as the sparks drove back the persistent darkness.

"Oh my word," I whispered as I blinked from the new flood of light. Before us stood the most exquisite locomotive I had ever seen. A normal locomotive was elegant and complicated enough, but this machine took craft and design to a new level.

Dark copper and bright gold shone through the thin layer of dust and cobwebs that wove among the thick spokes. The drive wheels were taller than I was, with caps larger than my head. Just above the wheels, huge gears wove their thick teeth into the axles and pistons. I ducked down to take a look at the underside of the engine.

I had seen mature trees with less girth in their trunks than the width of the axles. Each part, each gear, each rod, seamlessly came together in a puzzle so intricate and wonderful, I could have stared for a million years and still have something new to see.

"I love this so much," I mumbled to myself as I lifted my head, eager to climb into the locomotive to see how it functioned.

John and Will had gone to the back of the chamber and together turned a wheel. It connected to a machine that took up most of the back wall, save the tunnel that led to another large shadowy chamber. I wondered where it led, possibly to a turntable for the engine. A rattling and clanking racket filled the room as I hurried over to them.

Even beneath his heavy winter coat, I could see the power in Will's back and shoulders as he threw all his strength into turning the wheel. It was a sight to behold, and I felt myself flush.

"Meg, once this is taut, throw the switch there," Will said, his words coming out in puffs through his exertion.

Soon the wheel ground to a halt, and both Will and John grimaced and shouted in their efforts. It took all of my weight to pull down against the switch, but when it finally set into place, the men let go of the wheel.

They took a moment to catch their breath. Then John climbed up a ladder to the left of the locomotive and turned a new set of wheels. A long brass arm moved through the air and fixed over the boiler chamber. Will, without needing instruction, scaled the engine like a cat, swinging himself over rails and opening the boiler in spite of the fact that it probably hadn't been touched in years and was likely corroded shut. He had such an easy way with machines now, as if he understood them intuitively.

I fought with my skirts to reach the step up into the cab. The blasted things were always in my way. The least I could do was check the tender for fuel. We didn't have to go far. With a train traveling through a tunnel beneath the channel, we could be to Calais by nightfall. A small hill of coal waited for us in the tender. It was connected to the firebox with a machine that would pull the coal into the firebox without the use of shovels.

Will swung down into the cab, followed by John, who set his knit cap at an angle.

"Are we ready?" John asked.

"Brace yourselves," Will mumbled under his breath.

"Don't we need to light the fire?" I asked.

"Not yet we don't." John reached up and pulled a large red handle.

The train shuddered, and a resonant moan filled the chamber, followed by the squeal of grinding metal. I turned around to see the entire back half of the chamber collapsing.

No, not collapsing—lowering. It was an enormous counterweight designed to wind the gears.

The train vibrated beneath my feet as Will took another lever and pulled it with all his strength.

The engine surged forward by the power of the

clockwork gears. The massive wheels turned beneath us as the headlight blazed to life, illuminating the long tunnel ahead.

"We're coming, Papa," I said as I held on to the handrail at the door. The wind buffeted me as the golden engine found its stride charging into the darkness.

CHAPTER TWELVE

"OPEN THE FIREBOX. WE NEED MORE AIR FOR THE initial stoke," John shouted over the deafening noise of the train roaring through the tunnel. The wheels clacked against the rails, while the wind rushed through the cab.

I turned the handle on the firebox and pulled open the heavy door. If the outside of the train had been beautifully gilded, the inside looked like the pit of hell. The metal had been heavily charred. The machine that fed coal into the firebox dropped more and more onto the pile. John turned a switch, and a puff of coal dust rose out of the firebox.

"Watch the first flare. If it catches that dust, it can turn nasty," John shouted.

Will touched my arm and forced me back a step before grabbing yet another wheel to the left of the firebox and spinning it. Sparks showered through the firebox, and a ball of flame roared out of the engine. I felt the heat like a wave washing over my face and hands. If I had been any closer, I would have singed off my hair. Will swung the firebox door closed and turned the latch.

"Meg," Will yelled, his voice getting lost in the noise. "We need a spotter. If something's on the tracks, we could derail."

"Right!" I shouted back as loudly as I could, then looked around the cab for a safe perch. Will was more than capable of tending the engine. He was used to dealing with steam engines on the Foundry ship, and taming fire seemed like an inborn talent for him. Between Will and John, they would keep the train moving. I needed to be their eyes.

In the front of the cab was a wall of iron with shining brass pipes flowing over it. Various valves sprouted from the pipes toward the top. Between the pipes, levers and gauges decorated the iron like jewelry, even as the clockwork components of the train wove together seamlessly behind the pipes. The clockwork components spun, whirring with the speed and urgency of the train itself. At the very bottom was the firebox, already radiating heat as the channel beneath the grate in the floor fed it coal.

To the left of the firebox was a small space with a narrow window facing forward so I could see the tracks before us. There wasn't much room but I would be able to see straight along the boiler engine to the tunnel beyond. I bound up my skirts as best I could around my legs and climbed up into the space. The only problem was the window on the side of the cab. I wedged myself against a narrow riveted strip of metal next to the open window. If I wasn't careful, I could fall backward out of it.

I grabbed on to a long pipe running up through the corner of the cab and held on as the wind tore at my hair with frantic urgency.

The train was traveling at an unnatural speed. The clockworks must have had something to do with it. Holding on to the brass bar with one hand and pushing my hair out of my face with the other, I peered dutifully into the tunnel illuminated by the enormous beam of light coming from the headlamp.

It washed the tunnel immediately in front of the train in a bath of light, but beyond that lay the constant darkness. There was nothing ahead. Surely we weren't about to travel all the way to Dover underground.

Something flickered up ahead, then flashed. A light, but it wasn't the end of the tunnel. It wasn't steady enough.

We were coming up fast on something and I didn't know what it was.

With my stomach twisted in knots, I shouted, "There's something ahead. A flashing light."

"That's the signal," John called as he too grabbed hold of one of the brass pipes. "Better hold on. This might be rough."

I braced myself. Will climbed up in the back and held on to a bar. The tunnel walls that had been made of large dark bricks changed as we flew past a swinging mirror. The bricks seemed to melt away into enormous clockwork gears. The gears turned, spinning faster and faster as we barreled through the tunnel. The motion of the gears created a strange visual illusion. The tunnel looked as if it were shifting and twisting unnaturally.

Suddenly a light opened up before us. It began as a crack in the darkness and then widened, the power of it burning so brightly, I had to squint against it. The train shuddered and strained against the tracks as John pulled a handle and a piercing whistle filled the tunnel.

I let out a shout of pain as the sound split my ears. I couldn't cover them and hold on at the same time. The train surged upward, sending my insides flying into my throat. We burst into the light, leaving the tunnel behind. I squinted open my eyes at the barren fields before us.

Then I gasped in both shock and wonder as I watched a section of the ground split and a set of tracks rise up to meet the wheels of the train.

I pushed out of the nook and stumbled to the back of the cab. The split ground had been lifted on large metal plates, moved by gears. As the gears turned, the plates tipped and reformed the illusion of solid ground behind us. No one would ever suspect there were tracks hidden just beneath.

"This is incredible," I shouted to Will, but my voice sounded strange with my ears still ringing from the whistle. I climbed back up into the nook and held on as I watched the tracks rise to meet us, emerging from the patches of dark earth the shifting plates exposed.

"Watch for ice," John shouted. "If one of the sections of track doesn't rise, we'll have a lot of explaining to do. That is, if we survive the wreck."

I pulled myself closer to the window even as the freezing air whipped around me. The heat from the boiler radiated outward, but it did little to battle the bitter wind.

But I didn't care. I found it exhilarating. Surely no one

had ever traveled so quickly on all the earth. The train gleamed in the light that reflected off the patches of snow. The setting sun caught the cold world on fire, and the engine itself blended into the golden light.

The tracks flew beneath us, and it took no time at all before we were crossing wide sloping fields. It looked as if the earth ended on a sharp edge, with clouds rising straight from the ground. Those were the white cliffs. We were getting close.

As the next set of tracks revealed themselves, a pole rose with a swinging mirror that caught the light.

"Hold on tight. It's a long way down," John Frank yelled as the ground in front of us split, rising up like the doors to a root cellar. I clung to the bar in the corner and also to one of the pipes along the firebox. The front of the train reached the open hole, and then the entire engine tipped forward into the abyss.

The train screamed into the tunnel, gaining speed as it slid down the grade. John pulled hard on the brake. Sparks flew from the wheels, lighting the side of the train as the trapdoor closed back over us, shutting out the light from behind. Only the headlamp illuminated the way, but my eyes needed a moment to adjust. Everything ahead was a murky black.

John released the brake, and we gained momentum again as we sped through the dark. I heard a loud snap, then a crack and rattle. It sounded like a gunshot.

"What was that?" Will shouted.

"We hit a rock," John answered as he turned the steam release valve. "Let's hope that's the worst of it."

My eyes finally adjusted to the lack of light. Good Lord, we were in for trouble. "We're not out of the woods yet. The tracks are littered with bricks." On the walls of the tunnel ahead I could see large dark patches where the bricks had crumbled and fallen onto the tracks. "The mortar is falling apart."

I watched in horror as another brick hit the heavy pilot that protruded down from the front of the train. The plow-like object scooped the brick up and flung it toward the wall. Once the brick hit the wall, the shattered pieces flew back toward the train like grapeshot fired from a cannon.

"Meg, get down!" Will shouted. A piece of the brick hit the edge of the window opening near me. I threw my hands over my head and ducked, but I felt the sting of bits of brick as they peppered my arm and shoulder. "Quick, behind the boiler." Will reached out, and I grabbed his hand. He pulled me down near the firebox.

We were running blind, but I couldn't risk lifting my head.

More bricks shattered against the pilot and then rained down on the train in quick succession. We were under siege. I tried to keep my head down, but my arm stung from the places where I'd been struck, and the heat from the boiler burned my cheek.

We remained at the mercy of the flying pieces of brick for what felt like an eternity. The entire time, I remained braced for an impact. This was dangerous, but it was far too late to turn back now. I prayed we'd make it through in one piece.

Finally we leveled out deep beneath the English Channel. John stood to adjust the airflow in the firebox, and a piece of brick caught him in the face. He spun as he fell. Will caught him and pulled him back toward the tender. When John looked up again, blood poured down his face from a wound below his eye.

He grabbed his red cap and pressed it to his face. Dear Lord, the man was going to get a horrible infection and end up in a wooden box if he wasn't careful. I pulled a handkerchief from one of the pockets I had sewn into my skirts and handed it to him.

"Much obliged," he said. He pressed the white cloth to his face, then shouted into the dark, "Is that the best you can do?"

The train didn't strike any more bricks for a few moments. Like a mole crawling out of his hole, I pulled myself up from behind the boiler and dared to peek out the window once more.

"Perhaps it's over," I said as I touched the wounds on my arm and flinched. I wasn't bleeding, thank heaven, but the shattered pieces of brick had bruised deeply.

"Meg, you injured?" Will asked, holding on to the valves and wheels as he tried to reach me.

"I'll be fine. Nothing is broken. John is the one who needs aid." We began traveling up a grade and the train slowed significantly. I finally let out a breath. Will let go of the engine and moved toward John. He soaked my handkerchief in something from a flask, then passed the handkerchief back.

When John pressed it to his face again, he winced.

"How much farther?" I asked. Now that we were climbing, we had to be at least halfway to France.

John took a peek at a small pocket watch, squinting in the low light. "Not far now."

"Thank the Lord," I said, looking up at the tunnel ceiling. The steam and smoke from the stack curled along the bricks. I didn't like imagining an ocean above us. Still, I had a job to do. A dark streak on the ceiling marred the otherwise regular pattern.

"Oh no." I pulled myself to my feet and climbed into the gap where I could see the tracks. I peered as far as I could and prayed the headlamp could reach deeper into the darkness.

There was a crack in the ceiling.

My heart lodged in my throat.

Sure enough, bricks had dropped out once again onto the track, but I didn't duck away as the train struck them. There was something in the tunnel. Something massive and white.

White.

It was chalk.

"Brake!" I screeched, pulling myself around the controls and grabbing the heavy lever myself. "Brake! The tunnel's collapsed!"

Both Will and John Frank joined me, grasping the lever and pulling with all their weight. Together we strained against the engine brake. John pulled a second lever, and the gears within the cab strained as they shifted into a counter-rotation. The train screamed like a wounded beast as we fought against the momentum of the enormous monster.

It thundered toward the pile of rock and debris ahead of us.

We were going to slam into it. My arms shook with effort, and the entire engine shuddered with the force of the brakes. Sparks flew from the wheels.

Closer.

Closer.

We weren't going to stop in time.

The train was going to crash.

CHAPTER THIRTEEN

THE ENGINE WHINED, PULLING AGAINST US THE WAY A panicked horse strains against the reins. I felt the burn of my effort through my chest and shoulders as I used what weight I had to hold the brake tight.

The train squealed until the close-set bars of the pilot rammed into the pile of debris.

The impact hurled us forward. I slammed into Will, who crashed into the machinery in front of us. The train continued to move, pushing the debris forward until the locomotive finally groaned to a stop.

And like that, all became still. The train hissed in protest as I lifted my head. I lay across the top of Will, tangled in the small space to the side of the firebox.

"Will?" I whispered. I expected his arms to be wrapped protectively around me. Instead they lay limply at his sides.

"Will?" My voice sounded like a squeak as I pushed myself off him and took his face in my hands. His eyes were closed.

"Will!" I grasped him by the lapels of his coat, afraid to touch him too harshly. He couldn't be dead.

No. *No.*

Water from the boiler bubbled in the pipes. The heat from the firebox seared my cheek, and my ear felt on fire. Sweat dripped down my neck, and at the same time I felt cold, so very cold.

"Will, please," I whispered, my throat tight and aching. "Please wake."

Leaning forward, I touched his forehead. I lived a lifetime of pain and guilt in a single moment as I prayed I wouldn't lose him. Not like this, one minute alive, the next gone.

"Please." I stroked his face and placed my hand over his heart.

His chest rose beneath my palm. Oh, thank the dear Lord. He was alive.

I felt John's presence behind my shoulder. "Miss, are you harmed?"

"Will won't stir." I turned to the Guildsman, desperate for help. John pushed in next to me. He gingerly felt Will's head, then touched his neck and shoulders. "How bad is it?" I asked.

"He's taken quite a blow. Thankfully he hasn't shattered his crown." John pulled out his flask, and for a moment I thought he was going to force Will to drink from it, but instead he held it beneath Will's nose.

Will's eyes blinked but remained unfocused. He pulled in a sharp breath and tried to sit up.

John held him down with one arm. "Stay down. A knock to the head like that can kill. Can you move your feet?"

Will's boots turned side to side. He nodded, and then forcefully swallowed as if he felt ill.

"What's your name?" John asked.

Will took a deep breath. "MacDonald."

"Do you know what day it is?"

"Christmas." Will chuckled weakly. "One of my more eventful."

"He'll live. Keep him down as long as you are able," John announced, then left the cab. I became suddenly dizzy with my relief.

Will tried to focus on me, but his eyes looked strange. He reached up and touched my cheek. I took his hand and pressed my face into his palm. "Meg?"

"I'm not hurt." A hot tear slid onto his fingers before I could stop it. "Stay down. Everything will be fine in a moment."

I pulled my arms out of my coat. It didn't seem like enough, but I bunched it together and placed it gingerly under his head. John had said it wasn't cracked, but part of me didn't believe that.

"How is the engine? Can we still make it to France?" Will asked as he touched the back of his own head and winced.

"Blast it, Will. You could have died." My shock and fear from the crash rushed through me until I felt as if I were drowning. "We've wrecked the train. And needless to say, we're in a really bad state." We'd probably be expelled from the Order for this. It wasn't as if we could hide a train wreck.

"Hear, now," Will said, sitting up. He grimaced, then swallowed hard and looked at me with clear eyes. "A bad state never stopped us before."

I gave him a weak smile.

"That's my girl." He reached up and brushed my flyaway hair back from my face.

I stroked his cheek. All of the rules and the caution over my reputation meant nothing to me in the moment. I needed to feel connected, no matter the consequences.

Will heaved himself to his feet. He lost his balance for a moment and caught himself against the brake. "Where's John?"

"I think he's inspecting the damage." I reached out and helped Will down the step.

The tunnel was like pitch, with only the headlight shining like a beacon. Chalk dust, steam, and smoke from the stack drifted through the air, turning the beam of light into a nearly tangible thing.

John stood by the pile of rubble, scratching the back of his neck. "Well, this is a fine mess."

"How bad is it?" Will asked.

"The engine is still functional, thankfully. There's some surface damage to the boiler. We'll be able to hammer it out. The pilot is ruined, though. I may need a favor from the Foundry, or two." John laughed to himself, and I began to wonder about the older man's sanity. "Perhaps three."

"I'll put in a good word," Will said. "I guess we start digging."

John shook his head. "No, we start walking. I'll rally help from the French Guildsmen. We'll get the engine through to the turntable on the other side. Then we can bring everyone back for the oath at once."

"But what will you tell Leader Octavian?" I asked. I felt horrible that I had gotten him into this mess.

"Octavian?" John walked back to the cab. He climbed in and then came out with our bag, my coat, and his broken lantern. He tossed the bag and coat to me. I shrugged my coat on and looped the bag over my shoulder. "There's an old rule of the Guild, Miss Whitlock. If we're meant to keep a secret, we *keep* a secret. What Octavian doesn't know, is a good thing." He flashed me a smile and lifted the lantern. I had the feeling this wasn't the first time John Frank had been responsible for a large-scale disaster.

I took Will's hand and helped him balance as we climbed over the pile of rubble and began the long march on the other side.

What would have taken an hour or two in the speeding locomotive turned into a long hard climb that took ages.

We stumbled through the dark, keeping close to the

wall. None of us spoke. The silence began to seep into my consciousness. Thankfully, there were no rats, but with every unexplained sound that echoed through the tunnel, I expected the ceiling to come crashing down. If it had collapsed once, it could easily do it again.

And so we continued on until the rough brick turned into a mosaic of intricately laced gears. I ran my hands over the connections, feeling how they all fit so seamlessly together.

We reached a chamber much like the one where we'd found the locomotive, though this one seemed at once more pristine but also in worse disrepair. It looked as if no one had set foot in it since the moment of its creation. Lack of maintenance on the tunnel had led to a collapse. Any sort of disaster might await us here. John led us up a flight of stairs and through another locked door just like the first. A chill came over me. If neglect had sealed the door shut, we were well and truly trapped.

When the door creaked open, I didn't have long to enjoy my relief. Beyond the door was a shaft. I was never fond of ladders. I couldn't help the shudder that suddenly overcame me.

Will placed a steady hand on my shoulder. I needed to be out of the dark. John pulled a lever, and the ceiling above us disappeared, dropping down and then sliding into the floor of whatever was above us. Fresh air poured over us like cleansing water, and I breathed deep. It smelled like incense and candle wax.

I sent a quick prayer of thanks that we'd survived. Even the short ladder couldn't intimidate me as we climbed up to freedom, to France, and into a small country chapel, decorated for Christmas.

We snuck out onto an open lane amid sweeping grasses, dried and dead from winter. The stars shone above, a brilliant blanket of light in the deep night.

I wrapped my arms around myself, but I couldn't keep out the cold. Suddenly I felt Will's heavy coat on my shoulders. "Will, you're injured," I protested.

"The cold is good for my head. Keep it, at least until we find shelter." I wrapped myself in it, letting the heat still lingering from his body seep into mine. It was such a wonderful gift on this cold Christmas night. "John, do you know of an estate called Pensée?" Will asked. "We're looking for a man named Maurice Durant."

John let his gaze drop to the ground before his feet. His lips pressed tightly together. Then he shook his head, but it was such a slight motion, I almost didn't catch it. "No one has been to Pensée for years. Durant's retired from the Order, and now he lives alone, if he's still living at all. His mind is gone, which is a terrible shame. The last I heard he was no longer able to carry on a proper conversation. All he does anymore is peer at the stars." John looked around. Hopefully he would be able to gain his bearings.

"Can you take us there?" I asked.

"The last time I was at Pensée, I was newly sworn to the Order. I forget where it is exactly." He brightened a bit as he rubbed his thumb against one of his sideburns and smiled. "But there might be someone who can tell you more. We have to pay her a visit anyway. Come with me." He lifted his lantern, now flickering for lack of oil, and we followed him.

It was a long walk through the cold and quiet country-side. In spite of my excitement, I couldn't help feeling a sense of foreboding. I didn't know where it was coming from—the chill in the air, the desolation of the windswept fields so near the ocean.

We continued to walk for miles toward the sea. Eventually we came upon a small home on the edge of a large field. A lingering trail of inviting smoke hung like a wisp above the stone chimney. I heard flapping wings and looked up as a glimmering bird flew across the sky. John knocked loudly on the door.

There was no answer.

He knocked again, and I feared the hinges might break.

"She must be in the loft. Follow me." John motioned to us, and we turned around the corner of the small house to a large pigeon loft in the back, nearly the size of the house itself. The loft had been built against the side of the house so that the two structures shared a common wall, but while the house had a pitched roof, the tin covering the loft was perfectly flat, and there were no windows in the structure, only a small covered hatch for the birds to enter and exit. To my astonishment, about thirty small silver doves rested on the roof.

Real silver.

The metal birds shimmered in the moonlight, perched on small wheels instead of feet. Occasionally one would flap its wings as if restless, while the gears embedded in its chest turned.

"Gabrielle," John called as he knocked on the door. "I need to speak with you," he shouted into the shack. What shocked me is that he spoke perfect French.

The door swung open.

A striking woman with skin a shade or two lighter than

John's and thick hair tied back in a cloth stepped into the doorway. She stared at the Guildsman the way a viper stares at a mongoose.

"Tell me why I should not shut this door into your face?" she asked with a strange accent. I wondered if she came from the Caribbean.

John ducked his head in a courtly bow but ended up looking a bit like a jester. "Because you know you adore me, Gabrielle."

Gabrielle scowled in the way of a woman who had been putting up with nonsense a very long time. "Adore you? I've had greater affection for a pig." Her full lips turned up in an acerbic grin. "And he was delicious. What have you damaged beyond repair this time?"

In spite of her harsh words, she opened the door wider and allowed us in. Hundreds of pigeons waited in small boxes, each box neatly labeled with cities and sometimes the names of people. It was an astounding sight. Something thudded on the roof, and I jumped, until I realized it was the sound of another bird landing above me.

John removed his hat and had the sense to look contrite as he entered and faced Gabrielle. "I may have taken the loco-motive for a quick run to check the rails. It's half-buried in chalk beneath the channel. Oh, and Merry Christmas to you."

She threw up her hands. "And I suppose you want my help to dig it out, yes?" Her fists landed on her hips. One of the birds let out a trilling coo.

"Come now, Gabrielle. What would you have done if it had been languishing here on your side of the channel? It was a sin to leave it in disrepair, and you know it." John gave her a charming smile. "What is the use of keeping these inventors around if we cannot play with their toys?"

I was beginning to see the greater need for locking Amusements. John Frank was a menace.

Gabrielle rolled her eyes. "And so you wrecked it. This is nothing new. I suppose you also wish for me to prevent any communication about the *toy* from reaching London."

"That would be nice," John said.

"You can forget you even asked. I won't lose my position to save your hide." Gabrielle pulled out a small piece of paper, jotted a quick note upon it, and carefully considered all the names of the unusual birds before she settled on one. "I have already received a panicked note from the Duke of Chadwick asking me to watch for his wayward charge."

Will glanced at me, and I felt suddenly contrite. I hadn't meant to worry him. I should have known he'd be watching.

Gabrielle tucked the note into a pocket on the bird's belly, then walked outside. Once in the clear moonlight, Gabrielle threw her hands up, and the little silver bird took to the sky.

"Come inside, Mademoiselle Whitlock, Monsieur MacDonald."

We gratefully entered the little house as I wondered what the note had said. Even though the fire had grown cold in the hearth, the house retained its warmth well. I tried to shake the cold from my clothes as I glanced around at the small but well-cared-for furniture and belongings in the single room that served most daily purposes. The door to the left must have led to a bedroom.

Gabrielle stepped in front of me. "So, tell me, what brings you to France in such a desperate way that you would disobey the headmaster and seek the help of this imbecile?" she asked with a fair amount of censure in her voice and a sharp nod toward John Frank.

"We're searching for my grandfather." I said.

"Henry?" She switched over to English, though she pronounced my grandfather's name with a heavy French inflection. "And you believe he is alive?" Her dark eyes were wide as she looked at me intently.

"I believe so."

Gabrielle turned to the fire and built it back up until it blazed to life, but she didn't say another word.

"We need to call upon Maurice Durant. My grandfather may have visited him just before he disappeared," I explained.

"I do not know if Henry was ever at Pensée. I do know that for years the house was quiet but still open to visitors. Then suddenly it became a fortress. It is not wise to enter the gate." Gabrielle carelessly tossed a log on top of the fire, and a shower of dangerous sparks burst out, rolling over the stone toward the wood floor.

"Please, we don't have much time, and this is our only chance to save him. Can you lead us to Pensée?"

Gabrielle glanced down. Her brow creased. Then she looked back up, resigned.

"I cannot. There are too many letters coming over the channel," she said. I felt the sting of her words even as she said them. She stood and glanced out the window. "But my birds can."

CHAPTER FOURTEEN

GABRIELLE TURNED AND WALKED TO THE FIRE. SHE
stoked it with several hard jabs. "There is nothing to be done
for the night. You will need the light to track the bird, and it
is a long journey to Pensée." She smacked her hands together,
then came to stand by me. "You men sleep on the floor here
and be grateful. Meg, come with me." She ushered me into
the small bedroom, then turned back to the men. "And, John,
if I wake and all my cheese is suddenly missing, I blame you."

"It was the mice, I swear." John held his hand to his heart.

"Mice, my boot," Gabrielle grumbled before she shut the
door to the bedroom and locked it.

The next morning we packed provisions and met

Gabrielle out behind the loft. She held a small silver bird in one hand, and a large compass in the other. The bird had a fat little body that held a complicated set of gears in its breast. With a short copper beak and dark beady eyes, it was a cute little machine, but its long silver wings were delicate, and while the tenacity of a mechanical bird much like this one had saved my life once, it was still a fallible object. We had a long way to go, and if the bird failed, Will and I would be lost.

"The compass will show you the position of the bird. He will land at the gate. I cannot help you from there. I have many people to contact if we are to recover the engine. Good luck." She reached out and placed the compass in my hand. It felt heavy, and I could feel it ticking like a watch against my palm. Outwardly it looked much the same as any maritime compass, but the needle wasn't pointing north. It pointed at the bird without wavering.

Gabrielle wound the silver bird, then threw it high into the air. It flapped its wings, letting out a squealing noise with each stroke against the air.

It turned south, and Will and I were on the chase. At first we ran, trying to keep the tiny bird in sight as it winged its way through the clear winter sky. Our breath turned to tendrils of fog around our faces.

Will slowed to a stop ahead of me and placed his hands on his knees as he laughed while trying to catch his breath. "Must it always be like this?"

My boots crunched through a thin patch of frost as I joined him. It was wonderful to feel both dizzy from my exertion and free. There was nothing around us save fallow fields and thick stands of barren trees. No one to judge. No one to assume. No one at all. "I hope so."

I turned the compass over in my hands, feeling the seams and inspecting the gears under the face of the needle.

"Don't you dare pull that thing apart to see how it works," Will said.

"I would do no such thing," I protested.

Will smiled at me. "You were thinking about it."

I bowed my head and grinned, then stepped up next to him as we continued on. He was right, as always. The troll.

The day wore on while we talked as we crossed the frozen fields and wandered along the desolate country lanes. We conversed about nothing and everything at once. It was like we were speaking our letters aloud and letting our minds wander together.

The sun began to settle, low on the horizon, but we followed the compass toward the bird and Pensée.

Finally, after walking all day, I could see a large mansion atop a tall hill. Small pockets of forest tucked around the base of the hill, but even the loftiest branches didn't reach as high as the house itself. Light from the setting sun caught in the many windows. From the distinct peaked roof with its rows of gables, to the high arched windows with balconies, it was a house built for the sky. Everything about it seemed to reach toward the heavens, especially the central dome that towered over the rest of the house.

"Do you think that is Pensée?" I was stunned. "It's beautiful."

"Beautiful like a grave," Will muttered. "Come. We've a ways to go yet."

Before long we reached a high and smooth wall that surrounded the base of the hill. The forest had grown around it and had concealed it from a distance. Though both Will and I looked, there was no clear way over.

The gate was equally foreboding. Corrosion had turned the gate an eerie green. Two heavy knockers in the shape of wolf heads stared at us with hollowed-out eyes. The silver bird had landed on the top of the wall, and now chirped at us. I wasn't sure if it was in encouragement or warning.

Will pushed at the gate. "It's locked."

I tried the knocker, and it fell with a heavy thud against the perfectly round disk beneath the striker. I winced as the sound echoed off the hill.

There was no answer. The house remained still.

"There has to be some way in." I smoothed my hands over the door. There was no latch, which meant that the mechanism for locking the gate was either on the inside or within the gate itself.

"Perhaps there is a way we can climb over," Will suggested as he took a step back and inspected the wall. He ran at the wall and launched himself upward with a push of his boot against the smooth stone, but it was no use. He fell back to the ground like a cat, always on his feet. He turned and looked at me. "I could lift you."

"I have no way down on the other side, and we don't know what is behind the gate. Whatever it is, we should face it together." I took a deep breath.

"A fine point." Will removed his cap, rubbed his hair, and then pulled it back on. "For all we know, Durant is dead."

"What a pleasant thought." There had to be some way through. I just didn't see it. I took a closer look at the knockers, feeling the edge of the medallion beneath the swinging ring that hung from the wolf's mouth. It was the perfect size for my key.

I pushed and prodded at it, but it revealed nothing.

"What are you after?" Will asked, walking back toward me after making a second attempt to scale the wall.

"The strike plate for the knocker is the right size and shape to use my key, but it's useless. There's nothing there."

Will took a step back and cocked his head as he considered the gate. "Have you tried that one?" He pointed toward the knocker on the left.

I hadn't even thought of it. Usually a left knocker was only ornamental. Most of them weren't even able to move. Which is why no one would look for anything special there. Brilliant.

Quickly I inspected the knocker, combing over every inch of it.

Sure enough, there was a tiny latch below the strike plate. I placed my thumb on it and slid it as far as I could to the right.

Something inside it clicked, and hope surged through me. Though it was stiff with corrosion, the medallion swung to the side, revealing the cradle for my key.

I snatched the key from around my neck and pulled the cover open. The silver flower with slightly triangular petals rose out of the center of the watch exactly as it had the very first time Will and I had opened it.

I felt a tingle down my back as I fitted the silver flower into the lock. The other knocker slid sideways, revealing a tiny set of keys for a minuscule pianoforte set behind it. This was it, Papa's lock. All I needed was for the key to reveal the correct phrase from my grandfather's song, and the door would open. Only, my key didn't play the tune at all.

I would have to play the entire thing. Papa had definitely been here. No one else knew the entire song. He had locked the gate to everyone but himself.

"Papa set this lock. I have to play the whole song," I said to Will as he watched over my shoulder.

"Your grandfather was serious about keeping people out. We have to be careful." Will placed his hand on my shoulder as I played the wandering melody.

With each note, clicks, whirrs, and other mechanical noises emanated from the large gates. Will followed the muffled echoes of sounds along the walls. They couldn't have only been for a lock. They were too extensive.

"Meg, I think we're winding something," he said.

The last time we passed through such a gate, a mechanical Minotaur greeted us on the other side. Papa was both brilliant and determined to keep himself safe from a murderer. He would have no incentive to create something with restraint.

I took a deep breath. I didn't want to face the genius of my grandfather when he'd been bent on defending himself, but we had to. "Is there anything we can use as a weapon?"

Will reached up and pulled a pair of thick branches off a fallen limb just as I finished the song. The gates ominously opened before us.

I tried to swallow my fear as the crack between them widened. I waited for something to leap toward me from the other side. The crack grew, but all it revealed was a path through the woods. Everything fell still, even the bird atop the gate.

"Can you spare me a bit of your hem?" Will asked, pulling his knife from his sock and handing it to me. I used it to trim the lower frill of lace from my petticoat. I didn't wish to trip over it anyway.

Will cut the strip in half and wound one around each of the tops of the two limbs, then pulled a flask from his coat.

"Will?" He wasn't one for heavy drink.

"Duncan gave it to me," he said soberly. "It's still full."

The last thing we needed was a reminder of how quickly our adventures could turn deadly. Will poured the liquid onto the strips from my petticoat, then drew a match and lit them. "Hopefully if we find something, we can use these to distract it," Will said as he handed a torch to me. The Minotaur had used heat to find and track us, but we had been able to use fire to blind it. Will really was far more clever than many gave him credit for. "Ready?" he asked.

I nodded and held my torch aloft as the sun set in a wave of fire behind us. With my free hand I took his. "Let's go."

The gates now seemed eerily still as they stood wide open. We walked through hand in hand. The eyes of the wolves sculpted above the knockers seemed to follow us as we passed.

Once we were on the other side, the gates closed slowly. The rattling echoed off the hill, and the evening seemed much darker in the shadow of the gate. I held my torch high as we followed the path into the woods. With every step, I waited for the ambush. Every muscle in my back and neck felt tense, and Will held my hand tightly.

The gates closed with a heavy *boom*. Then suddenly the only sound in the still cool quiet of the evening was the crunch of our boots on the dried leaves and patches of ice on the path.

I could see my breath curling around my face in the flickering light of the torch. The hair on the back of my neck rose as I heard a twig break.

I turned, searching the shadows for something, anything. "Was that you?" I whispered.

"No."

My stomach tumbled through my middle. Will lifted his torch, and the light glinted off something in the shadow of the trees. Two points of light glowed red in the darkness. Then two more, then two more.

Oh God.

I lifted my torch and looked around frantically. Ten gleaming eyes, fixed on us. They moved closer, and the light shimmered against the metal faces of five large mechanical wolves.

One of them lifted his long snout, and his mouth fell open, revealing glinting silver teeth as sharp as knives. Metal fur covered his head and neck; it gleamed in deadly blades and spikes. A thick lens had been fixed over his left eye, and the outer ring of it turned, warping the red light of his mechanical iris as he focused on me. He growled, the sound a combination of a mechanical rattle and the grinding of gears.

Moving on instinct, I shifted, turning my back to Will's as the wolves surrounded us.

One by one the wolves lifted their heads and howled.

CHAPTER FIFTEEN

IT WAS THE ALARM. THEY WERE WARNING THE HOUSE we were there. I trembled, holding fast to my torch even though the flame wavered. The howls chilled me as they faded in the cold air. The wolves lowered their heads, and all their eyes fixed on us again.

Will waved his torch, but the wolves didn't follow the motion of his arm. Their eyes remained on us. These beasts were more sophisticated than the Minotaur had been.

I took a slow step back toward the gate. The wolves watched me, but they didn't move forward and they didn't attack.

"What are they waiting for?" I whispered.

All the wolves' heads shifted to focus on me.

"I think they're holding us here until someone can call them off," Will said. He leaned over and picked up a rock. "Brace yourself."

He threw the rock over the shoulder of one of the wolves. It clattered behind the pack, and their heads turned toward the noise.

"Are they following the sound?" I whispered. The conical curls of metal that made their ears turned back toward me, and they returned to their previous defensive stance. They *were* following sound, at least partly.

Will's posture had hunched forward, anticipating the attack, his body still and prepared. I shook inside, and he looked as steady as granite. "If they're anything like real wolves, they won't attack so long as we're facing them. But if we move, they'll run us down. If they can follow sound, they'll follow our steps. We need a distraction."

These were not real wolves. They had no fear, no sense of self-preservation. They could afford to be merciless in a way that a living thing could not. They scared me far worse than a real wolf ever could.

I shoved my hand deep into the pocket I had sewn into my skirts. I fumbled around in the thick fabric. It had to still be there. My numb fingers stung as I searched. Finally my hand closed around a small orb, one of my alarms. It was the one Will had tossed to me so carelessly in the shop. Thank heaven.

"Hold this," I whispered as I handed Will the torch. One of the wolves took another step forward, his mechanical paw sinking into the frozen leaves only a few feet from me. Will pointed the torch at the metal beast. With stiff fingers half-frozen from the cold, I twisted the two halves of the orb.

Immediately it let out a shrieking whistle. The heads of all the wolves snapped up as they surged forward.

"Here!" Will shouted as he moved both torches to one hand and held out the other. I tossed the orb into it, and he immediately flung it away from us. It sailed through the sky, the wail trailing along through the still evening.

The wolves turned and ran, loping through the woods with the power of the wheels and springs in their backs.

"Run!" Will shouted.

I grabbed my skirts and sprinted up the path, climbing the hill toward the house. The orb wouldn't wail forever. It had given us a head start, but it wouldn't last long.

Holding my skirts, I ran as best I could, but I couldn't swing my arms, and I couldn't breathe freely with my corset.

The hill turned steep, and the path twisted toward the house at the top. Will kept himself between me and the wolves, even though he could run freely.

Panting for breath, I heard the whistle die. I glanced back at Will behind me. We paused for the briefest of seconds.

Perhaps if we were quiet enough, the wolves would stay at the bottom of the hill. We didn't have much farther to go.

Just then I realized we were standing in two inches of frost-covered leaves. Will motioned forward, and I took a tentative step, easing my toe into the leaves as gingerly as I could, but they crunched down beneath my boot. It must have only been the slightest of noises, but to my ears it sounded like the crunch of a hundred breaking bones.

The howl sounded again.

They were coming.

Will leapt forward, grabbing my hand and pulling me with him as we ran for the top. I glanced back over my shoulder. The silver wolves raced straight up the hill toward us. They did not turn and they did not waver. I could hear the clattering of their joints, but somehow they managed not to distract one another as they followed us without err.

I had no luxury to wonder how this was accomplished. "Will! They're right on our heels!"

"Hurry! To the door!" He flung me forward, and the momentum carried me up over the crest of the hill and to the courtyard before the mansion. I ran over the barren front garden and the curving drive that led to the front steps. My face burned. I couldn't feel my feet, but I pushed forward as hard as I could.

Will's footsteps fell hard on the ground behind me, and I swore I could feel the phantom breath of the wolves as they snapped their vicious metal jaws together.

My momentum carried me straight into the hard surface of the closed door. I felt the impact of the crash deep in my shoulder and the bone beneath my cheek, but I had to shake off the pain. I furiously rapped on the knocker, then pounded on the door, screaming for someone to let us in—before I came to my senses. The knockers were identical to the ones on the gate.

"The left one," I gasped out as I slid to the side. As I did so, I caught sight of Will, with his twin torches blazing as he made his stand at the top of the steps.

The first wolf leapt at him. Will twisted, swinging the fiery branches up and under the body of the wolf. With a grunted shout he changed the beast's trajectory and sent it flying into the wall. The wolf crashed against the stone, damaging its spine. It kicked and struggled but couldn't find its feet.

I had to get us inside. With unsteady hands I reached for my key and fitted it into the left-hand striker. The other knocker opened, revealing the musical keys. I pressed my ear to the silver locket to try to hear the song and where it ended. Once again it was silent. I had to play the whole thing.

That would take minutes. We didn't have minutes.

Once again I spared a glance at Will as I moved back to the door on the right so I could play the tune. He brandished his torches at the wolves, holding them off, but they lunged and snapped, pressing into his space and forcing him back toward the door.

I played the melody as fast as I could, praying I wouldn't make a mistake and have to start over. "Why are they being so aggressive?" I shouted at Will as he landed a powerful kick against the lowered head of one of the wolves. "I thought they wouldn't attack so long as we faced them."

"I don't know!" Will shouted. "It's not like I created the blasted things. Hurry, would you?"

I continued to play, cringing at the sounds behind me. With every strike of metal on the stone stairs, I imagined the wolves overwhelming Will and tearing him apart.

"Meg!"

I jumped, then turned to the side as one of the wolves

charged forward and crashed into the door with its shoulder. The spikes and blades making up its fur bent with the impact. It held its head at a strange angle, and the light in one eye flickered out as it shook its head. It growled at me, lifting the silver blades around its neck. I kicked it in the snout and continued playing.

With a snarl it lunged and grabbed me by the arm. Its teeth cut into my flesh. Then it clamped down on the loose billows of my coat sleeve and held fast. I screamed, my arm on fire, hot and wet. I tugged against the wolf's hold. My eyes burned as I gritted my teeth. I could hear the fabric ripping, but I would *not* let the wolf pull me from the door.

Stretching back, I played the last two notes.

The moment I played them, the wolf suddenly released me.

The three wolves that remained lowered their heads, then turned and ran back down the hill. The one that had held me followed, limping along the path.

I cradled my wounded arm against my stomach as I doubled over.

Will rushed toward me and wrapped his arm over my shoulder as the door opened before us.

A man stood in the shadows behind the door. He was dressed in old livery, a butler perhaps?

"Sir, please, we're searching for Maurice Durant. Is he here?" I asked in French.

The butler reached up and grasped his lapel in one white-gloved hand, but made no other indication he'd heard me at all. His glove had faded and turned gray, and there was a hole in the back, where something glinted beneath, as if it were made of . . . metal?

He stepped out of the shadows, and I brought my gaze up to his face.

The face was blank, a smooth shield of polished metal with only the faintest contours of what a human face should be.

Gracious. It was an automaton. One of the finest I had ever seen.

He placed both his hands behind his back. Dust had settled on his black livery, and the powdered wig perched on his metal head had faded with dust and age.

"Good evening," the automaton stated in French. His voice sounded tinny as he gave me a stiff bow and said, "Welcome to Pensée, Monsieur Whitlock."

He had assumed I was my grandfather. There was no doubt. We were in the right place.

CHAPTER SIXTEEN

WILL SUPPORTED ME AS I CRADLED MY INJURED ARM and stepped inside. The heavy door eased shut behind us, throwing us into darkness.

The only light came from our torches. Will snatched a bouquet of dead flowers out of a heavy tarnished urn and set the torches in it. "Let me see your arm."

I held it out to him. The lower half of my coat sleeve had been badly torn and soaked in blood. He gently squeezed down my forearm. "Do you think it's broken?"

I winced. "No. The bones are fine." I gasped as he squeezed the wound.

He raised one eyebrow as he helped me pull my arm

from my coat. My dress beneath was soaked in blood. He drew his knife, then swiftly slit what was left of my sleeve, from wrist to elbow. There were three slashes cut deep into my forearm.

A new fear took hold as I watched my blood pooling out of them and trickling down to drip into Will's hands. If any piece of the cloth from my sleeve remained within the wound, it could fester and I would die of infection. "Do they need to be stitched?" My stomach knotted at the thought. We didn't have anything to sew them shut, and I didn't know if I had the fortitude not to faint as Will did it. I already felt light-headed.

"We need to make sure they're clean. They're going to scar." Will looked around desperately as my arm dripped with blood. I had nothing to staunch the bleeding. "You there!" he shouted at the automaton. Will seemed as surprised as I was when the mechanical man turned to him. "Fetch clean linens," he ordered.

"Will, that will never . . ."

The automaton gave us a bow, then walked down the pitch-black hall with a rigid and clanking gait.

Will touched a knuckle to his forehead, then looked desperate as he inspected the gashes again.

"What aren't you telling me?" I asked.

"We may need to cauterize."

"Oh God," I whispered.

I felt cold all of a sudden and sat on the smooth marble floor. I had to fight to keep from spilling my stomach. Our footsteps had left a scramble of smears in the fine dust. As soon as I began to shiver, the heavy weight of Will's coat enveloped my shoulders. He pulled out a handkerchief and soaked it in the whisky from his flask as he knelt next to me. "This is going to burn."

"It's only pain." I attempted to smile at him even though I dreaded what was to come. "It won't kill me." He pressed the cloth to the largest wound on my arm, and I hissed as every muscle in my side and stomach tensed, but I held still. "Or perhaps it will."

We both watched as he continued to dab the blood away with the soaked handkerchief, but it was no use. The blood kept pooling.

I caught Will's gaze. "Do it," I urged.

The color drained from his face. He let out a shaky breath, then cleaned his knife with the whisky. "It's okay if you faint."

I nodded, already feeling dizzy as the wounds dripped along my arm. Will grabbed one of the torches and held his knife in the heat of the fire until the blade grew red hot.

"Close your eyes. I'll be quick," he said, and I felt his broad palm cradle my wounded arm. "Do you want some of the whisky?"

"I'll be fine. Just do it," I said through gritted teeth.

The knife touched my arm, and I stifled a scream. I could feel the fire shooting up through my arm and shoulder. I swore my heart stopped beating with the shock and pain. Will's grip clamped down on my arm as he seared the other two wounds, and like that, it was done.

He dropped his knife onto the floor and gathered me in his arms, careful to cradle my wounded hand. "Breathe," he whispered to me.

I took a shaking gasp as tears streamed down my face. I couldn't help them; I didn't try.

"By God, you are a brave woman," he said as I wiped my face. I still trembled, and my arm stung from the burns, but at least the bleeding had stopped.

"What is our plan now?" I asked, my voice broken and shaking. I didn't feel brave. I was on the verge of falling apart.

"We find Durant," Will stated as he continued to tenderly touch my arm. We heard the rattle of metal in the distance, and to my surprise the butler returned with a large folded sheet without a trace of dust on it. Will took it and used his knife to slice a long strip from the linen.

"Will, you can't understand French," I said, still shaking. "I'm the only one who can speak with Durant."

"I don't want to leave you," he said. I noticed his hands were shaking as well.

"If Durant is angry at our intrusion, we may need to leave here quickly." Those wolves would be waiting for us. I shuddered at the thought. "You must find a way for us to escape while I speak with Durant. I don't want to linger a moment longer than we must."

Will considered this a moment. "Are you certain you'll be safe?"

I swallowed a lump in my throat. "No, but what choice do we have?"

Will shook his head slowly as a look of resignation passed over his features. "What of your grandfather?"

"I don't believe he's here." The house felt too empty. "He would have heard the commotion we made."

"Look for clues," he said. "I'll do the same. We can search more of the house if we are apart."

I nodded. "We know Papa was here. We need to know

why he may have left, and when, and where he could have—"

Will placed a finger on my lips. "Go speak with Durant. I'll take care of the rest."

"I don't want to face those wolves again." We'd barely made it into the house. If they'd been on us a moment longer, or if those jaws had found my neck—or worse, Will's . . . No. "There has to be a way around them, or some way to call them off. I know you will find it."

Will finished cleaning the wounds and bathing my arm in whisky before he wrapped it tightly in the strip of linen. As he tied off the bandage, the pain eased. The skimming touch of his fingers as he smoothed the linen, then cradled my small wrist in his hands, made my head feel light and floating.

Or perhaps it was the loss of blood. Will helped me to my feet, and I almost swooned. He held me, close and protected, against his chest until the world stopped spinning.

I needed my wits. "I'll be fine," I said as I found my feet. "I'll meet you back here." I took one of the torches. They had nearly burned out. I used it to light a small and dusty lamp.

Will shifted on his feet, seemingly uncomfortable, and his face held more color than usual.

He wouldn't meet my gaze as he looked around, but the harsh set of his lips gave away how distressed he really was.

He pulled a thick candle out of a holder with a jerk. "I prom-ise I'll find a way around those wolves. I don't want to see you hurt like that again."

I took his hand and brought it to my cheek. "Good luck," I said. "And be careful."

He gathered my hand and kissed the back of it like a gentleman. "You too." Then he disappeared into the shadows down a long and empty corridor.

I turned to the butler.

"Take me to Maurice Durant," I commanded in my clear-est voice. "Please," I added, because I couldn't help myself.

The automaton bowed to me, then turned on his heel and started walking the opposite way from the direction Will had gone down the long hall. I turned back to glance at the dark hall, where Will had disappeared. I prayed Will would remain safe, even as I walked into the unknown.

I followed the butler with my flickering lamp. It was strangely unsettling inside the house. Everything looked as it should have, but there was a very lifeless air in the halls. Like walking through a house populated by nothing but ghosts. It didn't help that I was following an automaton, who by his very nature was neither living nor dead.

I stifled a cough against the fine dust that hung in the air.

My wounded arm throbbed and ached, but I held the lamp fast. Papa had been right to hide here. No one in their right mind would come to this place, and with the house perched on the top of the hill, he would have been able to see anyone approaching the mansion. Between the view and those wolves, no one could enter the house without being noticed.

But if this place made the perfect fortress, why would he have left?

The butler moved through the darkness without much mind to it, since he didn't have eyes. The creaking and clanking of his stiffening joints rattled down the empty halls.

The mansion was enormous, and must have been a glory in its prime. Though the house itself was baroque, I didn't find the décor overbearing or gaudy in the way so many of the palaces of Europe tended to be. I never much cared for overly ornamental papers on the walls, or colorful porcelain tiles. Instead the walls had been painted a pale color I couldn't see so well in the terribly dim light, but the lower halves of the walls were delineated by elegant wainscoting that had been painted white.

We entered a smoking room before we crossed a corridor and found ourselves at a large set of double doors toward the back of the mansion.

The doors opened silently as the automaton approached, without the mechanical man ever reaching out to touch them. It was like magic, even though it seemed such a simple thing.

I felt as if the gates of heaven had parted before me. A golden light flooded into the hall. We passed through the doors into a gilded conservatory. The glass ceiling glowed with light from hanging lamps that drenched us in warmth.

I looked around and gasped. Delicate trees and flowers bloomed in profusion within the protection of the glass walls and ceiling. Heavy fruit hung from the branches and vines, and vegetables spilled out from containers and raised beds. The arrangement of them managed to be both productive and decorative at once.

Onions, tomatoes, potatoes, grapes, oranges, lemons— suddenly I felt starved, like Tantalus beneath the trees. A tendril of hair clung to my cheek in the humidity. I brushed it back as a fat chicken ran across the path and a goat bleated from somewhere in the corner.

A trio of enormous butterflies, easily the size of dinner plates, stretched their wings on a bush bearing exotic peppers. But no, they were machines. I looked more closely at the foliage and realized there was movement everywhere.

A mechanical peacock groomed his golden feathers,

then spread his tail. Patina on the copper gave it a blue-green sheen, and yet the ornamental swirls set in his rattling feathers shimmered with bright brass.

A monkey hung from a tree to my left, his jointed tail curled around a fat branch of an orange tree. He swung there, looking at me with lifeless black marble eyes.

An entire menagerie preened and strutted, moving through the protected garden and shining in the false sunlight, all clockwork, all beautiful, and yet nothing here could give me any answers as to what had happened to my grandfather.

I heard a growl, and I froze.

Beneath a bush a clockwork tiger bared his sharp fangs.

My heart stopped and I couldn't breathe. The wolf's teeth had been sharp and cutting; the tiger's teeth were three times the size.

He blinked his orb-like eyes, then prowled forward, keeping his head low.

I ran to catch up to the butler, desperate to leave the conservatory. Every fiber in my being urged me to flee as another set of doors opened, dragging across the rug on the other side. I slipped past the automaton into the hall and the doors closed again.

I found myself at the bottom of a twisting staircase. The butler began the ascent, and I darted ahead of him. There were no other passages, no doors. The stair led relentlessly upward until I finally reached a large arched door.

I passed through the doorway, unprepared for the sight before me.

Cold air washed over me as I looked up. The dome of the house split, opening to the clear dark winter sky shimmering with a million stars. A telescope easily the size of my toy shop tilted toward the deep night. As it moved, gears ranging in size from monstrous to tiny danced in a finely tuned ballet.

The entire structure was surrounded by rings the size of the room itself. Each ring held a model of one of the planets, and they spun and swirled around the central telescope, like a model of the cosmos taken to scale.

My Lord, I didn't have words. The heavens were there before me.

A very old man sat, reclined and motionless in a strange gear-laden chair beneath the telescope. He stared into the machine, peering into the depths of whatever lay beyond the stars.

I hesitated. I shouldn't have even been in the house. What should I say to him? "Sorry to disturb you, monsieur"?

Somehow that seemed like an uncomfortable introduction to someone I had never met, when I had intruded on his person without invitation.

What if he wished to call the constable? He'd have every right.

I took a deep breath and calmed my panic. Technically I was family, and Durant hadn't had any visitors in a very long time. All the same, I hoped Will had discovered a way to escape.

"Maurice Durant?" I said, as gently as I could so that I wouldn't startle or disturb him. "Monsieur?"

He didn't answer. I didn't know what to do. I took a tentative step forward, then another.

"Monsieur Durant?" I called again.

"What do you want?" he shouted in a voice that crackled and wheezed with age. "Can't you see I'm busy? Always bothering," he muttered.

This situation was the height of impropriety, and John Frank had already warned me that Durant's mind was half-gone. "Monsieur Durant, I beg your pardon for our intrusion, but I am searching for Henry Whitlock." He moved his chair, and the large gears and wheels above me turned, swinging the various planets in a coordinated dance around the main telescope. I took a step back, then ducked as the model of Mercury swooped overhead. "I am his granddaughter, Margaret."

Maurice Durant pulled back from his gazing, and the chair righted itself until it seemed like a throne set at the center of a shifting universe. He looked down at me. His eyes were rheumy and clouded with age, but I could have sworn there was something in them, some spark of a genius that used to be.

"Henri is not here, and so I have no use for his granddaughter. Be gone," he said, even as his gaze drifted back toward his telescope.

"Please, monsieur. I need to know where he went if he left of his own accord, or if he was taken from this place." I wouldn't leave, not without answers.

Durant's chair swung back around and lowered him beneath his telescope. "Thirty-seven degrees. Mark on the twenty-sixth of December at nine forty . . . seven."

"Please, monsieur!" I shouted.

Durant's chair made a grinding sound as he tilted it to look at me once more. "You're still here?"

I lifted my chin as I stared up at him. "I will not leave until you tell me what I need to know."

"Where is Henri?" Durant said with a frown. "He said he would be gone three days, but it is now two years, six weeks, eight hours—" He peered at a pocket watch.

"Monsieur, if you will. The time is not important to me," I said.

His weathered face turned red. "Not important!"

"All I wish to know is what drove him from this place." I fisted my hands at my sides.

Durant made a chewing motion, as if playing with the spaces where his teeth had once been. "Henri was chasing ghosts. No good will come of it," he muttered under his breath.

I stood straight and stared the old codger down. "Do you know where he went when he left here?"

Durant acted as if he hadn't heard my question. I didn't move from my spot, though I had to duck Mercury a second time. Durant gave me a sour look.

"He went looking for a truth that should have remained dark." Durant turned a large wheel next to him, and the entire mechanism shifted, lifting the telescope to a steeper pitch, and he peered back into it. "There are dark places, you know. A spiraling vortex that sweeps all light into it."

I didn't know what the old man was talking about. He

had lost all sense. Now I knew what John Frank had meant by his not being able to hold a conversation.

"Old flames burn the hottest," he continued as he stared at his precious stars. "Yet even that light cannot escape. It's the deadly spiral. It drew him in."

I climbed higher on the contraption in spite of the pain in my arm. "Get down from there. You'll damage the balance," he said.

"Do you know where Henry is now?" I asked again. If I had to ask it a thousand times, I would. Durant seemed to surmise this as he glared at me.

"He took a train." Durant turned the wheel again, then pulled a lever. "Vile contraptions. We never should have let some of their development leak to the masses. Now the rails are everywhere. The countryside gone. Locomotives belching smoke and blowing whistles. No more stars. Filthy skies."

I did my best to hold my patience.

"What city?" I asked.

Durant didn't bother to look at me. Instead he continued to stare into his telescope. "I never much cared for cities. Too many people. Too much light. Paris, bah. How could it compare to this?" Durant waved above him.

Paris.

"He went to Paris?"

"Get out of my house. You bother me." Durant glared down from his nest at the heart of the machine.

"Did he go to Paris?" I shouted.

"That's what he said. He also said he'd be back in three days. He lied." He tipped the pitch of the machine until it was nearly vertical. "The stars are constant. They never lie." His chair disappeared into the gears, leaving me staring up through the model of the swiftly tilting planets.

"Thank you, monsieur," I said as I jumped down.

"And don't disturb me again!" he shouted after me as I pushed through the heavy door. As I left, I could still hear him muttering a long string of numbers as he recorded his observations.

I ran down the stair in search of Will, and hoped his venture within the house had proved as fruitful.

CHAPTER SEVENTEEN

I TRACED MY PATH BACK THROUGH THE HOUSE, CAREFUL to tread as silently as I could through the clockwork conservatory. This place unsettled me, and I wanted to leave as soon as possible. When I finally reached the front door, Will was there waiting for me.

"Did you find him?" he asked. He was holding a contraption with a crank on the side, similar in size and shape to a jack-in-the-box.

I nodded. "My grandfather left for Paris about two years ago. He had only intended to be gone for three days, but he never returned."

"Did Durant say anything else of significance?" Will asked.

"He rambled quite a bit about the stars and darkness. He claimed my grandfather went looking for a truth."

Will gave me a nearly imperceptible nod. "I wonder if it has something to do with this."

Will pulled his hand from his pocket, and a woman's necklace dangled from his fingers. A pendant held a large jet-black stone nearly the size of an egg, surrounded by smoky crystals. "I found this in your grandfather's room. It seemed as if he left in a hurry. He'd burned a letter. Only a small piece remained on the hearth, but I couldn't make out any writing." Will lifted the necklace higher, and it reflected the dim light of his candle. "Do you recognize it?"

I looked closely at it. The stone in the center felt like it could draw me into and hold me in its depth. It felt as if the darkness there could hide any number of secrets.

"No." I had never seen it before. Not as a part of my mother's jewelry, nor in any family pictures. "I don't recognize it. Did you find a way past the wolves?"

Will closed his fist over the necklace and placed it back in his pocket. "I found Henry's plans for the wolves. They do respond to sound, but they're also called off by it. I removed the part that calls them off from the locking system within the door and installed it in this grinder. If we turn the crank, it should keep them at bay. I also found an old shawl we can wrap you in so no one notices your sleeve." He handed it to me, and I swung it over my shoulders.

"Will, you're a genius." The swell of pride that infused my heart surprised me with its intensity.

"We have a long way to go to the train station, but if we hurry, we can be in Paris by tomorrow afternoon. Unfortunately, if we take this"—he held up the grinder—"Durant will have no way to leave the house."

"I don't think he intends to ever leave the house again. We'll tell Oliver about this when we return. He'll know what to do for Durant," I said. "Let's go."

We walked nearly all night, and by the time we reached Calais, I was on the verge of collapsing. Luckily we arrived at the station just before dawn, early enough that we could pretend we had merely risen for the train.

We managed to buy two tickets to Paris, though the train was nearly booked. The tickets were very expensive. The only space left on the train was a private compartment, but Will paid for it anyway.

"Will?" I tried to protest, to offer what I could from my own meager earnings in the toy shop, but he stopped me.

He smiled. "I've taken care of it." He offered me his arm,

and I took it as we waited for the train to arrive. Many of the ladies were dressed in their finest, and I felt poor by comparison.

My own simple dress looked rumpled and soiled, with pale chalk dust still clinging to my hem, and the shawl hiding my torn and bloody sleeve. We looked like paupers, and yet we would be riding in our own compartment. I dozed off on the bench in the station, letting my chin fall against my chest, then tried to shake myself awake. Will told me to sleep while I could, and he vigilantly kept watch over us both.

Finally, several hours later, we boarded the carriage and found the door to our compartment. Will pulled the gilded handle and opened the dark wood-paneled door. The red velvet seats were thick and lovely, and the heavy curtains had been pulled back with a braid that had tiny golden tassels on the ends. I took a seat by the window and touched the polished brass arms of the lamp attached to the wall.

I had lived my youth in a house less fine than this. Will closed the curtains over the small window in the compartment door and sat across from me. "I hope this train ride is much less eventful than the last one," he said.

I let out a deep breath of relief. "Have we ever done anything so ordinary?"

"We shared a piece of tart once," Will said. The train jolted beneath us, then chugged forward into a comfortable and steady rhythm. I watched as the countryside passed by, sleepy French villages, woods, and farmland. I smiled softly to myself as I remembered how sticky the tart had been, and how Will had shoved half of it into his mouth at once. It seemed so long ago, and yet I could almost taste the forbidden treat.

However, now was not the time for gathering wool, even wool so fine as that. "What will we do once we reach Paris?" I asked. "We have no place to stay."

"We can stay at a boardinghouse or a hotel." Will reached across the compartment and placed a hand on my knee. My heart almost leapt out of my chest. I stared at his hand, so intimate. He withdrew it and gave me a glance, one of warmth and promise. I felt heat flushing through my cheeks. I had been trying to avoid intimacies as much as possible, trying to behave in a way that would protect my reputation. Now in the secure comfort of the cabin, I felt too tempted.

"A hotel will cost so much. This compartment was expensive." I folded my hands in my lap and looked down at them. "And it would be scandalous as well as dangerous. It is bad enough we're traveling alone together."

"That can't be helped." His soft brown eyes darkened, and I felt a terrifying thrill settle into my middle and dance around there until I lost my breath. "What do you propose we do?"

"I don't know, but we can't afford two rooms. You've already done too much. I shouldn't be in your debt this way. It is too generous." I met his eyes, and he actually chuckled softly to himself. I couldn't hear it so much as see the soft shaking in his chest.

"Do you know how good it feels for me to have money to spend?" He leaned back against the seat and crossed his arms.

"But you were saving that money for your future—"

"No," he interrupted. "I was saving it for us. If we use it now or we use it later, it doesn't matter."

"But it does matter. If we can't make it back to London for the Oath, you'll lose your position at the Foundry. Then what? It's too much to ask," I protested. "It is highly unlikely I'll survive this little holiday with my reputation intact. I can't ask you to tie yourself to a ruined woman and lose your position all at once."

Will didn't say anything, for a moment that felt uncomfortably long. He tilted his head, looking closely at me. I didn't want to meet his eyes. I couldn't see a way to escape this adventure unharmed, and it was unfair, because we had done nothing untoward.

He reached for me and tipped my chin up with a feather-like touch of his fingers. No man should have such eyes.

"As I recall, you never did ask. I offered." His voice sounded melodic and soft, the way it did when he used to work with his horses. "I want to do this for you. For us. I know you will never be free until we find your grandfather and stop the murderer who has him." He drew himself forward and cupped my cheek in his warm palm. I rested for a moment in the shelter of his touch. "I love you, Meg. If I can help you, I will. It is a gift freely given."

If I'd been starving, those words could have given me sustenance for a thousand years. If I'd felt alone, his words could have called armies to battle by my side. His words filled my heart, and at the same time terrified me because they meant so much.

I swallowed the sudden lump in my throat. "I don't doubt you. I only wonder if one day you will find that the cost is too much. I'm not free to marry for years yet, and thanks to me, you've nearly died several times. At what point does love become a hindrance instead of a blessing?" I sighed. "I can't help but wonder if one day you might meet a docile young lass up in Scotland without so many complications."

He tilted his head so I couldn't escape those eyes, soft and calm, deep like night and just as still. "Like a murderer attempting to kill her?" he asked.

"That."

He took a slow breath then dropped his gaze for the briefest of moments. With his head bowed, he looked as if he were in prayer. When he met my eyes again, there was something else there, truth and fear. "What makes you think I haven't had more promising prospects?" His voice dropped a tone.

I felt my heart stop.

I sat up straight, breaking his touch. He watched me, his expression still, but I knew him too well. His shoulders had stiffened, and he was bracing himself for my reaction.

My heart, when it chose to beat again, raced in panic. "Why haven't you mentioned this in your letters?"

"Because I've turned all the prospects down."

Turned them down. I felt drunk off the rush of relief, but then disbelief clouded my mind. I knew what Will meant to me. I knew what he had done for me. I also painfully knew every single time I had ever disappointed him, or taken him for granted, or turned away from all he was willing to give. I hated those moments. I hated that they existed. I hated that they made me feel I would never deserve the man who sat across from me. I wanted to feel I'd earned his love, and that I had more to give him than my own affections.

But I had nothing to give other than an uncertain life. He deserved happiness, not this madness. Not my rebellious passions. He deserved a woman who was worthy of his steadfast generosity, someone sweet and kind and good. I couldn't cling to him if I harmed him by doing so. If he wished for another, I had to be strong enough to let him find his own way.

"If you held affection for another, it's only right for you to consider her well. I'm only passingly fair, and I'm often trouble. I know there have been times I haven't done right by you."

Will crossed his arms, and his left eyebrow rose in that way it did when I was being either stubborn or difficult. "Haven't done right by me? You risked your reputation to seek me out in Rathford's stable when your reputation was all you had to survive. Then you treated me as if I were a person and not some dog rolling in manure, the way the rest of the servants in that house did. You were the first person *ever* to do something kind for me."

He remained steadfast and immovable in his conviction. "You forced me out of that bloody house and dragged me along into your schemes, where you relied on me, as if I had a keen mind, as if I were necessary. You had the audacity to turn down my proposal so you could do and be something great, something beyond my imagining, and then you continued to love and value me, even though I only work at the Foundry."

"You're brilliant at—"

"I'm not finished." His voice rose. "You risked your life to save not only mine but hundreds of my clansmen, my brothers. And lastly, but it's hardly the least of your apparent shortcomings, you've turned down the proposition of a blooming earl. A man you admire and respect. He's wealthy, he's nearly your intellectual equal, and he's handsome. Hell, if I were you, I'd marry him, and I can't stand the bastard!"

My heart felt so full, and free. I felt a hot tear slip over my cheek, and I let out an unladylike snort as I tried to compose myself. Will's expression softened, and he shook his head as if we had shared a witty confidence.

"What am I going to do with you?" he asked, his smile warming his deep eyes.

I didn't know, but I was so glad he was with me now. I couldn't help but tease him a little.

"So you had many a fair prospect in Scotland?" I touched my face with my handkerchief. The cloth felt like sand against my too sensitive skin.

"You are responsible for a river of broken hearts," he quipped, before reaching over and brushing my other cheek with the backs of his knuckles.

Damn but I loved this man. "Was Fiona at the inn horribly disappointed?" I asked. I had heard about the barmaid's ample portions of, well, portions.

"She cried for a month." Will's tension had drained out of him, but now I could feel another specter in the air, the memory of someone lost. I couldn't forget the young man who had initially teased me about Fiona's impressive bosom. Will looked down at his hands, then closed them and opened them as if he could feel something slipping through his fingers.

"You miss Duncan, don't you?" If only I had pieced things together sooner. We could have saved him. I still felt the sting of guilt that I hadn't been able to stop his murder. "I'm sorry."

Will met my eyes, and I could see the reflection of Duncan in them. As a young boy, Will had watched his father die, and then we both had had to watch his very best friend die, his blood flowing through my hands.

I never wanted to see death like that again. What I felt couldn't ever match the pain I could see in Will. I wished I could take the rest of it from him and bear it with my guilt, so Will could be left with only the love he had felt for his friend and brother.

"Duncan told me once to tie whatever bonds I could to you and never let go, because a woman of passion is a glory to behold." Will nodded his head, a slight movement I nearly didn't catch. "I have never met a woman as brave and bold as you. I told you once you were like a bird and I was like a stone. If that is true, then you make this stone look to the sky and know what it is to soar above the heavens. No docile and lovely lass in Scotland will ever make me feel the way I do for you."

I felt a tightness in my chest, a terrible and wonderful aching I never wanted to relieve. "If I am a bird and you are a stone, then you are my rock, the safe shelter I can return to again and again when my wings can no longer carry me. I love you, Will."

I could feel the air, thick and heavy around us, as he leaned closer to me, heated promise in his gaze. My longing for his touch became visceral, a hunger that threatened to consume me in fire. "And you will always return?" he asked.

"Yes. Always. Will you wait for me?" I whispered as he leaned even closer, stealing the distance between us.

"I'm a patient man," he murmured. "And stubborn," he added.

"Me too."

He pulled me into his arms, and his lips met mine with a hunger I couldn't tame. He kissed me with passion that could have burned through the cold of winter and set the world on fire. We fell together onto our knees on the floor of the little compartment. It was a private world for only the two of us, and the pleasure of a forbidden kiss. I pressed my body to his, wanting to be closer, knowing I could never be close enough as he took the air that I breathed and filled me with such wonder that I became the bird, and I soared, carrying him with me as I went.

A rhythmic tapping brought me to my senses.

Rap, rap, rap . . . "Tickets, please."

I gasped as I pushed myself onto the seat, my skirts in a jumble around my legs. I batted them down and swiftly brushed my hair back away from my face before straightening my shawl. I placed my hands primly in my lap and stared out the window.

My heart fluttered in my ears as I heard the compartment door slide open. "Tickets?" the conductor asked in French. Will produced them from his coat pocket. Will's waistcoat had been pulled askew, and his hair was wild from where I had tousled it in the back. His lips were full and glistening, and his hand shook as he handed the conductor the tickets.

The conductor cleared his throat, and I felt my face catch on fire. "Thank you, madame and monsieur," he said, this time in English. "Enjoy your stay here in France."

The man tipped his hat before giving us a wink and shutting the compartment door.

"Madame?" I still had enough decency to be affronted.

Will's eyes shone, bright and wicked. "He thinks we're married."

Dear heavens. If Will was in such a disheveled state, we had really crossed all bounds of propriety. "Or he thinks we're not." I must have looked like a trollop, with my hair flying away and my dress rumpled. "No wonder France has such a terrible reputation. He's practically condoning our indiscretion."

Will laughed. "Is that such a terrible thing?"

"Yes," I immediately protested. Then I gave him a wicked grin. "And no."

"You would have made a horrible countess." Will kissed his fingertip and touched it to my lip.

"I know." I leaned back against the seat. "Perhaps I am like my grandfather. I simply can't believe his past was so colorful."

"Describing your grandfather's rumored love life as 'colorful' is like describing a stained-glass window as 'a bit of glass.'" Will crossed his arms.

"It can't be as bad as that in truth. People love good gossip. I have a hard time believing my grandfather would behave so recklessly. At the time he went into hiding, he was fairly well along in years. What could a letter have said that would send him to Paris?" I asked. "And what does a necklace have to do with it? It doesn't make sense. He was so happily married to my grandmother."

Will steepled his fingers and placed them to his lips. "How can you know that for certain?" Will asked, choosing his words very carefully. "Things aren't always what they seem."

"I know," I snapped, perhaps more harshly than I should have. His words stung only because they matched my own thoughts too closely. I softened my tone. It wasn't Will I was angry with. "I know my Papa. He was a good and honest man."

"I'm not doubting that." Will pulled the necklace out of

his pocket. He watched it turn in the air. "It is as if we have several pieces gathered together, but they are all for different puzzles. You should keep this." He handed the necklace to me.

I looked at the large black stone and the chain. I couldn't bring myself to put it around my neck, not if it had once belonged to a woman in an unseemly arrangement with my grandfather. Instead I tucked it into the pocket I had sewn into the seam of my skirts.

The rest of the train ride to Paris was blessedly uneventful, and both Will and I caught some much needed sleep. We didn't have anything nearly so exciting as a tunnel collapse or a train wreck to throw us off course, although I wouldn't have minded another kiss. I felt my blood rush at the very thought, but I wasn't so bold as to initiate things, and Will had turned contemplative for the rest of the journey.

The worst of the adventure was our arrival five minutes late into a station that was half torn apart with construction.

It wasn't the most elegant entrance into Paris I could have imagined, but we had finally arrived.

We had little to claim as our own except a small sack of supplies. A sudden fear took hold of me. I didn't know where to go next.

I turned to see a man with a rounded face and neat beard watching Will and me. He wore pristine attire but had a look of mild reproach. I felt as if I had been caught cheating on an assignment by one of my instructors—not that I would ever do such a thing, but one could imagine.

I touched Will on the arm and nodded toward the man. He didn't look threatening yet but seemed far too interested in us. We had to pass by him.

Ducking my head in mock submission, I wished I had a proper bonnet to help hide my face. I fell into step behind Will, as if I were his dutiful young wife. I couldn't let myself stand out, not by my bearing or by holding my head high. As a woman I could disappear. All I needed to do was keep my eyes down and stay silent.

That is, until the man's foot came out between Will and me, stopping me in my tracks. I snapped my attention up to the man, fearful that he had put himself between me and Will.

Will turned quickly, but the man held his hand up to stop Will the way a constable does. Will paused only a second, but it was enough.

"It's a beautiful day in the garden," the man said, as if it were the most natural way in the world to greet a perfect stranger.

My shoes suddenly felt like lead, and my throat went dry. A million words I should not have known flew through my mind in a fit of vulgarity. I glanced down, and on his finger he wore a ring stamped with the seal of the Amusementists.

I gritted my teeth. There was no choice but to answer him. "Yes, when the sun shines behind the iris," I responded. As it turns out, my initial misgivings had been well founded.

The Frenchman smiled, and actually looked quite congenial as Will stepped around him and stood close by my side. "Hello, Apprentice Margaret. Welcome to Paris. Headmaster Oliver is beside himself." He smiled grimly. "Come with me. You too, MacDonald."

I gave Will a sidelong look.

We had been caught by one of the Order.

CHAPTER EIGHTEEN

WE FOLLOWED THE MAN OUTSIDE, WHERE HE WALKED A little way down the street to a less busy corner. A carriage waited nearby. I had never met this particular Amusementist before, and while he had the correct passwords to prove he was part of the Order, I was still wary.

"This is for you." He reached into his jacket and produced a crisply folded letter. I took it and inspected the wax seal.

It was Oliver's mark pressed into the wax.

I broke the seal with haste and read.

Dear Meg,

I would ask what you were thinking, traveling to Paris

with no one but Will, but I know what you were thinking, and I can't find it in myself to blame you. I am, however, running out of pigeons to send to Gabrielle, so I'll be brief. I am in no mood to lose my best student in my first year as headmaster, not to scandal, not to murder, and not to formality. You must return for the oath.

I know you feel we don't have time, but should our trail grow cold, I am certain we'll find it again. Your grandfather would not want you to destroy your life for this.

I expect to see you on the thirty-first. As for your reputation, I have explained the situation to Gustave. He's a trusted friend, and his new wife can act as your chaperone while you're in Paris. Take care.

I'll see you in London,

Oliver

P.S. Will, keep her safe.

P.P.S. Try not to drive poor Gustave into the madhouse.

P.P.P.S. The next time you ask John Frank for a favor, do tell him to leave the Amusements alone.

"I trust all is in order?" Gustave asked as he opened the door to the carriage.

"Indeed. Thank you for meeting us here." My misgivings

faded as we climbed inside. This had worked out better than I had hoped, and I was very glad to have friends who cared. Will sat next to me. I handed the letter to him so he could read it as well.

Once Gustave was seated, the carriage began to move through the wide avenues and boulevards of Paris. He straightened his jacket, and we had to look a fright compared to him. Will didn't look as disheveled as I did, but Gustave was clearly a very neat man. His dark clothing was meticulous, as was his short beard, which suited his wide face.

"I must apologize. English is not my best language," he began with a very heavy accent. "We have a way to drive yet."

"Where are we going?" I asked.

"To the home I have rented for the holiday for my wife and myself. Oliver suggested you may not have arranged for accommodations before you left London. He gave me the impression your departure was quite hasty." He crossed his arms over his barrel chest. "From the state of your attire, I see he was correct." He dropped his gaze to the pale dust on my hem, and I tucked the shawl more securely around my injured arm.

I did need to find something more suitable for Paris while we were here. Suffering judgment for not living as if I were a doll on the shelf was becoming very tedious. Gustave waved his hand in a nonchalant manner. "You are welcome to stay as our guests, but we will return to London in a matter of days. I ask for your promise that you will not run off again."

I nodded but kept silent. That was a difficult promise to make. I didn't know where the next clue would take me, but I now knew that asking for help from my friends was a much more convenient way to travel than trying to go on my own.

"We have no intention of traveling beyond Paris at this time," Will said. "Thank you for your hospitality. We are very grateful."

"I am only married this summer, and my bride is quite young. She is not a part of the Society as of yet. I would appreciate discretion," Gustave cautioned. The carriage suddenly rocked and shuddered as we rolled over a rough patch in the road. I glanced out the window at large work crews climbing scaffolding over the façade that stretched, unbroken, over the fronts of every building all the way down the boulevard. The façade made the street look very uniform and clean, but lacked character somehow. "MacDonald, it would be best not to mention that the two of you were traveling together."

"Of course," he assured.

"Now to the important matter at hand. You believe Henri

may be alive and in Paris?" Gustave leaned forward and wove his fingers together. "Oliver could say little."

Oliver had said Gustave was a trusted friend, and I realized I needed an ally here in Paris. I chose to take Oliver at his word. "I found a letter from my grandfather to Ulysses Rathford. It was posted after my grandfather's apparent death. He told Rathford he was going into hiding, and that the only person who knew where to find him was Rathford himself. Will and I searched Rathford's workshop and found a record of their last conversation. Rathford mentioned Pensée."

"So you paid old Maurice a visit," Gustave said. "And he is still alive?"

"Yes. He confirmed that Henry had indeed been at the estate, and that my grandfather had only intended to travel to Paris for three days, and then he should have returned," I explained.

"But he did not return."

"No." I took a deep breath. I didn't want to say what I was thinking aloud, but it couldn't be avoided. "During the summer the man who was responsible for the murder of my parents attempted to kidnap me. He mentioned he intended to reunite me with my grandfather. The ship he was traveling on frequently docked in Le Havre, and then continued up the river to Rouen. There's a possibility that he has been using the Seine to reach Paris by the waterways."

"That is a very weak connection," Gustave said.

"I know, except Durant has led us here as well. If we can discover evidence that the man who murdered my parents is in the city, then I will be certain my grandfather is still alive and here in Paris."

"But this man tried to kidnap you," Gustave stated.

"Which is why Oliver is beside himself." I smoothed my skirt.

"Do you know why Henri would wish to come to Paris?" Gustave asked.

"No, but we found this." I reached into my pocket and pulled out the necklace, letting the pendant hang from the chain. It felt cool against my fingers. "It was in my grandfather's room at Pensée. Do you know to whom it may belong?"

"It was near a letter that had been mostly burned in the hearth," Will added.

"It belongs to a woman," Gustave said as he took the necklace by the chain and let the large black stone twist in the light.

"We came to that conclusion, yes." I fervently wished we

could find my grandfather so I would no longer have to bear the weight of speculation about his less discreet dalliances in his youth.

"Perhaps he met an old lover and wished to rekindle the flame?"

"Do you know of any rumors of a love affair with a French woman?" I asked.

Gustave coughed and looked at me as if I had three heads, but then recovered his composure. I supposed it was a rather bold question. I was too used to discussing these things with Will.

Gustave cleared his throat. "That is too far before my time, and I never had any patience for the rumors of the Society women. I was not born into the Order. I was brought in due to my talent for engineering, and a certain need for structure in my schooling. I wasn't the best student before my time at the Academy." Gustave handed the necklace back and then pressed his back against the rigid seat. He glanced out the window. "We have time before we must travel to London. I will help you search Paris for your grandfather, but I refuse to knock on bedroom doors."

"Thank you." I felt the heat in my cheeks. I didn't wish to be poking around in bedrooms either, especially ones that may have been occupied by my grandfather, however briefly. I placed the necklace back in my pocket, then turned my attention to the window. Perhaps it was best that we moved off the subject. "What is that?"

I pulled myself closer to the window, craning so I could see as much as possible. A huge white arch rose up, like a great monument from the glorious days of Rome. It had been carved with depictions of triumphant angels in glory watching over men in battle. They had been sculpted with all the finesse of the masters of the Renaissance. It took my breath away. Even the street bowed around the arch in a wide circle.

"That monstrosity is the Arc de Triomphe." Gustave leaned away from the window so Will could look as well.

"Don't you like it?" I found it extraordinary. I wondered if perhaps the Amusementists had hidden something within it.

"So much of Paris has been torn down and built again in recent years. It is all fine in that the city is much more clean and orderly, but there is too much that is uniform about it, too much that is for the show of Paris." Gustave ran a contemplative hand over his short beard. "It is not Paris to me. Not Paris as it should be."

"And what is that?" Will asked him.

"Paris needs something unique," he began. He peered

back out the window, but instead of gazing at the Arc, he looked out on the horizon as if he could see something there, something grand. "It should be elegant, modern. An Amusement that stands out in the sun instead of sinking away and hidden to the world. Perhaps something that can facilitate communication between London and Paris, since receiving messages from the Order is so difficult here on the Continent."

"I'm sure you would be just the man to create such a thing," Will said.

Gustave waved his hand. "Ah, one day, perhaps."

We turned through some of the neat Paris streets until we came to a small square tucked away from the busy avenues and grandeur of the city.

Gustave exited the carriage and paid the driver before pounding the side of the coach and sending it on its way. "I apologize for our modest accommodations, but at least your reputation is safe beneath this roof."

We entered the narrow townhome and climbed a set of stairs before entering a modest parlor. A young woman came in to greet us. I was taken aback. We were very nearly the same age. She had a slightly squared face and very tidy hair that had been coifed in a strict fashion. While our ages were likely near enough, she seemed much older, or at least demonstrated a very serious disposition.

In spite of her cool expression, she smiled and placed dutiful kisses on Gustave's cheeks before turning to us. "I see you have found your associate, and recovered your friend's ward. It has been a busy day."

She spoke in a soft voice in French, though she threw a suspicious glance at Will.

"Yes. I'm afraid I had to wait quite a long time between the two trains," Gustave replied. "I'm sorry it took most of the day. My darling wife, allow me to introduce Mademoiselle Margaret Whitlock and also my associate Monsieur William MacDonald. This is my wife, Marie Marguerite." Gustave took his wife's hand and led her toward me, while Will very subtly faded back, as was his habit in polite company. Gustave's wife didn't spare him another glance as she came forward, took me by the shoulders, and kissed both my cheeks.

"How wonderful to meet you. I'm certain we should be good friends." She nodded primly at Will, who returned the gesture with a brief bow. "I'm sure you would appreciate the opportunity to freshen up. Then we may share something to eat and drink. It is a long journey from London."

She had no idea. "Thank you," I said as she led me

upstairs to a neat but sparse room. A small bed with a thick feather mattress and a warm cover occupied the corner, while a simple chest of drawers with a small mirror atop faced the bed at the foot. There was no other furniture save a worn knotted rug that covered the gouged wood of the floor.

I didn't realize I was so tired until I saw the bed. I didn't feel as if I had slept properly in a bed in ages. Marie Marguerite clasped her hands together as if she couldn't decide what she should do with them. "You may stay here. Where are your trunks?"

It was a simple question, but the truth didn't paint me in a very good light. I didn't know how Gustave had explained my sudden arrival to his wife, but her gaze kept flickering to my hem. She must have thought I had run away from my protector, and my lack of trunks would do little to spare her that conclusion. Still, it wasn't as if my trunks would suddenly arrive. "I don't have any." I caught a glimpse of myself in the mirror. My hair had become disheveled, I didn't have a bonnet, and I looked a fright.

"Did you run away?" She squinted her eyes, clearly suspicious of me.

"Not precisely."

"Did you plan to elope?" Her hand came up to her throat.

"No, not at all." I had to think of some explanation for all this, but my mind felt jumbled, and there simply was no good explanation for my appearance or my presence in France.

Her face brightened somewhat. "Do you run away from a marriage your protector has arranged for you?"

"Yes," I lied. "Yes, that is it exactly. I do not wish to marry." At least that much was the truth.

I thought about the kiss on the train. Well, perhaps I did wish to be married a little, but Marie Marguerite hardly needed to know about that. This was my best explanation, and I needed to abide by it.

"Oh, my," she exclaimed, taking a place on the bed and pulling me down next to her. I shifted my injured arm away. "Marriage is not so terrible. I had misgivings as well when my mother told me I was to marry Gustave, but I knew him from my childhood, and he is a very kind husband. Perhaps it will be the same for you."

I had to swallow the tightness in my throat. How did I find myself in this conversation? "I don't believe it will be the same for me." Actually, I was quite sure it wouldn't.

"You are a ward, no?" she asked.

"I am."

She seemed to relax a bit, now that she had taken on the

role of the wise madam who already knew everything there was to know about matrimony, though she had only herself been married for less than a year. "It must be hard not to have a family of your own."

I scooted an inch to put a small distance between us. "Yes, it is."

And it was. I tried not to let my longing for my family overcome me too often, but there were times I couldn't escape it.

Marie placed her hand on mine. "Then why should you not wish to begin a family of your own? You could have six children before the end of the decade, and then you'd have a very large family to care for."

By heaven, that was the last thing I needed. "Thank you for your concern, but this situation really is untenable," I protested. I felt the heat in my cheeks. I wished to marry Will eventually, but it wasn't our time. I had too much I needed to accomplish, and so did he.

"Is there something the matter with your betrothed?"

"No."

"Is he old?"

"No."

"Poor, unattractive, unkind?" She seemed genuinely

concerned for me, which only made me feel worse about this entire ruse. Perhaps it wasn't wise to mention that I had turned down an offer from a young, wealthy, handsome—if irritating—earl. "No, it is nothing like that."

Her lips pinched tightly together, making her face seem that much more stark. "Allow me to give you some advice. If a girl does not have a wealthy dowry, it is best to take the offer one is given. You would not wish to be on the shelf forever. You would never have a life of your own."

I blinked, speechless. For the life of me, I had never met anyone so intent upon my private circumstances. "What of you?" I suddenly realized I didn't know Gustave's last name, and it would hardly be proper to address her husband by first name. "Did you have any misgivings before you wed?" I asked.

She laughed, but it wasn't a joyous sound. There was something hollow and uncomfortable about it. "He was in need of a wife, and now here I am, Madame Eiffel." She patted me on my hand. "Do not fret. I'm sure you shall come to your senses soon. Your protector will not wish to keep you as a ward forever, and what will you do when he turns you out on your own? I will ask my husband if we can have an outing. We can go shopping for a new dress for you in the morning, and a bonnet. I'm sure his friend will not mind. Then when you return to London, perhaps you will be in better spirits."

A chill ran down my back. Marie Marguerite's words felt so foreign to me, and not because they were spoken in French.

"That would be lovely," I said, feeling very deeply uncomfortable in the presence of the young woman. She was the same age as I, and yet Gustave was older than Oliver. However, that was hardly uncommon. Most families wished to marry off their daughters to men who had already established themselves enough to care for their wives, especially if the girl had little dowry.

I had no dowry, but that didn't matter. I had something more. I thought about the toy shop and all I had accomplished in the Academy. To be kept as a wife felt so confining to me. I had none of these thoughts when Will and I were careening through dilapidated tunnels, or exploring the mansion of a senile old man. And yet, this world of Marie Marguerite was the world I lived in. This was the expectation on my shoulders.

It was as if I were staring into a curved mirror. I could not recognize the girl in the reflection.

Only two years ago, married like Marie Marguerite was all I had ever aspired to be. I had been preparing for my debut into society, where the mirage of choice would have been put before me in the form of fancy parties and dances, but in the end the man who wanted me would have chosen me. The wedding would have been arranged, and I would have settled into a life alongside Marie Marguerite, where my world would never have been any larger than the confines of my *place*.

"Perhaps I have a dress you may borrow for our supper so you can make yourself presentable. I'll return shortly," Marie Marguerite said. She touched her middle lightly as she rose, and I wondered if she carried a child already. How many more would she carry in her life? Would she do anything else of note? Did she secretly wish to? Or would she become nothing more than a note in the story of her husband's accomplishments?

Marie Marguerite left the room to retrieve her dress, while I turned to the mirror. I straightened my hair until it was neatly confined in its braids and a knot at the back of my neck once more.

A slight bruise from the flying pieces of brick had appeared on my cheek near my ear. I touched it. It was tender but did not hurt. I placed my hand over the bandage on my arm and the scars I knew I would always bear there.

They made me feel alive.

CHAPTER NINETEEN

SUPPER HAD TO BE ONE OF THE MOST SURREAL EXPERI-
ences of my life. Marie Marguerite's dress fit me well enough,
though it bound me beneath the arms, and the weight of the
fabric was enormous. The sleeves billowed out, and I had to
take extra care to eat with my very best graces, so as not to
place a sleeve into the sauce on my plate.

Gustave took to discussing the finer points of metal-
lurgy with Will in English, which was well enough for our
ruse. Marie Marguerite assumed Will and I didn't know
one another at all, and instead she occupied me with small
talk about the weather in France, and her predictions for the
weather come spring. Occasionally she added some variation

to the conversation by discussing the quality of the cheese that had been served, or complaining about the lack of proper linens in the house.

I had to bite my tongue to keep from joining into conversation with the men, but I had to play my part. Instead I tried to draw out some of Marie Marguerite's interests or even opinions, but whenever I broached any topic of conversation other than the weather or the quality of the linens, she brushed it off and turned our conversation back toward the mundane.

I was ready to scream.

When my hostess retired for the evening, I breathed a sigh of relief. Will retired as well, so as not to appear unseemly.

It frustrated me that I couldn't even bid him good night.

When we were finally alone, Gustave addressed me directly.

"Marie Marguerite asked me to talk some sense into you," he said, taking his glass of wine in hand. "It seems she's under the impression you're running away from a forced marriage." He chuckled. "Poor thing."

I sipped my cup of coffee. Oliver had helped me discover a taste for it, and this particular cup was very fine indeed. I placed it on its saucer.

There was something I wished to discuss with him, but it was a risk. Gustave was new to the Order, and so the traditions of the Amusementists didn't seem so tightly imprinted on him. I hoped to discuss Haddock with him but wasn't sure if he would reprimand me for mentioning the forbidden name.

I decided to be direct.

"What do you know of Haddock?" I asked.

Gustave choked on his wine. He coughed, pounding his chest as he looked at me through squinted eyes. "That name is forbidden." He grimaced, as if he too were at war with himself over whether or not to have this conversation.

"I know, which is my difficulty, because I believe Haddock is the one holding my grandfather hostage." I turned my cup on its saucer, then slowly turned it back again. "Punish me if you must, but I can't get to the truth of the matter if I cannot speak freely. If Haddock is dead, his punishment is complete. He won't care one way or the other if we have this conversation."

Gustave shifted uneasily. Eventually his eyes met mine, and there was a gravity in his expression that hadn't been there before. "Haddock is well and truly dead. He's buried in Père Lachaise. He cannot be the one holding your grandfather."

"Logically I know that, but that scandal seems to be the only thing in my grandfather's past fraught with enough hostility to lead to murder." I scooted back in my chair. Someone had to know something so I could put the Haddock name to rest once and for all.

"I know little. Only rumor. The incident was before my time. During my apprenticeship, he was whispered about among my peers. A cautionary tale." Gustave took another sip of wine.

"Do you believe he could still be alive?" I asked. "That he could somehow resurrect himself through mechanical means?"

He shook his head, as if I had just asked him if it were possible for an elephant to sprout wings and fly. "That is impossible. He is dead and buried. If you know what is best, you'd leave that name be, before you offend someone with more reason to reprimand you than I. You must take care, Apprentice." Gustave cleared his throat. "A man cannot reach beyond the grave. He had no heir. His name is as dead as he is."

"The man who attacked me wears a clockwork mask embedded in his flesh," I said.

Gustave's eyebrows rose. "How can that be?"

"Are you certain there is no way to mechanically resurrect

someone? My kidnapper used a bomb bearing Haddock's mark to attack me." I took another sip of coffee even though my hands felt unsteady.

Gustave tapped his wineglass in a thoughtful manner. "He created terrible things. Perhaps the one who wishes you harm merely knew where some of the dead man's old abominations were kept and wishes to claim them."

Lord knows I had discovered enough old Amusements on my own. "That is possible." I had considered that the man in the clockwork mask may have simply uncovered an old workshop and used the bomb for his own devices. There was only one problem with that line of reasoning. "But if that is the case, then the man in the clockwork mask must still be connected to Haddock in some way, or he wouldn't have known how to set one of Haddock's bombs. It's not as if these things are left around unprotected, not bombs anyway."

Gustave's expression tightened. "Please, do not say his name again. We understand one another. It's not necessary."

I realized the Black Mark was supposed to be a punishment. It would be dreadful to have your entire existence erased among a group of people who valued their contributions and their reputations so dearly.

Gustave placed his wineglass down and scratched his

beard on his right cheek in a slow and thoughtful manner. "Where would you like to begin your search tomorrow?"

"I have no possible link to the Frenchwoman who may have owned the necklace we found. The best clue I have at the moment is the one who bears the Mark. I'd like to visit his grave," I said.

Gustave leaned back and cocked his head slightly to the side, much in the same way that a horse does when it balks at a jump. "There are many connected to the Order in the city as we speak, preparing to travel to London for the oath. If they catch you, the consequences within the Order are not to be taken lightly."

"Thank you, Gustave. I understand the risk." I stood, ready to retire for the evening. "I deeply appreciate all that you've done for me."

"Do not thank me if you are caught. I want nothing to do with that cursed name." He rose as well and gave me a bow. "I regret I can do no more to help."

"I understand." The closer I came to Haddock, the less help I would find.

That night I had trouble falling asleep. I was warm, I was comfortable, I was clean, and yet I could find no peace.

The heavy feather mattress surrounded me, and with every breath, I felt myself sinking deeper and deeper into it as I stared at the ceiling. Too many things plagued my mind for me to find rest.

Every sound in the house sounded amplified in my ears. I tried to force myself to sleep. I needed to keep my mind sharp in order to find Haddock's grave.

I turned to my side. The wall held my interest as much as the ceiling. I closed my eyes and refused to open them.

Visions danced through my head, drawings, designs, and mathematical formulae. I often used the time just before sleep to try to piece together my grandest ideas. I pictured the clues I had thus far. In my mind I could see a puzzle, but the center was missing. It was an enormous dark hole that no amount of knowledge could fill.

The vision shifted and swirled until I lost hold on the control over my mind and fell into dreams.

I saw Will walking some distance ahead of me in the shadowy dark. It was as if we were back in the tunnel once more. I didn't know how I knew it to be Will, something about his walk and the way he held his shoulders. There was no mistake; I simply knew it was him.

"Will!" I called, but my voice caught in my throat and

wouldn't come out. I tried to run, but my feet felt stuck in mud. All the while he kept walking, drawing farther and farther away from me.

"Wait," I shouted, though the sound died in the darkness. I pushed forward, trying to drag myself toward him, but the invisible murk that had captured my legs stole up through my body and would not release me. I couldn't move.

Then I saw a light—warm and flickering at the end of the tunnel. My throat constricted as I tried to scream Will's name, but no sound would come out. The light was fire.

The flames reached up, growing and stretching until they became a massive wall of flame. Will continued to walk as if he didn't see it.

"No!" I screamed. I fought at my bonds. "No. Will, stop! Turn back!"

I fell forward onto my knees as Will reached the flames. I fought and fought, throwing myself on the ground and clawing forward, but it was no use.

He stepped into the inferno.

"Will!" I screamed. I watched the blaze consume him. The wall of fire circled around him, and he writhed in the center of a maelstrom of flame. He twisted and reached back to me, but his hand and arm had turned to ash. His entire body became gray, breaking apart and crumbling before my eyes.

He blew away in a ravaging wind.

I sat upright in my bed, sweat clinging to my chest and soaking the hair at my brow. I panted in fear as my heart raced. My throat felt dry and strained, as if I hadn't had a drink of water in years.

I threw my cover back and swung my feet to the floor. Without thinking, I padded across the room on my bare feet without a candle and cracked open the door. The wood floor felt like ice, but I still felt hot in spite of it.

Without hesitation I snuck down the narrow hall until I found the door to Will's room.

I had to see him. I lifted my hand to knock, but stopped myself.

If I were caught in front of his door—or worse, in his bedroom—my reputation would be in shambles and we'd be forced to marry under inauspicious circumstances. I opened my hand and pressed it to the wood. I leaned in close until my forehead touched the door as well.

A tear slipped from my eye as I forced myself to calm the lingering effects of my panic. In the quiet of the night, I could hear Will snoring softly while he slept.

I hated the separation. I hated all the blasted barriers that stood between the two of us. I wanted to pound on the door in frustration, or forget all bounds of respectability. I wanted to crawl into the warmth and safety of Will's arms and finally find my peace.

On shaking legs I turned away and crept back to my own room.

I didn't sleep the rest of the night. I felt I had survived ten full years by the time the sun rose again.

CHAPTER TWENTY

WE LEFT NOT LONG AFTER DAWN FOR THE PÈRE LACHAISE Cemetery. Thankfully, there was no snow, but it was still a bitterly cold morning. I could see my breath floating in the air as we climbed into the small open carriage Gustave had borrowed from a friend. He took the reins, and I sat beside him, while Will swung himself up onto a small luggage platform on the back.

I gripped my satchel more tightly. Marie Marguerite had been kind enough to lend me her dress for a second day, as well as a proper bonnet, but the skirts had no pockets. I was reduced to carrying around a satchel with my things instead of having both my hands free. I couldn't seem to get used to the hindrance.

Unfortunately—or fortunately, depending on how one

looked upon it—Marie Marguerite woke feeling quite unwell, and so she didn't accompany us. Perhaps she was already carrying her first child. It was an unsettling thought, though I didn't know why it should be. Besides, there was no room for her in the carriage. We would have had to take a taxi. That would have been quite expensive, considering Gustave's house was on the west end and we had to cross the whole of the city to reach the eastern side.

In spite of the cold morning, I loved the carriage ride. We followed the Seine east through the city. The river shone, silver in the cold morning light. To my left the entire city seemed to be made of nothing but palaces. There was a fine and elegant air to Paris that made it uniquely romantic. I wished we could have stopped so I could take in all the sights, especially as we passed near the island that was home to Notre Dame. I strained to see the roof of the cathedral, but couldn't make it out over the rooftops of the city.

Gustave snapped the reins next to me. "The city is beautiful this morning, no?" he asked, clearly pleased with my infatuation.

Will shifted behind me, then crouched on the platform, twisting so he could speak softly between us. "I think we are being followed."

I immediately turned my head, but Will stopped me with a sharp, "Be still!" It was hardly more than an urgent whisper, but I froze. "If you turn around, they'll know we're watching. It's a covered coach, not far behind us."

Gustave straightened but didn't give any other indication that something was wrong. "How long have they been behind us?"

"Since we came along the river," Will said. He adjusted his position so his arm looped lazily over the back of the seat, not a care in the world.

"They may be touring the city. It's natural to follow the river," I said. I really hoped that was the case, but even I doubted my words. Will was cautious, but he was hardly ever wrong about these things.

"Let's hope so," Will said.

An unsettled feeling consumed my middle as I gripped the edge of the seat. During the summer the man in the clockwork mask had proven himself a patient predator as he'd waited for moments of confusion or distraction to strike.

If he'd discovered our presence in the city, he would have the clear advantage in a game of cat and mouse. He was familiar with Paris and we were not. I pulled a small round mirror out of my satchel and used it to peer behind me. There was a fair amount of traffic on the streets, and the jostling of the carriage made it impossible for me to hold the mirror steady enough to get a good look.

My nemesis had planted a bomb in my toy shop to try to flush me out into the open. There's no telling what he could do to poor Marie Marguerite if he knew where we were staying. She was alone in the home.

Gustave turned to the left so suddenly, it jolted me into the side of the seat. I braced myself as he snapped the reins and urged the horse into a brisk trot. At a wide boulevard we turned again to the right, and the force of it pushed me into Gustave's side. I righted myself as he snapped the reins again. Will had managed to hang on and was now on his feet on the platform, crouched behind us again. "They're still following," he said.

Gustave didn't look away from the street before him. His eyes squinted into the sun and he scowled. "When we reach the gates, go inside the cemetery quickly." Gustave raised his voice so that we could hear him above the clatter of the wheels. "Will, be on guard. I'll do my best to draw whoever it is away. The grave you are searching for is near the tomb of Héloïse and Abelard. When you enter the promenade, turn to the right. It is not far. The grave you seek is a black stone on the ground. You will know when you see it."

We passed by a tall pillar, green with patina, with a winged golden figure atop the high column. We continued straight on past the monument, driving faster up a long straight road that passed between two ominous fortresses. They loomed over us like great castles, except the air around them was heavy with misery and death. Before the gate to the building on the left was an open area. Only then did I realize that we had crossed between two prisons, and the area was meant for crowds of onlookers to watch those doomed to the guillotine.

I ducked down, as if I could escape the heavy feel of death in the air, but it only thickened as we reached the high wall of the cemetery. Gustave turned the carriage sharply into the open curved area before the main gates.

Will leapt off the back of the carriage before it had fully stopped. He held his arms up to me, and I jumped to him without hesitation. He swung me to the ground, held my hand tightly, and we ran.

At the center of the curve in the wall stood a gate flanked by two enormous stone pillars. The top of each was a circle carved from arched blocks. In the center of each circle, a winged hourglass had been carved in relief. Large carvings of eternal torches decorated the sides of each pillar, with a garland defining the lower edge of the circle. Beneath the garland something had been written in Latin. We ran through the gate and turned immediately to the right.

"Do you think it's the man in the mask?" I asked breathlessly as we stood in the shadow of the massive pillar. A wide promenade cut straight into the heart of the cemetery, flanked by elegant mausoleums and young trees.

Will fought to catch his breath. "It must be."

A chill came over me. Yes, we had been searching for him, but now that I was faced with him, I only wished to run.

"Come on," Will urged. We ran together up the promenade, then squeezed between two of the mausoleums, hiding in the gap. He put his finger to his lips and a protective arm in front of me.

He backed us both up, and we hunched behind a narrow mausoleum. I tried to peek through the gap, tucking myself close to Will's side. A man passed on the far side of the promenade. He had a dark cloak with an unusually high collar and a brimmed hat that dipped low over his face.

He walked with slow, carefully placed steps. I held my breath, and Will pressed closer to me. He urged me back behind the mausoleum, but not before I saw a glint of light beneath the dark brim of the man's hat.

That was no monocle.

His face was wrapped in cloth, but I could see the edge of gears turning around a cold mechanical eye. My blood turned to ice.

"It's him," I whispered, pressing my body against the smooth stone of the crypt. "How did he find us?"

Will didn't answer. Instead he watched the man with the intensity of an alley cat. The man in the clockwork mask passed us, continuing on along the promenade. "I'm going after him," Will said.

I grabbed his arm. "Will, he's a murderer. He'll kill you if he sees you."

He took my hand and held it before glancing back toward the man walking steadily away from us. "He doesn't know where we are. This is the first time we've ever had the advantage. If I follow him, he could lead me to where your grandfather is hidden."

An image flashed through my mind of Will walking away from me and into the fire. It terrified me. "Will . . ." I wanted to tell him it wasn't worth the risk, but he was right. This was our one chance.

Will reached up and brushed a loose tendril of hair across my forehead. "He's not after me. He's after you. I will not wait around for him to strike any longer. He won't be watching for me. If I stay close to him, it will give you the chance to find Haddock's grave. If I am following, he can't sneak up on you the way he has before." Will reached down and removed the short blade he always carried in his boot. Then he took another quick look over his shoulder. "This place is a labyrinth. We're going to lose this chance."

"Don't you dare confront him." My heart was in my throat.

"I won't."

"How will I find you again?" I asked as he pulled away from me, skillfully concealing himself in the shadows behind another crypt.

"I'll meet you at the tomb of Héloïse and Abelard. He's turning. Meg?"

I closed my eyes against my terror. "Go."

Will surged forward and shocked me with a quick and passionate kiss before he pulled away. "I'll return soon."

I blinked, touching my hand to my tender lips. He darted through the tall monuments and mausoleums that lined the main promenade. I sent a quick prayer to the dear Lord for his safety and gathered my skirts before turning down a narrow lane lined on either side by trees. I hurried through the shadows, grateful to sink deeper into this quiet part of the cemetery.

When Haddock had been buried, the cemetery had been new and not crowded, but in the time since, the popularity of the cemetery had swelled, like a flood of the dead. I turned around. There were tens of thousands of graves, many elegant monuments to wealth and prestige.

The graveyard was full of faces, sculpted visages both beautiful and haunting, portraits of the dead in stone. Even in death, this was a place where one would wish to be seen, and I was searching for a shadow.

I reached a dead end, the wall cutting off the lane in front of me, so I turned to the left down another neat tree-lined path. The mausoleums began to feel like a village of tiny houses whose doors never opened.

A large building loomed to my right, so I walked alongside it, trying to keep to the wall. I found myself in front of another small gate, and the exit to the city made me nervous. I could see the towers of the prisons in the distance. I had to remain hidden, and I had to hurry.

My path had taken me in the opposite direction from Will, and though I glanced back over my shoulder, I knew every step took me farther from him. To my right was a narrow path lined by thick trees that had grown taller than the others in the cemetery. I darted down it and found myself in a crowded corner of graves. Many of the ones tucked into the corner by the wall weren't as ornate or as monumental as some of the ones near the promenade.

To my left I could see the crossed peaks of the roof of the Gothic chapel that held the remains of Héloïse and Abelard. I was in the right place. I just needed to find the right stone.

I picked up my skirts and stepped around and among the graves.

"Black stone, black stone, black stone," I whispered. Finally my gaze settled on a plain black slab resting on the ground. There was no name, no date on the marker.

Nothing.

I inched closer, my heart thumping so heavily that I could hear the sound in my ears. The plain black slab lay flat, large enough to cover a man completely. It felt like a hole in the ground, a pocket of darkness I could have fallen into. There was no escaping it.

It was the cruelest grave I had ever seen.

Until this moment I had thought the man in the clockwork mask was Haddock. I remembered the look in his eyes when he had attempted to kidnap me. He'd wanted to *destroy* my family. There was malice there that was acute and personal, and the only man I had found who had reason to hate us that much was Haddock.

But there was a feeling near this grave, something chilling and horrible. It was as if I could feel the spirit of Haddock beneath that terrible stone, trapped, erased for all time.

A patch of sunlight shone over the wall and through the dappled trees, hitting the dusty surface of the flawless black stone. I glanced around. There was no one in this narrow corner of the cemetery.

I knelt beside the stone, dusting it off with my fingertips. There had to be a clue here, something that would help me find the connection that eluded me. I pulled out the piece of paper and the crayon I had tucked into my satchel to make a rubbing of Haddock's grave in case it yielded a clue, but there was nothing engraved on the stone, so I stashed them away again.

My fingertips had left streaks in the dust, and the surface beneath shone like obsidian. I wiped a large streak across the stone, then another, eventually succumbing to a compulsion to clean it completely.

With my palm I stroked the stone, brushing off the dust, until my hand passed over the center where the heart of the corpse should have been lying directly beneath.

Tiny streaks of color followed my hand.

I pulled my hand back, afraid I had something on my palm, but aside from dust from the grave, there was nothing. Turning my attention to the stone, I noticed a pale brown color fading again to black.

Curious, I reached out and pressed my finger to where I saw the mysterious brown streak. I held my finger there for a moment, then pulled it down slowly. My finger left a trail of red in its wake.

Again I lifted my finger, and again the color faded back to black.

Whatever had been embedded in the stone, it reacted to the heat in my hand.

Spreading my fingers, I planted my palm on the stone. I held my hand there, counting to ten. Tension thrummed through every part of my body as I felt the stone warm to my touch.

I lifted my hand away, and there, glowing in orange and red, was the spiraling ram's horn.

It was Haddock's mark.

CHAPTER TWENTY-ONE

I LEAPT TO MY FEET, STUMBLING BACKWARD. I ALMOST tripped over a gravestone behind me and lost my balance. I had to catch myself against a tree.

"You should come away from there, dear," an old woman's voice said. "You wouldn't want to be caught somewhere you shouldn't be."

I staggered out of the graves and onto the path that passed in front of the tomb of Héloïse and Abelard. Hastily I tried to brush the dust off my skirt and tuck my loose hair back under the brim of my bonnet. "I apologize. I don't believe we've met."

The thin woman stood slightly hunched. Her stark white

hair had been done up in an older fashion beneath the brim of her hat. She reminded me a bit of Mrs. Brindle. She smiled at me and stepped closer on the path. "I haven't seen you since you were a child. I was good friends with your grandmother. My, you have grown. You look just like your father, a Whitlock through and through." The old woman had a sweet, round face and keen intelligence in her eyes. "You have made quite a name for yourself in the Order. Here on the Continent we have followed your exploits quite carefully. Allow me to introduce myself. My name is Madame Boucher, and I am a matron of the Society."

My heart hadn't stopped pounding from the moment I'd entered the cemetery, and yet somehow it managed to beat harder and more urgently. I felt quite ill. "Are you going to report me to the Order?" I asked, folding my hands and standing the way I had used to as a little girl when my mother chided me.

"My God, no." She gave me a sweet, motherly smile. "What good would that serve? However, it would be wise to stay on the path when visiting Père Lachaise."

"Of course." I took a hasty breath and tried to settle the rolling feeling in my stomach. I had to breathe, to think. The madam seemed more amused with my predicament than angry or offended. And truly, it was a comfort to have another person to talk to. "What brings you to the cemetery?"

She waved her hand idly toward the pillars and roof of the monument up the path. "I come every morning to leave a note with Héloïse and Abelard. They haven't answered my prayer quite yet, so I return each day. I also like to visit old friends. Unfortunately, when you have seen as many years as I have, most of your friends reside here. It is a good thing I found you. You must be very careful, my dear. I'd hate to see you ruin your family name. The name Whitlock holds a great deal of power." The frail little woman began walking down the path, but moved so slowly. I offered her my hand, and she leaned on me. "Thank you, dear."

It was then that I noticed how fine the material of the old woman's dress was. I had never seen such immaculately woven cloth, and the lace adorning her cuff could have bought the entire inventory of my toy shop outright. She must have inherited very well from her late husband.

The tomb was only a short distance away, and as we passed beneath a spindly tree, I looked up at the Gothic chapel. The roof seemed to float above the statues of the nun and the monk lying in repose. Their hands were pressed together in prayer as they chastely lay side by side for all eternity. It struck me as ironic, considering they had been rather scandalous lovers in their time.

The points on the roof seemed to reach toward the heavens, while the spire in the center of the crossed peaks gave the tomb the look of a wedding chapel. In the peaks a clover-like motif bound circles to circles, unbroken yet not whole either. They were empty spaces, cut away from the stone.

I wondered where Will was, and if he were safe. He was supposed to meet me here, and I longed to see him walking up the path. I had told him to go. I'd had to do it, but still. I worried. He would not give up on his task easily, and it might be a long wait before he could join me again.

Madame Boucher stood at the steps to the tomb and extracted a neat envelope from her reticule. She then leaned forward and dropped it onto the white stone steps of the monument.

She claimed to have known my grandparents, and she was a part of the Society here in France. She had to have been privy to rumors, including ones about my grandfather. Perhaps she could be the key to unlocking this mystery.

"It's very romantic," I mentioned, looking up at the two statues lying on their cold stone altars.

"Romantic? More of a tragedy, I would say." Madame

Boucher gazed at the tomb, and the warmth in her expression faded. "Young Héloïse, seduced by a charismatic scholar who was trusted by her own family. After she found herself with child, she was sent away to bear her son alone. He sought to protect his reputation, and so destroyed their future."

"That is not quite the story I heard," I mentioned, though now that I thought about it, Madame Boucher's version was probably the more accurate account of what had happened. "Poor Abelard ended up the worse for it."

The old woman smiled. "Indeed."

I glanced down at the bits of paper and messages littering the steps of the tomb. Now that she'd delivered her letter, Madame Boucher probably wouldn't linger much longer. It was a cold and bitter day, and I could feel the chill settling over me. "You say you knew my grandparents?"

"Oh yes, quite well, actually," she admitted as she turned away from the tomb and walked back down the path. I stepped forward and took her arm again to support her. "Your grandmother was a talented painter. I still have a small picture of a garden she painted for me in our youth."

"You do?" I had loved my grandmother's paintings, but they had all been destroyed in the fire. "I would love to see it."

Madame Boucher brightened. "Why don't you join me

for some tea? This cold is settling into my bones, and it is time I returned. I can show you the painting and tell you more about your grandparents."

I felt suddenly lighter, my heart quickening. This was my chance. Madame Boucher would know whom my grandfather had flirted with in his youth. She clearly had a keen mind and had been steeped in Society gossip for decades. Haddock's grave hadn't borne much fruit. When I met with Will again, I wanted to contribute something to our task. He was on the far more dangerous adventure.

"I really shouldn't leave the cemetery before my chaperone comes to collect me," I said. Though in my heart I knew it would be a long and risky wait. I didn't know where Gustave had gone, and Will could be relentless. He'd follow the man in the clockwork mask to the gates of hell if he had to.

The old woman waved her bony hand. "Nonsense. My home is on Île Saint-Louis. After refreshments it would be no trouble to send you home. After all, it is the center of the city. Come. It's getting late for luncheon, and I'm certain I have a fine selection of pastries for us."

Could I take this chance? I knew it wasn't anything as risky as chasing down a murderer, but Will was expecting to meet me here. Still, Madame Boucher could prove to be a font of illicit knowledge. The longer I waited in the cemetery, the greater danger I was in. I needed to find safety, and with Madame Boucher I could kill two birds with one stone. I needed to tell Will where he could find me.

"Go on ahead. I think I'd like to leave a letter for Héloïse and Abelard as well. I can catch up." I retrieved the paper and a red crayon from my satchel and quickly jotted a note to Will about joining Madame Boucher for luncheon on Île Saint-Louis, and that I'd meet him back at Gustave's. Then I folded the paper and stared at the clean back of it. There would be no way he could tell the note was intended for him.

Quickly I sketched a bird with her wings outstretched, perched on a round stone. I felt a flush of warmth as I remembered our conversation on the train and his passionate kiss. A bird and a stone. He would remember.

I placed the letter among the other plain envelopes. The red bird stood out in sharp relief. Satisfied it would catch his eye and he'd know it was for him, I stood, and then jogged through the graves to join Madame Boucher. I was very glad to be leaving the cemetery. I didn't like feeling surrounded by death.

When we reached the gates, I looked for Gustave, but he was nowhere to be found. Instead a large coach waited, pulled by a heavy black horse with a thick forelock falling over a wide white blaze. The horse's shoulders were wet with sweat. Vapor rose off the beast's body and clung to his thick winter coat.

A fair-faced boy sat at the reins looking bored or, rather, irritated with his situation. His dark hair stuck out in thick curls around the brim of his cap.

Madame Boucher approached him. "Did you do as I instructed?" she asked, but there was something different in her tone, a sharp edge that hadn't been there before.

The boy nodded but didn't speak.

"Good. Take us home then."

I helped Madame Boucher into the coach, then climbed in myself. The heavy door shut behind me, closing us in. We pulled swiftly away from the cemetery, the horse trotting down the boulevard with a loud clatter of his hooves.

Staring out the window, I sent up a quick prayer for Will. I wouldn't feel right until I saw him again, but for the first time since we'd begun this adventure, I felt hopeful. Will knew what he was doing, and I trusted his abilities.

We had found the man in the clockwork mask. He was in Paris, which meant that my grandfather had to be some-where in the city as well.

My heart ached. I was in the same city as my papa. I was close to him once more. I glanced at Madame Boucher—she watched me with eyes hooded with age but not dulled. With her help I'd finally put together the pieces that were missing and find him. I knew I would.

I'd bring him home. With luck perhaps I could even bring him back for the oath.

I let myself picture our happy reunion and glorious return to the Order. He would be next in line to assume leadership of the Amusementists, and with his power and protection, I would be able to fully be all I wished I could be.

I clung tightly to that hope as the carriage clattered past the fountain in the center of the plaza where the Bastille had once stood.

The farther we traveled away from the cemetery, the more hopeful I felt. The rocking of the large coach was soothing, so soothing in fact, I wasn't certain if Madame Boucher was still awake. She had her chin propped on her chest and didn't speak a word. The poor woman was probably exhausted. The monument to Héloïse and Abelard wasn't on the far side of the cemetery or up the large hill in the center, but the old woman had probably wandered a great deal while visiting the graves of friends.

The mark on Haddock's grave had baffled me. On the one hand, it had been hidden rather ingeniously. On the other, it felt as if someone had embedded it in the marker to rebel against the soulless nature of the stone.

It was a delicate piece of work, a forbidden one. The Black Mark was supposed to erase everything. The inlay on the grave proved that Haddock had someone who cared about him enough to give him a secret mark on his stone. That someone would have to have the technical knowledge to create something so flawless and delicate.

I wouldn't put it beyond the man in the clockwork mask. If the man in the mask cared about Haddock enough to alter his grave in defiance of the Black Mark, I had to discover how they were connected.

It could have been a mentor situation, something akin to what Oliver and I had forged. Perhaps they were related somehow. It had been difficult to piece anything together from the inked-over family trees in Simon's notes.

The disturbing thing was, there seemed to be a connection to me. I had been shocked last summer to discover that the man in the mask bore a resemblance to my father. I didn't like to think about it because it made me think of the moment I'd been kidnapped. In the safety of the coach, my heart accelerated and I could have sworn I could smell and taste chloroform. It choked me and fed the echoes of my fear. Perhaps it was time to consider that connection. Perhaps Haddock had nothing to do with this at all.

Maybe I was hunting in the wrong family. The man who had shed our blood could share it. Any number of deep family secrets or wrongs could have led to a discontented cousin seeking his revenge. Only, I had no family left who could reveal such secrets.

The coach shuddered as it hit a hole in the road. Madame Boucher jostled awake.

I didn't have my family, but I did have a new ally, one who might know things my family wished to hide.

"Thank you for inviting me to your home," I said. "I appreciate your taking me in."

She smiled at me. "The pleasure is all mine, my dear." She touched her neck at her collar. "I am so glad to have you."

CHAPTER TWENTY-TWO

I KNEW I HAD MADE THE RIGHT DECISION WHEN WE crossed the bridge onto Île Saint-Louis. Fine townhomes lined the street, built so closely next to one another that they seemed to form one single creation of fine stone and polished glass windows.

The carriage brought us around to the northern side of the island, then turned before stopping near the point. I stepped down from the carriage and gasped. Across the river stood Notre Dame. The light of the noon sun caught on the glorious flying buttresses winging off from the cathedral. The two towers stood like the gates to heaven itself, with the sun pouring down in a clear winter sky.

I stood, dumbstruck in the road, until Madame Boucher cleared her throat. She seemed bemused as she allowed me to help her down.

"Do you like the view?" she asked.

"It's wonderful." I tried not to let my voice sound too breathy, but I couldn't help it.

Madame Boucher's eyes lit up, as if she were sharing the most delightful confidence. "It's even lovelier from the tea room. Come."

We entered the foyer, and I was shocked for a moment that no butler or footman opened the door. It was strange that there were no servants to greet us. In a home as large as this, there should have been six footmen, at least. The interior looked as if it had been carved from pure marble and painted with gold. There was no mistaking the wealth on display— from the modern paintings to the crystal chandelier hanging in the foyer. Even the heavy blue velvet draperies spoke of money, and a lot of it.

I had been wrong. The madam had not inherited well; she had inherited *very* well.

The madam didn't call for anyone as she led me through the foyer and up a flight of stairs. I caught a glimpse of a courtyard in the center of the house. The trees and plants that had once grown there were dead from the winter cold, or perhaps from neglect. Some of the remnants of the foliage seemed badly overgrown, as if the courtyard hadn't been tended in years.

We reached a cheery room that had been painted with creamy yellow. Madame Boucher sat upon a dark green settee and watched as I gravitated toward the windows and the stunning view of the cathedral.

"I apologize, but it may be a moment before our luncheon is served." Madame Boucher folded her hands primly in her lap.

"That's quite fine." I was glad to be in a house again. It felt safer than standing around alone in a cemetery all day. "What did your husband do as an occupation?" I asked. "This home is lovely." Small portraits and pictures decorated the walls, and I turned to get a better look at them. Perhaps my grandmother's painting was here in this room.

"My— Ah, yes. This fortune was built on textiles. I manage the business on my own." She turned a figurine of a shepherdess so the porcelain girl faced the settee.

"You do?" I sat down across from her, eager for conversation. It was no wonder she had such fine sleeves. Business must have been doing well, for her to be able to afford all of this. "How is that possible? I didn't think that a woman could inherit in such a way. Wouldn't the business have passed to your husband's heirs?"

Madame Boucher remained impassive as she watched me. "He had no heir, and even if he had, it wouldn't have mattered. The company is mine. As you can see, I've done well."

"Very well. How remarkable." I was so honored to have met this woman. It was one thing to run a small shop in Mayfair, but it was another entirely to develop an industry and manage such a large endeavor. "I work very hard in a toy shop. I can't imagine how difficult it must be to control a mill or a factory. However do you manage?"

"My dear, the stories I could tell." She gave me a matronly smile. Perhaps after this was over, I could visit with Madame Boucher and count her as a mentor. She patted my knee. "You're a clever girl," she said. "Let me give you a piece of advice."

I leaned forward, eager to hear her words even as I glowed a bit inside at her kindness.

The wrinkles in the corners of her eyes creased more deeply with sudden seriousness. "Never let anything get in the way of your aim. Be flexible if you must, but never accept defeat."

I nodded. I let her words sink deep into my mind, determined to keep them there like a precious gem of knowledge. Madame Boucher turned around and lifted a small chess set from the table nearby. The squares of the board were inlaid ebony and creamy alabaster set on the lid of a box with sculpted edges. Silver vines and leaves adorned the edges above delicately painted pastoral scenes. Madame Boucher collected the pieces. She turned the black side to herself and waved her hand over the board.

"They say chess was created to teach strategy in war without real men coming to arms." She placed the king on the board. Something in her demeanor changed. Her expression grew heavy. "If only men could settle their differences through a game instead of blood."

"Did you lose someone to war?" I asked as gently as I could.

"A son." She placed the row of pawns, a neat rank of easily sacrificed soldiers. "He went to war against my wishes and returned a broken man. No mother should lose a son in such a way."

"True, but what can be done?" I set my rook on the board. "There will always be war."

"For all their inventions, I've often wondered why the

Amusementists haven't found a solution," she said as she placed her dark queen.

"That seems an impossible task. You can't change the nature of man." With the pieces set, I folded my hands.

"Men respond to many things," she said as she leaned back and waited for me to make my first move. "Greed, power, lust." I reached forward and moved my first pawn. She gave me a subtle grin. "Fear."

"What is there to fear greater than war itself?" I asked as she brought out her dark knight.

"That is the question, isn't it? As I recall, your grandfather was a fine chess player. Did he teach you as a child?" she asked.

I moved another pawn. "Of course."

She smiled at me. "Be warned. He never won a match against me." She made her countermove.

"You must have known my grandfather well." I had to think through the various chess strategies I knew to determine my next move. "Can you tell me about him?"

"Your grandfather was a man who commanded attention, which is why half the Society adored him. In his youth he knew little restraint, but he was a keenly intelligent man. If he had one fault, it was his ambition. He was never quite satisfied with what was before him. It was unfortunate, really. He could be very reckless," she admitted. "And he didn't often think of what that recklessness could produce."

"I'm not sure what you mean." I watched Madame Boucher's hands as they smoothly moved her queen forward. I didn't understand what she was doing. Didn't she see my rook?

"Here is another piece of advice for you," she said as she crossed her arms and waited for me to make my move. "Always think about the consequences of your actions. What brought you to the forbidden grave?" she asked.

"Curiosity," I said. I wasn't sure how much I should admit. Members of the Society were known for their gossip, and I had to be careful with what I revealed. I also had to be careful of a looming trap. I didn't trust that dark queen. Madame Boucher had probably changed the topic to distract me from the game, and at the same time I desperately wanted her to continue to tell me more.

"I find it interesting that you searched out that particular grave, considering." She glanced out the window as a black bird flew by. "Your grandfather was very closely aligned with the man buried at that grave. He was a part of the family, really," the old woman said. She moved a pawn. "It was inevitable."

I leaned forward, feeling I was on the cusp of something I

needed to know. I moved my knight to take the pawn. "What was?"

"That the daughter of the man you sought would fall in love with him." The old woman's eyes met mine. "They tried to keep it secret. They were very discreet, but some things cannot be hidden forever."

I let my hand fall away from the piece I was about to move. My heart beat faster. I was so close to the answers I sought. I could feel it. "I heard she had been sent off to protect her from her father's scandal."

Madame Boucher took my knight with her rook. "That is only partly true. There were other circumstances that required discretion."

Other circumstances? What other circumstances would require a girl to be sent so far away from her home? A knock pounded on a door below us, and the old woman rose.

"If you would excuse me. I have a matter to attend to."

She left the room and shut the door behind her. I wasn't quite sure what she'd been implying, unless— Oh my goodness. She couldn't have meant the girl was carrying a child. Certainly someone would have heard of the birth. I couldn't believe that a scandal of that magnitude would have escaped Oliver's grandmother's shrewd ears.

I took a close look at the chess board.

"Blast," I whispered. My king was in check.

Feeling fidgety, I stood and circled the room, busying myself with the various portraits and paintings hanging on the walls. A particularly lovely one of a vase of flowers and a bowl of oranges caught my attention. Next to it was a portrait of a young woman.

I realized with delight and surprise that it must have been a portrait of Madame Boucher. The woman in the portrait had the same round face, though her features were softer, with rosy cheeks and full lips, and hair that had to have been the envy of all around her.

She was a remarkably beautiful woman, and she was wearing a dark pendant at her throat. The pendant was small in the portrait, and wasn't completely clear, but . . .

I walked to my satchel and rummaged around in the bottom of the sack. Finally I caught the chain of the pendant in my hand. I had lifted it out of my satchel to compare it to the portrait, when the door opened.

A young housemaid appeared with a tray of food for our meal. She was dressed in a proper uniform with her hair tucked under a frilly white cap, but she looked directly at me as she placed the tray down and then approached me.

I took a step back. It was very odd behavior for a maid. I would have never approached a houseguest in such a way when I had been a maid, if we'd ever had any guests, which we had not. But that was hardly the point.

"You should not be here," she said quite frankly, squaring herself to me.

Aside from her olive complexion, we had remarkably similar features—the same height, build, even the same shape to our jaw and similar eyebrows. With her maid's uniform, I felt I might have been staring at a mirror of who I'd been only a year ago.

"What is the meaning of this?"

"You must leave, now." She grabbed my hand and pulled me toward the door. Affronted by her rudeness, I tugged my hand away and then reached up and grabbed her cap from her head. Short black curls tumbled out.

"You were the boy who drove the carriage!" I dropped the cap to the floor. "What is going on here?"

Her expression turned desperate. "There is no time to explain. You are in danger."

I felt a quickening in my blood. A tingling behind my ears. A voice in the back of my mind told me to run, and I listened to it. Something was very wrong here.

I had to get out.

I ran toward the door.

It opened, and I nearly collided with Madame Boucher.

Backing up, I did my best to give her a calm and pleasant smile. The maid retreated quickly into the corner and cast her eyes down. Her cap was still on the floor, her short hair wild around her ears. "Oh dear. I'm so sorry. I was going to tell you our luncheon had arrived," I said, attempting to turn to the side so Madame Boucher would step out of the doorway. As soon as a gap appeared, I intended to run. The old woman wouldn't be able to catch me.

I could feel the sweat gathering at my brow. My throat went suddenly dry. "Won't you sit down?" I asked.

Instead she looked at my hand, still clutching the pendant.

She tilted her head much in the way a cat does when it has discovered a mouse. Then she smiled just as she had when she'd moved her last chess piece.

"I see you found my necklace," she said, taking a step forward. I didn't know how it was possible, but she straightened, turning herself from what had been a bent old woman to an imposing wall.

She took the pendant from my hand, and in my shock I let it go. With steady hands she then placed it triumphantly around her neck. "I didn't expect to see it again. You see, I sent it to Henry to lure him here. How kind of you to return it."

She covered the pendant with her palm, pressing it against her bare throat. Boucher closed her eyes and took a deep breath as if she'd just found a long-lost treasure. When she drew her hand away, the dark stone had come alive. Shimmering from the heat of her skin, the spiraling ram's horn glowed with bright red and orange.

It was Haddock's mark.

"You're Haddock's daughter." I braced myself on the back of the settee for support.

Whatever had been sweet and motherly in the old woman's face vanished in that moment, as if she had peeled away a mask. The eyes that met mine were as hard as steel.

"I knew you were a clever girl," she cooed. "I'd like you to meet my son." A large figure filled the doorway. His black cloak swished against the clean white wainscoting as he looked up.

I fought my panic as I stared into the mechanical eye of the man in the clockwork mask.

Madame Boucher gave me a cruel grin. "Don't be rude. Say hello to your uncle, Honoré."

CHAPTER TWENTY-THREE

"TAKE HER," BOUCHER ORDERED.

I didn't have the chance to scream. I threw myself backward, crashing into the table and sending the chess pieces sailing across the floor.

The man in the mask, my grandfather's bastard son, surged forward. He slammed into me, and my body was crushed against the wall. I called for help, but there was no one who could save me. The maid who had tried to warn me slipped out the door.

The man in the mask wrenched my arms behind me. He squeezed the wound on my forearm, and my legs buckled with pain. He bound my wrists as Madame Boucher stepped calmly forward and placed a sack over my head.

In an instant my world had narrowed to what little light could pass through the weave of the cloth. I could see the folds in front of my eyes, but couldn't escape them. With each panting breath the sack grew hot. I tried to shake it off, but it was no use. I couldn't move. I couldn't see. My heart raced, and I tried to hold my breath as the rough cloth abraded my cheek. There was no escape.

I struggled and fought, flailing against my attacker and digging my heels into the floor. The bastard was too large and strong, and my dress restricted my movement. He muscled me forward, and there was nothing I could do to stop it. I kept grabbing for him, pinching and scratching what I could, but I never caught anything more substantial than his thick clothing. The sack smelled like rancid smoke and onions, and my eyes watered as I coughed.

"Really, my dear. It is unbecoming to put up such a fuss. You'll ruin your dress," Madame Boucher said.

It had been a trap. All of it. They had worked together to lure my friends from me, then sent the one person I wouldn't suspect to draw me in like the pied piper. I had fallen for it.

The dampness from my breath caught against my face as my half uncle knocked me against a wall.

He dragged me down a stair. The floor disappeared from

beneath my feet. I tried to find purchase again, but my uncle kept me pinned to his side. Only the tips of my toes brushed the stair as he hauled me down. I felt with every step as if I were about to fall.

That idea had merit. I tried to throw my weight so as to tip us off balance and send us crashing down the stair. I didn't succeed before my uncle lifted me off my feet entirely. I lost the tactile connection to the ground and suddenly felt dizzy as the bastard tucked me under his arm and dragged me down like a wet sack. I tried to bite him in spite of the heavy cloth covering my head. Every jolt, every step sent some part of his body colliding with mine.

I fought as hard as I could, because I knew that if I didn't escape now, I never would. I had to do whatever it took, but my uncle's body felt like a machine—cold, hard, and unyielding. I couldn't break his grip, or even throw him off balance. We descended deeper and deeper into whatever hell the old woman had in store for me.

I felt faint, unable to breathe. Bile rose in my throat, but I couldn't succumb. I had to be strong.

He threw me to the ground. The side of my head hit hard on the stone, before he ruthlessly grabbed my upper arm and dragged me back to standing.

"Henry, my darling. We have brought you a visitor," the old woman called, her voice echoing off the walls. Then she ripped the bag from my face.

I found myself in a dank cellar. I could see clearly. My eyes had already primed for the darkness in the sack. The room had been cut in half by the most terrifying wall of prison bars I had ever seen. Gears like spinning saw-blades moved around tracks fixed onto the bars of the cage-like device. No, they weren't gears. They *were* saw blades. They moved up and down the bars and over the prison's door. My heart caught in my throat as I felt alight with the fire of pure panic. Every muscle moved at once, taken with the instinct to fly as quickly as I could away from the monstrosity.

My bastard uncle held me fast, laughing low near my ear as I struggled against him.

A shadowy form emerged from the darkness.

His face appeared thin and wan, but his smooth bald head remained unbowed as he came forward into the light. The sharp angles of his brow made his eyes appear like narrow angry slits in his otherwise calm face, but there was no mistaking the fury in the set of his jaw or his proud shoulders.

"Papa!" I screamed.

He broke his composure. His gray eyes widened as he

rushed toward the killing wall. He stopped just shy of the spinning blades. "Margaret?" he shouted. "Can it be?"

I felt the sharp edge of a cold knife press against my throat.

"Back away from the door. If you make one move forward, she dies," Boucher said. Her hand was firm and I had no doubt she meant it. I didn't dare breathe for fear that the air passing through my throat would push my skin against the blade and cut me. A tear slipped out from my eye.

I had never seen such a fearful expression on my grandfather's face before. He backed away with his hands held up in surrender. "I will do whatever you wish, Cressida. Just don't harm her."

The old woman handed Honoré the knife. He pressed even harder into my skin. I felt the trickle of something slide down my neck and prayed it was only sweat.

"You will give me anything I wish?" She offered my grandfather a wicked smile. "You shouldn't make such tempting promises, my love."

She glided over to a panel in the wall and opened it. I saw a set of dials. She twisted them in a pattern, but out of the corner of my eye, I couldn't make out the combination of turns.

The spinning blades on the prison bars moved off the bars of the door, then slowed and stopped.

"If you move at all, Honoré won't stay his hand. He's already killed your son. Don't think he'd hesitate to kill her, too."

Honoré ushered me forward. Before we reached the deadly prison bars, Boucher grabbed the clockwork key. "You won't be needing this anymore."

She snapped the chain, and I felt the sharp sting across the back of my neck. Then all at once she opened the door to the prison and my bastard uncle threw me into the arms of my grandfather, sending us both tumbling backward.

The door slammed shut with a heavy crash, and then clanked and rattled as the blades whirred once more, resuming their pattern over the bars of the prison cell. My grandfather's arms held me tight. Then he sat up and hastily unbound my wrists. "Are you harmed at all? Did they hurt you?"

As soon as my hands were free, I flung my arms around his neck and held him so tightly, my shoulders ached with the embrace. I tucked my head against him and shook as he stroked my hair and clung to me.

He pulled me back and inspected my neck, but even that small a distance was too much. "I'm unharmed," I said, choking on the tears that quickly formed in my throat. He was alive. Thank God, he was alive.

He wrapped me in his arms and held me, pressing his rough cheek against the top of my head. "They told me you were dead. And George? Is he alive as well?"

My tears finally spilled over my cheeks. I didn't think I had the strength to say the words, but they came out in spite of it. "They killed him. Father and Mother both. They murdered them."

Even as I said it, I broke into sobs, racking tears that felt ripped from my soul as I cried in the arms of my grandfather. He was shaking. I could feel his own tears in my hair as he held me, but he didn't make a sound, and I finally succumbed to all the terrible grief I had been holding deep within my heart.

My mother was gone, taken from me by these evil people. She would never help to sew my wedding dress, or hold my child one day. Whatever children I had would have no grandparents to spoil and dote on them. My father had always been the center of our family, protecting me and teasing me when I became too serious or too full of my own pride.

I needed his guidance. I needed his love. I wanted for him to know Will. I wanted him to know that the reasons I loved Will came from the reasons I had loved him. My father had been steadfast and solid, but he, too, was gone for all time.

When I had been alone, my grief had been a terrible thing, but at the same time, it had felt as if I were the one who was lost, not my family. Now that my Papa was here holding me, the hole in my family seemed all the larger. My parents were never coming back. I could no longer share my life with them. I loved them so much. I needed them. I missed them. They were gone.

Gone.

And there was nothing I could do to ever bring them back. Papa couldn't either. In that, we had each other. Finally my tears turned to shaking breaths, and I couldn't cry any longer.

"I'm sorry," I mumbled against my grandfather's damp shirt. The clean scent of lemon mixed with rosemary that had always lingered on him was gone. His clothes smelled like mold and dust, or a grave. "I tried to find you."

"My darling girl," he said, and in his voice I could hear all the love he'd ever held for me. "You succeeded." He gave me a smile. He stood and helped me to my feet.

He was alive. I had found him alive. I wiped my nose on my sleeve and looked around. I couldn't see much in the dark. The only light came from a single lamp burning near the stair. The room we were in was sparsely furnished with a single bed and a chair in the corner. There was not much else. Nothing we could use to escape. The walls were thick stone, and the cage holding us terrified me. "It would have been better if I hadn't ended up in here with you."

"It was much more comfortable initially," my grandfather explained, "but I used most of the décor to try to escape."

I took his hands and noticed the scars crossing them. "What does that horrible woman want?"

Papa led me to the bed and helped me to sit, then took his place in the chair. "I would say revenge," he said, "but I'm afraid the situation is more dire than that."

"Tell me."

Papa's mouth set in a grim line. "She believes she can prevent mankind from ever waging another war if she can give the world a weapon so terrifying, no man would dare fight against it."

"That's madness." I rubbed my sore arm as I struggled with my disbelief. "She wants to use her father's invention, doesn't she? What is it?"

He stood and paced only a step away from me, then turned back. "A juggernaut."

I felt the impact of the word deep inside my chest, as if I had taken a terrible blow.

"What does it do?" I asked as the hairs stood up on the back of my neck.

"It's a vehicle." Papa ran a hand over the lower part of his face, then turned his tight circle again. "At least it was supposed to be. Haddock corrupted the original design. Originally it was intended to clear land. It could knock over and cut down trees, and rip the ground apart in its wake, leaving a blank canvas for building."

"You helped to design it?" I watched Papa's face closely. The corners of his thin mouth were as downcast as his eyes. After my encounter with the wolves, I could see a dark side to my grandfather's genius. Had he always taken things to a ruthless extreme?

I hated that I knew the answer to that question. He had abandoned his young lover to her fate, turned against his mentor, then allowed his family to believe he was dead while he'd hidden in France. Our family's downfall had been his making, and I hated it. I hated not being able to look at him the way I always had, as if he were a hero.

I didn't want to face my disillusion. Not yet. He was alive, and in spite of his faults, I did love him. "Did you know what the juggernaut could do?"

"I did," he admitted with a note of frustration in his voice.

"I was in the midst of my apprenticeship, and at the time, it was common for apprentices to pair with older members of the Order for special instruction. It was often difficult to meet at the Academy during that period, and so, like true apprentices, we lived under the roof of our master. Haddock was like a father to me, much more of a father than my own blood." He looked toward the spinning blades of the cage holding us prisoner. "I was young and headstrong and never imagined things would come to this."

"What happened?" I was ready to know the whole truth. I had been dancing around the edge of it for far too long.

Papa sighed and crossed his arms. One hand rubbed his elbow in a contemplative way. "We were in the midst of the Napoleonic Wars. Richard became fearful that Napoleon would be successful in his desire to invade England, and then the war of 1812 began. He went rogue on the project. Breaking the most fundamental laws of the Order, he took the design for the land-clearing device and turned it to a weapon for the benefit of the Crown in spite of such things being strictly forbidden."

"That's terrible." I had my own experiences with Amusementists gone rogue. It never turned out well.

Papa's brow furrowed as he watched the spinning saw

blades move along the surface of the cage. "I overheard his intention to sell modified plans for the device to a contact he had within the military. If he had succeeded, it would have exposed us, and embroiled us in the wars. I foiled his plot by locking the plans within the inner workings of the machine so that he couldn't sell them. Fearing he might break my locking mechanism and access the plans, I confessed everything I knew to the head of the Order." Papa turned his ring around his finger. The seal of the Amusementists flashed between his fingertips. "I only intended to alert the others to Richard's darker nature so they could talk with him. He could have been saved, if given the chance."

"You don't know that," I murmured. Papa turned to look at me and gave me a weary grin. No wonder he had been so intent on saving Rathford as well.

"There was no evidence at his trial of what he had done. When I tried to lead others to the juggernaut, the chamber was empty. The Order found nothing except for one vague message to his illicit contact. My testimony at the trial marked him. It shattered both his life and that of Cressida, which I'd never intended." He ran a hand over his face and fell back into the chair. I left the bed to sit at his feet, then laid my hand on his knee.

"You told the Order the truth," I said as he stroked my hair. "It should be the truth that matters."

"Truth is a slippery beast. I didn't know Cressida was with child. Had I known, I might have done things differently." He pinched the bridge of his nose, pressing his fingers to his eyes, then inhaled quickly as he lifted his head and steeled his expression once more. "I loved her once. Now she has taken everything."

"What does she intend to do with the juggernaut?" I had to get him off the subject of all we had lost. We were together at last, and together we would find our way out again.

"It's not the machine she's after. It's the modified plans." Papa stood from the chair and walked toward the deadly cage. "As I said, she intends to use the machine to attempt to stop a war."

The *Méduse* was sailing to the United States on the New Year. "She wishes to interfere in the War Between the States? What good would that do? Neither England nor France is closely allied in that war."

"No, but her business fortunes are dependent on a plentiful supply of cotton. She has some very lucrative contracts with certain plantation owners. Should the South be defeated in their civil war, Cressida would lose a great deal of money, and she won't stand for that. She intends to sell the plans for the juggernaut to the Confederate army and has deluded herself into believing she's serving the greater good."

Greater good? She had to be the most coldly ruthless woman I'd ever met. She'd killed my mother and father to reach her ends, and for what? "All this time, all she wanted was the key so she could retrieve her plans?"

"Not only the key," Papa stated as he crossed his arms. "She also needs someone who can use it."

CHAPTER TWENTY-FOUR

IF MADAME BOUCHER NEEDED SOMEONE WHO COULD use the key, that put us both in terrible danger. "Now she has two of us," I said, swallowing the lump in my throat.

Papa's eyes lit up as if he had seen the fruition of a carefully laid plan. "So, you discovered how to use my key. I knew you would. You always were clever. How did you figure it out?"

I didn't feel clever as we sat side by side on a thin feather mattress in our dark cell. We were no longer at home in our parlor discussing childish things like how I'd fared on my music lessons. The world had become very dark. My childhood seemed like a dream by comparison. I thought about the song, and all my memories of Papa singing it to me in more carefree times. "I discovered the key when Rathford attempted to use me to unlock his time machine," I said.

"Rathford? So he was responsible for the murders, then?" Papa asked, his brow furrowing into a disappointed scowl. "I had hoped it wasn't true."

"It wasn't." I forgot for a moment that he didn't know anything that had happened in the last few years. I told him how Rathford had taken me in as a housemaid after the fire, in the hopes that I would reveal the key. I told him about Lucinda, and meeting Oliver, flying with the Icarus wings, and battling the Minotaur. He seemed amused at times, and in awe at others, especially when I told him about the battle with the mechanical lake monster.

I told him about Strompton using Rathford's madness as a means to deflect suspicion while he committed murder for his political ambitions and his pride. I even confessed the horrible choice I'd had to make in the heart of Rathford's machine to leave my parents' deaths in the past.

Through it all, I left Will out of the story. I wasn't ready to let my grandfather into that part of my life yet. If Papa didn't accept him, I didn't know what I would do.

"I'm so proud of you, my girl." Papa smoothed my hair,

and I could see the love shining in his eyes. "You have done far more than I had ever imagined you would."

His words reached into me and filled me with a deep satisfaction, like gorging myself on all the Christmas feasts of a lifetime. "It doesn't change our fundamental problem. Since Boucher knows that both of us can use the key, that makes one of us expendable."

"That is true." Papa's brow furrowed over his sharply defined nose. He brought his knuckle near to his mouth and tapped it forward in a contemplative way. "We have to be prepared for the worst and look for any means of escape given the opportunity." Papa let his hand drop as he looked at me, then placed his arm over my shoulders. "We're together now, and we'll find a way out of this."

"Our hopes seem so bleak." Really our only hope was Will. I prayed that he discovered my note, that he would find some way to reach us here.

Papa pulled me more tightly to his side. "Nothing will seem bleak to me again. You're alive. They told me you had died in the fire, and it destroyed me. After that I told Cressida I would gladly die as well before I helped her use the key."

"Was that during the summer?" I asked.

Papa let out a heavy sigh. "I don't know for certain. I

haven't seen the sky in years, but it was warmer than it is now," he said.

I stood. That was it. It all made sense now. I had wondered about the reason for the sudden shift in tactics when I'd become a student at the Academy. Up until that point Honoré had been willing to kill me to get the key. After that point, it hadn't been merely the key he'd wanted. It had been me. If they couldn't force my grandfather to use the key, they needed an upper hand.

I was the pawn that had put the king in check.

"Dammit," I whispered.

"Margaret, I raised you better," Papa scolded. Then he rubbed his face and let out a resigned huff. "Though, I can't say it isn't fitting in this situation."

I paced, unable to contain the restlessness gnawing at my mind. So much weighed upon our shoulders. There was only one thing I knew for certain. "No matter what, we cannot unlock the juggernaut. It doesn't matter what they do to us. Those plans must never come to light."

War was bad enough, but the slaughter that would come should the juggernaut be unleashed would stain the world for generations. It could turn the tide of the war in favor of those keeping people like John and Gabrielle in slavery. Thousands, if not millions, of lives were at stake.

Papa's lips grew thin. He gave a subtle nod, though there was no mistaking the worry in his gaze. He placed his hand on his knee and braced himself to rise. The bones stood out on the back of his hand, and cuts and bruises had turned dark and discolored against his pale skin.

His hand shook as he pushed himself to standing. He straightened to his full height, and then his head fell forward. He stumbled and crashed against the bed before collapsing.

"Papa!" I ran to his side.

He blinked as he struggled to sit up. "I'm fine. I'm quite fine."

He didn't look fine. He was wan and pale. It couldn't have been healthy for him to be so thin.

He wasn't the towering, invincible man I remembered from my childhood. The man that stood before me seemed like a shadow compared with the man he had once been.

"You're exhausted." I helped him up by the arm and onto the bed. "You need your rest. You have to save your strength."

"I can't rest," he said, even as I pushed him back against the pillow. "I have to keep watch." His voice sounded thin.

I gathered his hand in mine. "Let me take a turn at the watch," I said. "Get some sleep now. I'll wake you if there's need."

It took a long time for Papa to settle down. He didn't seem to want to stop looking at me. He fought his exhaustion as his chin dipped toward his chest. I continued to hold his hand, not wanting to break the connection between us until he finally gave in. His breathing became even, and I was certain he had fallen into a deep sleep, perhaps for the first time in years.

"I'll watch over you," I said as I placed a gentle kiss on his forehead. I realized suddenly that those words were what my mother used to say to me when I had too many worries and couldn't sleep. I wasn't ready to be the one to bear the weight of it all, but as I looked at Papa, I knew he could not. I had to find the strength in me somewhere. He was my family. I would be strong for him.

I sat at the foot of the bed, but I couldn't still my mind. I wondered how many endless days and nights Papa had stared at the cage holding him prisoner. If there was a weakness in it, he would have found it by now. Papa was a mechanical genius, and I had no doubt of his desperation to escape. I felt it all too acutely. Time ticked on, punctuated by the rattling saw blades.

The blades spun through the bars of the cage, an endless, deadly ballet of moving parts. The rest of the walls were solid stone blocks. Trying to burrow through them would be as useless as bashing my head against them. The only way out was through the door in the prison bars, and yet those perpetually moving saw blades had me at an impasse. With the cage door shut, the tracks aligned to allow the saws to move freely over the bars of the door. I couldn't touch or inspect the bars in any way so long as I feared losing my hand to those saws.

I had to stop the saws. Papa was fading, and we wouldn't have long before our captors returned. There had to be a way to dismantle the cage somehow. It was an extremely complex structure, between the bars and the tracks for the spinning blades. Complex structures always had weaknesses. I needed enough time to find that weakness and exploit it. I had to try even if it seemed impossible.

I walked straight toward my opponent. The blades gleamed in reply. The light from the lantern flickered. There was a strange beauty to the blades, in spite of their macabre nature. They almost looked like falling snowflakes as they moved along the tracks.

If I could stop the saws, that would give me time to figure out how to open the door. I needed something I could use. I had only once felt this trapped in my life. I'd been locked in a trunk, and I'd managed to escape by breaking the hinges on the lid with the tools I'd had tucked in my pockets.

This time I had no tools, for I had no pockets. My only resources lay upon my person, and my clothing wasn't even my own. It was Marie Marguerite's and far too confining for my tastes.

They weren't my clothes.

I looked down at my skirts. I wore a cage crinoline! Thank the Lord for impractical fashion. It was modest, but it would do. Though I had to contort myself in an unseemly way, I managed to struggle free from the cage that held my skirts aloft. Working quickly, I ripped and tore at the crinoline until I had freed one of the bands of steel running through the hooped skirt. With the fabric covering it, it would cause quite a muddle if it tangled up with the saws.

At least, I hoped it would. The steel bands in the crinoline were meant to be flexible and light, not strong. I didn't know if the band would hold, but it was the best idea I had.

I bent part of the hoop from the skirt into a small loop and brought it toward the largest of the blades as it moved to the right. I could feel my heart fluttering in my throat. If I weren't careful, I could end this venture with no fingers. The loop had barely touched the blade when the teeth caught it and jerked my hand toward the saw. I let go, falling backward as the metal strand from the hoop whipped wildly about. I ducked and it nearly slashed me in the face.

A grinding noise filled our small chamber, and the gears and saw blade strained. Still, the machine pulled more and more of the metal into it, devouring the band as bits of metal and fabric flew out from the saw teeth. I covered my head until the grinding squeal eased to a constant high whine and the loud cracks and snaps of whipping steel slapping against the metal cage bars ceased.

Lifting my head, I peered cautiously through my fingers. The large saw blade trembled as it pulled against the binding I had inflicted upon it. Pushing myself from the floor, I held my breath and waited for the bonds to snap and the blade to start whirring again. The rest of the saws vibrated as well. Some turned as if trying to cheat the constraints that tied all the blades mechanically together. They slowed to a halt.

It had worked.

I couldn't believe it had worked.

Now I had to get past the lock and we'd be free. Hopefully the racket I had made hadn't caught the notice of anyone above us. I glanced back at Papa. He stirred and mumbled something incoherent. I hurried to him and soothed him back to sleep. He settled again, clearly exhausted. Breathing a sigh of relief, I ran a hand over my head, smoothing the hair that had flown from its confines. Hopefully, no one else had woken.

Something loud clicked, and then I heard a loud *thunk* behind me. A gear clattered, followed by an ominous scraping on the floor.

I desperately prayed it was the final death throes of the cage. Instinct told me it wasn't.

Somehow my heart managed to pound faster as I peered over my shoulder.

The wall had advanced!

I jumped back as the cage-wall with the tethered saw blades inched steadily forward, sliding over the stone floor.

Dear God, it was coming toward me.

"Papa!" I screamed, stumbling backward over my elongated skirts and landing against my grandfather. He woke, his whole body tensed.

"The wall." The large saw blade groaned as it strained against the metal wound around it. Twice it slipped and buzzed at us like an angry wasp. All the while the wall inched closer. The saw blades turned in short bursts of motion every time the hoop slipped. It wasn't stopping. By God in heaven, it could crush us if it didn't stop.

Papa leapt forward. "What happened?"

"I tried to stop the blades." The large blade slipped on the shredded hoop again, flinging a piece of the hoop right at our heads. We both shied away from one another, and it struck the wall right between us. The cage reached the halfway point of the room. With the saws spinning, the wall would tear us to shreds. I grabbed a loop of the fabric-covered steel trapped in the gears and pulled.

Papa grabbed it as well and unwound it from the axle of the blade as fast as he could. With eyes wide and his teeth gritted, he pulled, then drew his hand back to keep from being cut.

I wrapped the steel band as well as I could around my hand and tugged, but it wasn't easy with the bars constantly moving toward me. I threw my weight back, and the saw spun more freely, slowing the press of the cage.

"We need to brace the cage wall," Papa said. He reached back and tipped over the chair, then pushed the bed so the foot was facing the cage to give us as much room as possible.

The cage wall reached the foot of the bed and continued to press until the wood of the bed frame creaked and moaned from the pressure.

"It's going to snap," I warned, but I was too late. The side board of the bed fractured. Shards of splintered wood flew at us. One of the pieces struck me on the forearm hard enough to feel like the sting of a whip across my already wounded arm.

The cage wall lurched forward.

"We don't have much time. Pull together on my count," Papa ordered as he found a good hold on the flexible steel. "One, two . . ."

My heels hit the back wall, and I panicked. The cage had pressed the remnants of the bed and chair into a ghastly heap. Feathers flew everywhere as the saw caught the mattress and ripped into the filling. I nearly lost my footing. I needed room to pull, but there was no room left—in another few seconds the cage would press me into the stone. The saw buzzed too near my face. Sweat trickled down near my ear.

"Now!" Papa shouted.

We pulled, and the band of metal came free. The saw squealed as it came to life, becoming a smooth pale disk and masking its cutting teeth with its speed, but the cage still moved toward us. I scrambled backward, pressing myself against the stone wall.

The rest of the saw blades whirred back to full speed. One of the blades spun as it passed so near my cheek, I could feel it catch the wayward strands of my hair.

This was it. We were going to die, and it was my fault.

"I'm sorry Papa." I grabbed his hand against the stone and held it tight. "I love you so much."

"I love you too, my girl."

I closed my eyes, my breath coming in quick pants as I waited for the burning pain of the saws catching my flesh. I had stared into the eye of death before, but never like this. I was about to be ripped apart. I squeezed Papa's hand more tightly, dreading that first terrible bite of metal to my skin.

I heard another loud *thunk*. I blinked open my eyes as the press of the wall creaked to a stop, the blades still spinning near my ear.

I didn't dare breathe. I was about to faint. If I did, I would fall against the blades.

In the corner of my eye, the blade slowed. I dared to gasp a breath, but then the blade spun in the opposite direction. By the Lord! That wouldn't do any good. It was equally deadly one way as the other. The grinding started again, and I winced, waiting for the slicing to come. But suddenly I could see more of the blade from the corner of my eye. I blinked again, unable to believe my eyes as I now had enough room to turn my head.

The wall was in retreat.

A squeak escaped my parched throat.

Thank heaven. The cage wall was moving back.

Once I had enough room, I collapsed to the floor, pulling in great gasps of air as I tried to settle my innards. I was about to be ill.

Papa's chest heaved as he braced his hands on his knees with his head hung low, as if he'd just run across half of England.

My throat felt too dry for me to speak. I placed a hand to my chest where the key should have been.

"Are you hurt?" Papa finally asked. I shook my head, unable to form words, even though I could see a red stain seeping into my sleeve. I must have opened one of my wounds. There was nothing I could do for it, except let it bleed. I glanced around at the shredded timber, canvas, and feathers. We'd be sleeping on the floor, if I ever managed to sleep again.

Papa put a hand on my shoulder. Then huffed. "The juggernaut is not here in France. If they wish for us to use the key, they will have to take us to it. That is the moment we should strike, when they are vulnerable at last." Papa gave me a hard pat.

The bars looked dark against the light coming from the

lantern, and the saw blades pitched high and whined as the wall settled back into its original position.

I heard a footstep on the stair.

"Oh no. Honoré and Boucher must have heard the racket. What are they going to do?" I asked, turning to Papa.

"Well, they're not going to give us a new bed," Papa said.

I held on to Papa's arm the way I had always done as a little girl. We watched the stair, forced to wait helplessly to meet our fate. I trembled, but I had to be brave. I didn't want Papa to feel he had to protect me from fear.

"Meg, are you in here?" a soft voice whispered.

There, standing in the light of the lantern, looking haggard and sick with worry, was Will.

CHAPTER TWENTY-FIVE

"WILL!" I GASPED, UNABLE TO CONTAIN MY SHOCK AND elation.

He rushed toward us. "Thank God you're alive." Will skidded to a stop. "What in the good name is this?"

I ran toward the blades that only moments ago had nearly ended my life. "It's nothing to be trifled with, believe me."

We faced one another, only feet apart but separated by the terrible cage.

I longed to reach for him, to let him hold me in his arms. I had nearly died. I would have never seen him again. Now here he was, and yet there was no way to breach the atrocity between us. "How did you find me?"

"You left me a note, remember?" He didn't smile as he inspected the cage.

"It only said that I would be on the island. However did you find the house?" I'd thought there was no hope, and yet somehow Will had found a way. He always did.

"I crept into every single mews on this island until I found the horse and carriage that had followed us."

"Leave it to a stable boy." I never would have thought of that.

"Meg," Papa said. "Who is this young man?"

I took a small step back and ducked my chin. I felt suddenly on edge with nerves. "Papa, this is William MacDonald. He was Rathford's stable hand when I was a maid in his house, and now he's a member of the Foundry. I would never have found you without his help. Will, I'd like for you to meet my grandfather."

Will gave Papa a respectful bow. "I'd shake your hand, sir, but I'm afraid that under the circumstances, we'll have to wait on good manners." Will took a step to the side and raised up to get a closer look at the corner of the cage. "If we can stop the blades, we can get you out."

"No," Papa and I called at once. Will stared at us as if we'd lost our wits.

"I've already tried that," I explained. "If you tamper with the blades, the cage will crush us against the back wall." There was no way to escape. Not until we could defeat Boucher and her son. "There's no way out. Rally the Amusementists and bring them here. You have to stop Madame Boucher."

"Who is this Madame Boucher?" Will looked at the center of the cage, then drew his attention to the lower left corner.

Papa stepped forward. "Boucher is Richard Haddock's daughter. The man in the clockwork mask is her son." He paused, then hung his head. "He's *my* son."

That caught Will's attention, and he looked up at Papa with a wary expression. They didn't say anything, and I felt uncomfortable in the silence.

"What does Boucher want with you?" Will finally asked.

"She's seeking a set of plans Papa locked away inside her father's juggernaut. She hopes to sell them to the rebel army in America," I said, the words tumbling out of me like a sudden flood. "She's ruthless and prepared to kill. You must leave before you are caught. Boucher must be stopped before she can travel back to London."

I didn't want for him to go, but he couldn't stay. We had made a terrible amount of noise. Boucher could come down the stairs at any moment, and they would have no reason to lock Will up. He was of no use to them. He only posed a threat. They would kill him.

"I'm not leaving without you." He backed up a step, his eyes darting as he followed the pattern of blades around the cage.

"Please, Will. There's nothing you can do for us here. You have to escape." I looked into his eyes. "Save yourself so you can return."

Will removed the knife from his boot.

I thought he was going to jam it into the gears, and I surged forward—only to balk as I came too close to a blade that slid on a diagonal in front of my face.

"Will, don't," I said, but he stepped as close as he could to the bars and knelt. Then, with a quick jab, he pushed his hand through. "Take it," he insisted. "Use it if you have to."

I clasped my hands on his, taking the knife and putting it on the ground as I fell to my knees before him. The blades passed dangerously close to his wrist, but he didn't flinch. He'd found the single gap in the pattern.

"Will." I felt dizzy and breathless as warmth and hope did battle with the cold fear running like ice in my blood. I pressed my face against his palm, trying desperately to feel closer to that warmth that kept me whole and brave. His fingers combed into my hair around my ear. I kissed his palm, uncaring if my grandfather saw. The blades passed dangerously close again, slicing through the sleeve of Will's coat beneath his arm. Still he didn't falter. "I love you," I whispered. I had come dangerously close to death, and if I didn't make it out of this, I wanted him to know. He had to know without a doubt.

"I will come for you," he said, his dark eyes unwavering. "I promise. I will come for you."

"I know you will." I let go of his hand. He pulled it out from the cage, moments before a new blade slid down in front of me.

I picked up his knife as he grabbed his lantern and jogged to the steps. He looked back over his shoulder and nodded to me before disappearing silently up the stair as quickly as he had come.

I didn't move. The leather sheath of the knife still felt warm from being pressed against his body. I held it tightly against my heart as I listened and waited. With every effort of my soul I prayed for his safety, and that he would be able to find Gustave and the others.

Help would be here soon. We just needed to wait.

Finally Papa broke the silence. "So, you have a young man in your life."

I felt raw and exposed as I turned to face my grandfather. "I do."

"And I suppose you wish to marry him?" One of Papa's eyebrows rose as he crossed his arms.

"Not at this time, but perhaps one day, if he'll still have me." I bent and secured Will's knife in my own boot. It was uncomfortable pressing against my ankle, but the pressure was also reassuring in its own way.

"I beg your pardon?" Papa stepped closer to me and took my elbow in hand, forcing me to rise. "Clearly you have feelings for this boy. Has he compromised you?"

"What?" I stared up at him in disbelief.

Papa cocked his head, and his eyebrows drew close over his eyes. The expression made his already hawk-like features even more intimidating. "Because if he has, I will insist upon your marriage as soon as we are free. Now, has he compromised your reputation?"

I yanked my elbow from Papa's grasp. My face grew suddenly hot. I had been through too much to have this argument now. "That's a fine question coming from the man who sired a bastard while still an apprentice."

Papa looked as if a snake had risen up in front of him. "Margaret Anne Whitlock! You will not speak to me in such a way. I asked you a question, and I expect an answer."

It didn't matter to him that Will and I had done very little that was unseemly. It only mattered what others would say about us. I'd been through too much to care one whit what anyone else thought anymore. "Well, then expect to be disappointed, because I don't feel like giving it." It wouldn't matter if I did. He'd already drawn his own conclusions.

I turned away from him to the crushed and splintered bed and began stacking the larger pieces of wood against the wall. There was no real point to it, but I needed something to do. I slammed a piece of the wood to the ground and turned to him. "You may attempt to force my hand, but I will not marry."

"I am your grandfather and guardian. You are to obey me in all things, and I demand your respect." He stiffened, rising to his full height, but I stood up straighter.

"Then you should have earned it instead of fostering a reputation that nearly burned my ears clean off my head. To accuse me of some moral failing now is the grossest hypocrisy." My hands shook, and I couldn't stop them. All the tension of the last day took hold, and I felt like a pressure vessel with a dangerous crack in the casing.

"I am a man." My grandfather pointed to the ground as if his gender entitled him to the entire world he stood upon. "You are a young lady. The consequences of a lack of morality are much more severe for you."

I held my hands out to my sides and gestured to the cell we were in. "Are they? Because I can't imagine consequences much more severe than this."

"Your tongue has grown sharp." Papa scowled at me, and in that moment I really saw the similarity in our features. I was a Whitlock through and through.

"It's not the only thing that has," I muttered. I had grown much in the last year. I'd had to, because I had spent the last year alone, facing unimaginable danger, all because he had chosen to abandon his family and fake his own death.

Yes. I knew he'd had his reasons, and they were good reasons. But a small part of me could not abide him forcing me to live on my own in this crazy world of his invention, and then expect me to remain as fragile and untarnished as a porcelain doll on a shelf. I ripped open the buttons on my cuff and pushed back the heavy mutton sleeves to inspect the wounds on my forearm. The burned scabs were seeping blood, the dark stain growing as blood soaked into the linen. I yanked the bandage tighter.

Thankfully, Papa let the argument settle for a moment or two, and I was able to cool my head. When he spoke again, his voice was more gentle.

"I don't understand. You care for this boy. So why would you refuse to marry him? Is it because he is a Foundry man?" he asked in a conciliatory tone. "Because I'll admit I had higher ambitions for you, but if this is what you want, I'm willing to consider him."

I let out a heavy sigh and faced my grandfather. He knew about Will. I might as well confess the other weight upon my shoulders. Though, should we escape, he had very real power to take the thing I loved away from me.

"No, Papa," I said. My voice cracked. "It's because I'm an apprentice to the Order."

Papa took a step backward as if the room had suddenly shifted beneath his feet. "You're what!"

I had never seen a look of such disbelief on a person's face.

Just then we heard a noise on the stair.

I straightened and moved instinctively closer to my grandfather. Whatever shock my grandfather suffered, he shoved it away in an instant, stepping in front of me and shielding me from the stair.

I watched as the light caught on the pale hem of Madame

Boucher's skirts. She entered the room, with her son quick on her heels. I swallowed and remembered that salvation was on its way. In no time Will would bring others who could help. Then this all would be over.

Madame Boucher's lips pulled together in a slight purse of disapproval as she looked at the destroyed bed. She clucked her tongue, but then her eyes gleamed with an evil humor.

"I see you wasted no time in trying to escape." She stepped over to the panel that she had used to unlock the cage. She turned the dials, and the blades finally halted their incessant motion for real this time. Then she pulled out a pistol and pointed it directly at my heart. "If only you had been more patient, my dear. We had no intention of leaving you here. We're going on a little journey. Won't that be delightful?"

I spit at her.

She cocked the gun.

I didn't care. Every moment was another moment bringing Will back to me. My heart raced, but it wasn't due to the pistol trained on it. If they moved us, Will wouldn't be able to bring help. We'd be lost and on our own once more. I couldn't let that happen.

"Meg. Please. Do what they say," Papa urged as Honoré opened the door. I wanted to run, to fly straight up the stair and away from all this horror. Papa, too, stared at the open door.

Boucher turned her attention to him. "I had no idea you had raised such a rude and ill-mannered brat," she said as Honoré fastened heavy manacles on Papa's wrists behind his back. "If there's one thing I can't abide, it is a girl with poor manners. You should teach her some, before my finger slips."

I glared at the old woman as my uncle fastened a second set of irons on my wrists. I wanted to fight, but I wasn't willing to die. Not yet. I had to find a way to stall them.

"Move them out," Madame Boucher barked.

"No!" I fought as Honoré dragged me forward by the elbow. He caught me by the hair and forced a cloth over my mouth. The now familiar taste of chloroform filled my mouth and nose. I tried to struggle as the horrible chemical took effect. My head swam, and I collapsed, unable to fight any longer.

The last thought that crossed my mind was that I had failed.

I was lost, and Will would never find me again.

CHAPTER TWENTY-SIX

I WOKE COUGHING AND FEELING AS IF THE WORLD WERE spinning and shifting beneath me. Suddenly ill, I took shallow breaths through my nose. Thankfully, there was a little bit of light. I pushed my feet out, and they slid along a smooth floor. At least I wasn't in a trunk.

My innards roiled. I didn't know where I was, and now Will wouldn't know either. We'd been so close to rescue, only to be snatched away.

"Papa?" I blinked to clear my vision. I attempted to reach my hand out to brace myself so I could sit up, but my wrists were bound in heavy manacles. Using my elbow, I managed to right myself. It was slow going, since the chain between my wrists was looped around a pipe. With a deal of struggle, I managed to brace my back against the wall.

To my left, Papa slumped in a corner with his head hanging lifelessly to his chest.

"Papa!" I kicked my feet, trying to find some purchase as my throat went dry. My shoulders ached from pulling against the manacles.

"Hush. He's not dead."

I immediately turned to the voice coming from the corner. The housemaid with the short dark hair was once again dressed as a boy in plain trousers and a heavy coat. A faded gray cap covered most of her carelessly cropped hair. A dim lantern flickered near her hip.

"Who are you?" I asked, both wary of and curious about the girl. She had tried to warn me in the house. If only I had heeded her more quickly. There was no way to discern if she was friend or foe, but either way, it was best to know more about her.

"I'm supposed to keep you sleeping until we arrive," she said, shaking the dark bottle of chloroform. "Do us both a favor and keep your voice quiet, or I'll have to use this."

"You let me wake?" I had never seen a girl sit so still. She had her knees propped up immodestly in her trousers, with her elbows resting carelessly on them the way a boy would. Even her gaze was steady and watchful. "Why?"

"I'm not the best at following orders." She still didn't move, or reveal any expression at all on her face. She would be an extremely difficult opponent at cards.

"What is your name?" I asked. The more she talked, the more time I could give myself before she used the chloroform again.

"Josephine," she said.

"I'm Meg Whitlock. It's a—"

"I know who you are." Her thumb moved back and forth, a contemplative motion that revealed nothing.

Speaking with her was like speaking with my own shadow. "I'm assuming there's something you wish to say to me, or some information you want, or you wouldn't have let me wake." The floor shifted again, and I realized it had nothing to do with the chloroform. "We're on a ship, aren't we?"

She nodded, a single dip of her chin.

"I suppose your mistress is taking us back to London, then." It seemed that if I wanted any information at all, I was going to have to tease it out of her.

"She's not my mistress. She's my grandmother." Again

her expression remained still, but this time her gaze flicked to Papa sleeping in the corner.

"You're a Haddock." I felt the floor dip and surge again. My heart rose and fell with it. She was the daughter of the man in the mask. My half uncle. That made us . . . "We're cousins."

For the first time her face came alive with emotion, a flash of anger, then deep fear and sadness. Her dark eyes glinted in the light of the lantern, and her jaw set as she seemed to catch hold of the anger. "There is no bond of family between us. I owe no loyalty to you, or any Whitlock." She scowled and pulled her arms more tightly around her knees, crossing her forearms in front of her.

"Then why did you try to warn me?" There was something here. She hid it well, but there was a desperation in her. I couldn't see it so much as I could feel it, even from across whatever small and dank hold we were in.

For the first time she looked away.

"They treat you like a servant." I had to find some way to break through to her.

"Once madam captured him"—she nodded her head toward Papa—"she dismissed all the servants. She couldn't risk rumors."

So the girl had had to play every part from kitchen maid

to coachman for the last two years. I thought my own experience as a maid had been hinged on insanity. Josephine's situation had been even worse than mine.

"But—"

"Hush." Josephine jumped to her feet with the agility born of split-legged clothing. "She's coming. Pretend you're asleep."

I immediately collapsed to the floor and closed my eyes. With my face slack and my mouth open, I feigned sleep even though my heart was beating like the wings of a panicked bird.

Madame Boucher's boots clicked down a set of metal stairs. "Where have you been?" she snapped. I stayed still.

"I've been doing as you asked, keeping them asleep." Josephine's voice sounded very different, higher pitched and meek.

"If they're asleep, there's no need for you to remain. Speak with your father. He'll put you to work." Madame Boucher's voice was chilling. There was no love between the two of them, that much was clear, and it was a piece of information I might be able to use.

"He hasn't been my father since you did that horrible thing to his face. He no longer has a thought on his own, only does your bidding," Josephine said.

A loud smack crackled in the silence. I inhaled quickly through my nose, then prayed Boucher didn't notice that I had flinched. The blow had landed hard, and while I was thankful Boucher hadn't struck me, I felt terrible for Josephine.

"You would do well to be more obedient," Boucher said. "And less like that Turkish whore you called a mother. If it weren't for her, my son never would have gone to war. He never would have been wounded. I was forced to repair him. He should have listened to me from the start. I always know what is best."

Josephine didn't say a word. I wondered if she was also thinking about her grandmother's wording. *Repair him.*

Boucher's boots clicked on the floor, and I felt the vibration in my cheek. "Now Honoré's the perfect son. He's loyal, unquestioning, and flawlessly obedient. Don't worry, my dear. Soon no mother will ever have to lose another son to war. I'll make sure of that." Her footsteps clattered once more on the stair that led out of the hold. "Be quick!"

As soon as I was certain she was gone, I opened my eyes and struggled against my chains. "Josephine, are you injured?"

She turned to me, the side of her face tinged red even through her darker skin. I could see the fury in her eyes.

"Please," I begged. "You have to help us. I know you want to do what is right. We can stop her. We can stop them both."

She took a step toward me as I struggled to sit up. She crouched down, balancing on the balls of her feet as she looked me in the eye.

"I don't *have* to do anything." She stood again, and my heart sank. She crossed the room back to the bottle of chloroform, and for a moment I feared she would use it. I was helpless to stop her.

Instead she put her boot on the bottom stair. She turned and looked back at me over her shoulder. "My father was a good man once. All he wanted was to make a life for me and my mother. Your grandfather would have been proud of him, if he had ever bothered to know him." She lifted her chin, then turned and walked up the stair, taking the lantern with her. "Now it's too late," she said as the light disappeared. My hope was lost.

Every day of the last two years had to have been mental torture for Papa. It was as if we were being held hostage by Cain. A damaged Cain that had been pieced together in a way God had never intended. It bothered me that Honoré bore such a striking resemblance to my father. For Papa it had to be ten times worse.

I collapsed onto the floor, feeling it surge beneath me. In the dark the motion felt greater and it made me ill. Papa groaned behind me.

"Papa, stay down and stay quiet. We're on a ship. They don't know we're awake." Again I pushed my heels against the slick floor, but I found no purchase, so I gave up and lay still. "Are you well?" I whispered.

"I'm fine," Papa said, but his voice sounded weak. "Do you know how long we've been on this ship?"

"No." We were completely at our captor's mercy, even if there seemed to be a chink in Madame Boucher's armor. Josephine would not be an easy ally to win over.

And now she was beyond our reach.

"Meg?" Papa whispered in the inky darkness. I wished I could reach out to him. I didn't like feeling so disconnected, in spite of our argument.

"What is it, Papa?" I closed my eyes and let my head rest on the cold metal floor.

"I am so very sorry for everything that has happened." His voice cracked as he whispered. A lump formed in my throat. "You were right to condemn me. All of this is my own doing, and I deserve to suffer for it. You should not."

"Oh, Papa." My voice broke as I said his name. "You didn't know."

"But I should have. What did I expect? Every day for the last two years, I kept thinking about a boy just like Georgie who grew up with no father. Now I see myself in Honoré, but that terrible mask distorts him. He's a monster now, with no humanity left. What sort of life is that? *That* is my fault. I should have married Cressida, even if it would have ruined me. I wanted to be ignorant because my responsibility didn't feel like my burden at the time. I didn't ask. I didn't want to know, and so long as I didn't seek an answer, I could pretend I had no responsibility. I didn't wish to be burdened then. It's my burden now."

"We all have burdens. If you had married Boucher, I would not exist," I said, to take his mind off his misery.

He let out a heavy breath. "Indeed, and what a tragedy that would have been, my remarkable girl. Please forgive me," he said. "Even if I never forgive myself."

"I do," I said. "Of course I do."

"Thank you," he whispered. "I would have hated to think that I'd lost the love of my only grandchild."

"But I'm not." I searched for his face in the dark. He must not have known about Honoré's daughter.

"I beg your pardon?" His chains rattled, and his voice took on a strange pitch.

"The servant girl, Josephine. She's your granddaughter too."

Papa breathed heavily through his nose. It took him a

long time to speak. "What is this? No servant girl has revealed herself to me."

I wished I could hold Papa and comfort him. It must have been a terrible blow to learn of Honoré, but in some respects this seemed much worse. "Don't worry, Papa. We're together. We'll find a way through this. Let's not think on things we cannot change just now."

We fell silent. Hours passed. The rolling of the waves beneath us took up a steady rhythm. I allowed my mind to wander in the dark and remember the family I'd once had, then contemplate the distorted family I found myself in now.

Finally Papa whispered, "What upstart had the gall to nominate my granddaughter as an apprentice?"

The question shocked me out of my reverie, but I needed it like air. I chuckled, trying hard not to let the laugh out and reveal to Boucher we were awake. It hurt to hold it in. "That honor would belong to Oliver."

"I should have known. He always did like to cause a stir, even as a young boy." I could hear the amusement in Papa's voice, which felt so strange considering our situation, but I supposed we had felt absolutely everything else, and the only thing left was to laugh in the face of our impending doom.

Here in the dark and quiet, it felt safe to do so. Papa let out a sigh. "I'm proud of you. I hope you know that. It must have been no easy feat trying to survive the Academy on your own."

I couldn't say anything in return. I had desperately hoped that Papa wouldn't force me to leave the Academy. Even if I didn't make it back for the oath, even if I were forced to leave it all behind and marry Will, my struggles would have been worth it to know I'd made my grandfather proud.

"So, tell me all you have done," he said.

And I did. I whispered the entire story of the bomb, and my nomination, Headmaster Lawrence's betrayal, and how David and I saved the Foundry.

Papa asked questions and was eager to offer advice from his own experiences as I told him about my struggles with the automatons. In the silent dark, with my hands shackled, unable to see or touch, I connected with my grandfather and for the first time truly felt as if I had a family once more.

Something banged against the hull, and the ship we were on shuddered.

I propped myself up on my elbow to peer into the dark.

"Pretend you're asleep," Papa whispered, and I eased

myself back down onto the floor. "Wait for the right moment, and then run. Your legs are free."

I nodded even though it would have been impossible for him to see me.

Run.

I could feel the sharp jolt of anticipation as a crack of light opened up from the hatch.

CHAPTER TWENTY-SEVEN

THAT LITTLE BIT OF LIGHT TAUNTED ME. AT THE SAME time it terrified me. While I could see an opening, a means of escape, I knew our captors would be coming down the stairs any moment.

Each second that they did not descend felt simultaneously like relief and torture. I lay as still as I could on the floor, counting my breaths and hoping I wasn't counting the last of them.

Just when I thought I couldn't stand pretending to be asleep any longer, the sharp heels of Madame Boucher's boots clanked on the metal floor near my head.

"Get up," she snapped, but I didn't move or twitch.

She kicked me hard in the middle. "I said wake!" White light flashed behind my eyes as the blow punched the air from my lungs, then turned to a deep and throbbing ache that made me wish my entire inside could be expelled, simply to make the pain go away.

I coughed and curled into as tight a ball as I could with my hands still bound to the pipe behind my back. Honoré knelt behind me and unlocked the chain. I tried to struggle away from him but I didn't have the breath or the strength. He yanked my arms back hard, and a new pain blossomed in my shoulders.

He latched the chain to a metal ring attached to his belt. He locked Papa to his belt as well, then pushed us both in front of him. I heard the ominous click of a flintlock setting behind me.

"If they try to escape, shoot them. Preferably some-place painful, but do try to keep at least one of them alive," Boucher said. I turned and watched the gears revolving in Honoré's face. His head trembled as he grimaced and winced. He looked as if he were trying to fight. The mechanical eye glowed red, then he stilled and nodded. I had been terrified by the man in the mask for a long time, but I had never been as terrified as this. I had just watched a man's will stolen.

Boucher cocked her head, satisfied as she addressed us. "It would take very little effort for Honoré to throw your dead body into the river. I suggest you don't try my patience. Now walk."

Papa and I stumbled after Boucher, climbing up the stair onto the modest deck of a small, mechanically altered steamship. I glanced around as surreptitiously as I could, keenly aware of the gun pointed at my back. We were at the London docks. It was late, and my vision was still blurry from the lingering effects of the chloroform.

We crossed a narrow gangplank. Then Honoré pulled up a hatch and pushed us down a spiral stair. I slipped, only staying on my feet when my chains pulled taut against Honoré. I stumbled on the heavy skirts as they caught under my boots. They were too long now that they weren't held aloft by the hoops, and they tangled hopelessly around my ankles.

The rotting wooden stairs creaked and moaned beneath us as Josephine went ahead dressed as a boy. Papa froze, and nearly caused us to fall when he saw her. He glanced at me with a question in his eyes, but I shook my head. The hope in his eyes died. I hated deceiving him, but now was not the time. Boucher already had the upper hand, and while she was reluctant to kill me outright, I had no doubt she'd kill Josephine if Papa showed any bond to her—to spite them both.

The light from Josephine's lantern swayed against the curved walls of the tightly spiraled stair. When we reached the bottom, we came up against a small landing and a heavy wooden door. Honoré produced a ring of keys and unlocked it. He pushed us through, and I found myself suddenly in someplace very familiar.

It was the tunnel that Will and I had taken with John Frank to reach the train. The enormous locked door stood before us, and behind was the passage to the canal that led to the catacombs and the Academy. We had come down the stairs that had been used to smuggle foreign Order members into the Academy.

We were so close to safety, to help, and yet we were trapped. I couldn't escape yet, but now I felt I had something of an advantage. They had to make a mistake at some point, and when they did, I knew the way home.

I watched as Honoré unlocked the larger door, moving the parts of the door in the right sequence. No wonder he'd been able to sneak into the catacombs of the Academy at will. He had the keys to the kingdom, and no one was the wiser.

Sometimes the insufferable arrogance of the Amusementists really was their Achilles' heel. They were men, not gods, and they too made mistakes.

The door shut behind us, locking us into the dark. Josephine lifted her lantern, but the small light did little to illuminate the long tunnel. It did reveal the hind ends of several rats as they scurried out of view.

I shuddered. We began the long walk down the corridor that led to the chambers beneath the Royal Observatory. Our footsteps echoed in the corridor as Madame Boucher stepped up beside me with a spring in her step as if she were suddenly a much younger woman.

"To think, no more war. No more death. It will be a perfect world soon." Boucher turned a wistful smile to Papa.

He glared at her. "Your actions will cause bloodshed on a scale the world has never known." He softened his expression. "Stop this insanity. You are not this cruel, Cressida. You had a beautiful heart once."

"And you broke it!" she snapped. "You broke it when you killed my father. You broke it when you abandoned me. And you broke it when I had to hold the body of my son, ripped apart by war. But I used what you taught me. I repaired him. Without me he would have died. He never needed you. And to think, now he's your only heir."

Papa's face was stiff with fury. "I have my heir." He moved closer to me. Josephine's light wavered as she glanced back at me. Her eyes glowed with bitterness, and then she turned ahead again.

I pulled away from my grandfather. If he placed too much value on me, Boucher would have more incentive to kill me. It was likely a moot point. She knew I was all Papa cared for. That was why she had captured me to begin with.

Boucher grinned, watching me the way a spider stares at a fly, waiting for it to weaken. She stroked my hair, and I flinched away from her. "Yes, and what a lovely heiress you have, for now."

We moved on in silence for a moment or two, but clearly she wasn't done tormenting us. "You and I are a lot alike, Meg. I, too, spent many hours reading the notes of a mentor and studying what I could copy from the archives. It is quite a peaceful way to learn. Of course, the most useful information that comes through these tunnels is never written down. You can achieve quite a lot if you listen carefully, even mask one's involvement in murder, if you wish. Such a tragedy, your parents."

That was the final straw. I threw myself toward her, straining against my chains. "I know that you ordered Honoré to kill them," I said, jerking the chain that connected me to my bastard uncle.

"Yes, but no one else in the Order figured it out, did they?

They were so quick to assume there was only one murderer on the night the Duke of Chadwick died. With a poisoning to distract them, no one looked into the origins of a fire." She lifted her head. "In fact, they still don't believe you. And so we're free to do what we wish right beneath their feet."

"You evil witch!" I pulled against my chains, but Honoré yanked me back. I fell against Papa.

She was responsible. It had been her all the time, from the very beginning.

"Keep quiet. Don't give her a reason to shoot," Papa whispered, but there was no dousing the burning rage that had taken hold of me.

Madame Boucher reached out and lovingly stroked my cheek. "Say what you will, my dear. You're at my mercy." She tapped my cheek in warning, letting her fingernails graze my skin. "Now be a good girl. Keep walking."

I fell into step beside my grandfather. I didn't say a thing. Papa and I glanced at one another. In his eyes I could see the same determination I felt. We would defeat her. We had to.

We finally came to the end of the corridor, where it opened up into the elephant graveyard. Once again mechanical eyes stared at me in the dark. Instead of continuing on to the train, we turned and entered the darkness.

Josephine's light stretched upward, growing weaker as it attempted to fight the gloom of the enormous room. The light caught on the dusty metal of the machines around us, then found gaps in the joints and gears, projecting enormous moving shadows onto the arched ceiling.

I stared in awe at the machines looming over us. The ones in front were mechanical replicas of several animals, including two enormous bears. Within their metal chests there was a gap with controls, just large enough to hold a man.

Towering above them was a war elephant with an articulated trunk. It was beautiful and haunting, with intricate Indian designs. The howdah on its back glittered with gold. I had never seen anything quite so beautiful and terrifying all at once.

As we continued, the machines turned to the fantastic. A Chinese dragon slept with its orb-like eyes closed near the feet of a manticore. In the dragon's paws was an enormous golden egg.

There were others as well, animals large and small, random engines and mechanisms, all languishing forever in the darkness.

At the back of the chamber we came to a third door, larger than the one at the end of the corridor.

Honoré opened this one as well, but he did it quickly, as if he had done it a thousand times before. Perhaps he had. The rat had been living in the sewers long enough. I glanced at Josephine. She was watching her father's hands.

She was learning the locks.

Perhaps she already knew them. Our gazes met for the briefest moment, and I wished I knew what she was thinking.

The door opened. If this chamber was the place where Amusements went to die, what were we passing into?

Honoré pushed me forward, and we entered a second chamber, deeper and darker than the first.

Madame Boucher seemed to forget we were there as she stepped into the room. But it was empty. There was a large raised platform deep in the back, much like a stage made of stone, and some pillars, but other than that, there was nothing.

Josephine lit a torch with her lamp, then went around the room quickly lighting more. The light didn't miraculously reveal the room's secrets. There was nothing there.

A ramp led up to the platform, and Boucher walked up beside it. She removed a loose brick from the side of the ramp, then reached inside. A rumble sounded beneath the platform.

I gasped as what had been empty space twisted and

flashed. Mirrors—enormous mirrors—had formed a magician's veil reflecting the wall behind us, as if it were the wall behind the platform. I had never seen such a large and convincing illusion. What had been emptiness became a curtain of moving glass slowly pulling back to reveal a monstrosity.

The machine hidden behind the curtain of mirrors was easily the size of a house, a smooth metal building with a round armored turret set staunchly atop it. Great blades protruded from the front. Each one had a diameter of easily fifteen to twenty feet. They had been attached to large gear structures that reminded me of the blades of our prison cage. When in motion they would spin, rotating around like the mouth of a giant mechanical crab that pulled everything into the blades.

The entire machine rested on giant wheels, the treads studded with sharp metal spikes.

It was a machine that looked like it could both crush and slice through an army of men. There would be no stopping it. No musket, no cannon would break the armor. It was death in mechanical form.

"Lovely, isn't it?" Boucher said as she climbed the ramp and patted one of the terrible wheels as if the machine were her favorite horse.

"No," I said. "It's rather juvenile, actually. Shoddy design, and it lacks finesse. No wonder your family influcnce waned, if this is the finest the Haddock line could produce."

Boucher marched back to me and grabbed me by the throat. Papa called out and tried to throw his shoulder into her, but Honoré blocked him.

I looked Boucher in the eye without blinking, even though I couldn't breathe.

"Let her go," Papa demanded.

"You have a lot of cheek," Boucher said. "Throw them into the maze until I have the boiler ready."

Honoré pulled us away. We stumbled through the door and back into the first chamber that was filled with mechanical monsters. Honoré dragged us into a large alcove off the main chamber. Filling the alcove were mirrored panels much like the ones that had hidden the juggernaut. The mirrors were oppressively tall, easily ten feet or more.

Honoré pushed us down a long corridor where the mirrors were perfectly aligned to create a long hall, with a tightly sealed polyhedron room at the end.

The mirrors reflected our small party as we passed along them. Our images appeared smoky in the dust that had settled on the glass. Honoré unlatched our hands and pushed us forward toward the room at the end of the long hall.

I landed hard on the metal floor that was set with deep channels and grooves. The edge of one groove dug into my hand as I pulled myself to my feet.

"Go to the center before I shoot," he warned, brandishing a pistol.

Papa took my hand and pulled me into the small room of mirrors. Honoré retreated back down the hall without ever taking us out of the sight of the pistol. Once he made it clear of the mirrors, he pulled a lever protruding from the floor.

I threw myself forward, determined to run back down the mirrored corridor. From somewhere beneath me the floor began to shake. The glass around me vibrated. A ratcheting sound clattered against the harsh squeal of old gears grinding, and suddenly the walls began to move.

"Meg, step back," Papa warned as two of the panels slid together right in front of me. Had I been another foot forward, I would have been crushed between the heavy mirrors.

I stumbled back into the small angular room, tripping on my hem, until I came face-to-face with my own reflection in the dusty glass. Long lines of me trailed into infinity as the angles of the mirrors reflected my image over and over.

Papa stood and took my hand. "Stay in the center and keep your eyes down when you can. The mirrors don't move here."

"What?" To my horror, the panels of mirrors making up the twists and turns of this terrifying labyrinth shifted, moving along the grooves of the floor to arrange themselves in a new way. Where I was looking at one side of myself, suddenly I could see from a different perspective. Thousands of images of me flashed in and out as the mirrors danced like ballerinas in a troupe, synchronized and mystifying.

"We're trapped here until they decide to let us out. You cannot move between panels without being crushed," Papa said.

"How does one defeat this?" I asked him. I did my best to focus only on him. It was so strange to see myself moving in and out of my vision as the mirrors surrounding us turned. They created pathways, then let those pathways fall apart as they shifted once again.

"I'm afraid it's impossible. There's no way out so long as the mirrors are shifting. It doesn't take long for the maze of mirrors to turn one completely mad," he answered.

CHAPTER TWENTY-EIGHT

"I CAN SEE THE WAY OUT," I SAID, POINTING TO MY LEFT. Every couple of moments the darkness beyond this terrible maze teased me as gaps opened up when the panels spun and shifted. "We simply need to make it through the spaces between the panes as they move."

Papa shook his head. "That's not going to work. This maze was very well designed. If you move out of the center and into the shifting glass, the paths that open up in front of you will always lead you back here eventually. There is no way to reach the outside unless someone activates the main corridor again."

"Who created this awful thing?" I asked as Papa watched the mirrors.

He gave me a rueful smile. "This was not one of my better ideas."

"You invented *this*?" I turned around, beginning to feel dizzy. "Had you lost your mind completely?"

He shook his head. "Perhaps." He turned his attention back to me. "But I won the wager."

"Dear Lord, what was the wager?"

Papa threw his hands up, the way one does when they don't know what else they should do. "I was challenged to make an impossible maze. So I did. In hindsight, teasing the person with glimpses of the outside is a bit cruel, but trust me, it's all an illusion. No man can fit through those gaps." He took a step forward and peered out, only to have a panel shift suddenly and turn, forcing him to face himself. "More than half the Order tried to escape this maze. A fair purse hinged on it. Not a single one did. We are trapped until Boucher lets us out."

I watched the mirrors move, some of them with surprising quickness. If a man got caught between them, he'd be crushed.

But then, I was not a man.

"I'm small," I whispered. I'd have to be careful, and I'd have to be quick.

"What was that?" Papa asked over the din of the moving machine. I didn't heed him. Instead I followed Will's lead. He had found the single space that had allowed him to put a hand through the blades in our cage. If I observed carefully enough, perhaps I could find the precise timing, the correct gap to allow me to squeeze through.

I walked a slow circle, watching, counting. Planes of dusty glass and metal drifted before me, taunting me with my own image. I looked a fright. My hair had come completely undone and was sticking out in tufts from its pins. Poor Marie Marguerite's dress was in tatters. Even so, I didn't look nearly as horrible as Papa. I worried he would collapse again. My throat was parched. We hadn't had water in ages. It had taken its toll on Papa.

We didn't have much time. Boucher would be back for us as soon as the boiler was steaming. I took a deep breath. I couldn't let the pressure get to me. I had to have a clear head.

I exhaled, and fixed my gaze on a spot through the maze as one of the larger gaps opened. I could see a torch flickering on a pillar beyond. I kept hold of it with my gaze, watching as mirrors cut it off, then revealed it again. Maintaining the rhythm, I tapped my foot in time with the machine.

Like the flow of notes over the page, the mechanical beat revealed itself to me. I moved my hand now, tapping the air as I noted the beats of rest, those pauses in motion where my path was clear.

"What are you doing?" Papa asked.

I had it. I could do this. I turned toward Papa. "I'm going through."

"Meg, you'll be crushed." He took me by both arms and pulled me away from the gap. "I cannot allow you to do this."

"You have to, or they'll kill both of us before they're through. This is our only chance. I can make it." I stepped back to face the gap. My toe caught on my hem. But I couldn't do it like this.

I bent over and pulled Will's knife from my boot, then used it to free myself of my overly long skirts and slash the heavy sleeves of my dress.

"Meg, what on earth are you doing?" Papa said, clearly appalled that he could see the lace of the cuffs of my drawers hanging over my knees. I shed fabric the way a butterfly sheds a cocoon. Soon a pool of it lay at my feet.

"I can't afford to catch my dress or stumble." I ripped through the last bit of my sleeves and then cut a thin strip and used it to tie up my hair. Suddenly I felt more myself.

"I don't have the strength to follow you." Papa took my hand in his. His eyes burned bright with concern.

"I'll release the lever as soon as I am out. Don't fret, Papa. I can do this." I kept the rhythm in my head as I turned back to my torch. I flexed my legs, feeling the strength in them as I pulsed up and down with the beat of the shifting glass.

"Be careful," Papa said, but before he could say more, I sprang forward into the gap.

A panel of mirror twisted in front of me. I spun a half turn, then slid, making my body as tight and thin as I could while a second panel grazed along my back. I'd barely pulled my arm up before the panels closed in together, nearly trapping my hand within the tight seam.

I didn't have time to panic. Another gap. Another twist. I nearly lost my balance as I jumped to the side, then darted forward. I had to keep the torch in my sights, remember the rhythm.

A mirror passed in front of me. *Go! No, wait!* Another panel spun and stopped in front of me. I had nearly slammed into it. *Now go.* I jumped again, then stopped short. *Go. Wait. One, two, hold, jump!*

The mirrors aligned to create a long channel, and I broke into a run. My boots pounded hard on the metal floor as I flew toward the closing gap. The edges of the mirrors inched closer and closer to the torch, threatening to cut off my only escape.

I felt the knife come loose from my boot, then heard a clatter on the floor. I flinched, the briefest hesitation, but it stopped my momentum. I didn't want to lose my only weapon. In that moment an unexpected mirror swung into the path in front of me. I glanced back, hoping to grab the knife before the panel turned again, but another panel swung in and crushed the knife in one of the seams.

No.

I felt as though the last connection I had with Will had shattered.

The panel before me moved, and so did I.

Pulling in my breath, I ran. My timing was off, but I had to make it through one more gap. It narrowed, dangerously thin. I reached out my arm, then pressed my back to the mirror and slid through moments before the seam slammed shut, catching my skirt and holding it fast, unwilling to let me go.

I grabbed on to the already shorn fabric and ripped, cutting a long slit up the side of the skirt.

Falling to the ground, I gasped and felt as if my lungs were afire.

I did it.

"Meg?" Papa's voice sounded so distant. I had to hurry.

I ran to the lever Honoré had used to open the corridor into the maze, but I stopped short.

"Oh no." He had wrapped our chains and manacles through the lever. A heavy lock held the lever fast. I gave it a shake. It couldn't move, with the chain threaded through the gears at the base. Papa was still trapped. "Papa?" I called, terrified I was going to alert the Haddocks that I was free.

"Papa, the lever is locked. I can't get you out."

I didn't know if he could hear me. I didn't want to shout any louder. I found another shifting gap and stared back at him. There was shock and relief on his face. Then he smiled, and I saw the pride there. He shook his head as if in awe or disbelief and said something. I couldn't hear his words, but before the gap closed, I saw the movement of his lips. "Go."

I had to find help. I turned my back to the spinning maze, and suddenly found myself face-to-face with Josephine. She looked as surprised as I felt, with her hands out, as if I'd caught her off balance.

We stared at one another, unmoving, for a moment that felt like three lifetimes.

A million thoughts raced through my head. The loudest

of them told me to rush forward, grab her, throw her to the ground and silence her before she could call a warning to the others. That instinct to attack screamed at me. I remained frozen, unable to move, the way a deer goes still in the face of the hounds.

The corner of her lip turned up, just a hint. The Mona Lisa grinned like a fool compared to the subtle slip in Josephine's stone visage. "You escaped," Josephine said, her voice breathy.

I still had a chance. We were equally matched, and with my dress in tatters, I could move as freely as she did. I balled my fist. "I'm going for help. I won't let you stop me."

She shifted, widening her stance with a subtle slide of her boot on the stone.

Josephine glanced to the side toward the entrance to the elephant graveyard. "You won't make it through the tunnels," she said.

I couldn't tell if it was a warning or a threat. I had nothing left to lose. Holding out my hands in a conciliatory manner, I implored her. "Help me. If I can reach the Academy, I can stop this, but if Boucher succeeds, no one will be saved. Thousands will die. How many daughters will be condemned to lose their fathers?"

Josephine's brown eyes widened, a flash of expression that revealed little, but it was something. Something was there. Pain, and I could have sworn I saw anger. If she didn't feel it, then she was less human than her father, because I felt it on her behalf. She'd been gravely mistreated, and it wasn't fair. "You know what it is like to lose those you love," I pushed, digging into the wound.

She drew in a slow breath.

"As do I," I added. I felt the sting of the admission in my heart. Her father had killed mine, yet I needed an ally, not another enemy.

A high-pitched whistle sounded from the other room. Josephine looked up, and I did as well. The boiler was ready. We were out of time. I inched forward. If she wasn't with me, I'd have to keep her from warning the others somehow. I couldn't afford to linger any longer.

Our eyes met.

I shifted my weight, preparing to grab her.

As I surged toward her, she turned with surprising adroitness and ran like a fox with the hounds on her heels. She outpaced me, sprinting for the entrance to the tunnels.

"Dammit," I muttered under my breath as I charged after her, stumbling forward and trying to shift my momentum enough to get my feet under me. I should never have trusted her, not even enough to consider trusting her. My hesitation had led to my ruin. She'd tell the others. I had to get out as quickly as possible. So much was at stake, and help was so close.

If I caught her again, I would give her no pause.

I chased after Josephine through the Amusement graveyard, pausing only to yank an ornamental spine from the back of the dragon. The end of the spine formed a sharp spike and a hook, typical of the designs of the East, but it made an excellent pike for my purposes.

I ran forward toward the archway but didn't see Josephine anywhere. Slowing down, I listened.

Instead of the frantic steps of a running girl, I heard a squeaking noise driven forward by the sound of heavy footsteps.

I glanced down the tunnel that led to the room where we had boarded the clockwork train, then immediately pulled myself back and into the shadows.

Honoré was pushing a handcart full of fuel straight toward me.

I tucked myself behind one of the large mechanical bears. Honoré didn't seem in a hurry. He must not have spoken to Josephine. It was as if she had disappeared into thin air. But she hadn't found and warned Honoré. That was something. Boucher was behind me in the room with the juggernaut.

Neither of them knew I was free.

It was my only advantage.

If I could get past Honoré, I could make it down the long tunnel to the Academy and find help.

But Papa was still trapped in the mirrors, and the boiler on the juggernaut was primed and ready. They would do untold atrocities to him, and he wouldn't survive it. Boucher was waiting for her moment to do so. I could see it in her eyes. She wanted revenge.

Boucher, for all her evil machinations, wasn't strong enough to do any of it without her puppet.

I watched my uncle pass before me, completely unsuspecting. I couldn't let him harm Papa anymore.

My hands tightened on the pike. The weight of it felt solid, steady. He had killed my family. He deserved no mercy.

With a shout I leapt forward, swinging the pike above me and bringing it down toward the back of his head with a swift strike that landed on the back of his shoulder.

I expected to hear the crack of a bone. Instead the pike clanged loudly, and the shock of the reverberating force nearly knocked it from my hands.

The monster swung his head around, his mechanical eye burning red as it watched me stumble backward. The pike had caught on his shirt and was ripping the fabric as it tangled and fell.

Half of his back had been plated in smooth metal that encompassed his shoulder and flowed over his chest to cover his heart. It was like looking at a suit of armor, but more precisely molded. He turned, and the shifting plates of metal seemed alive as they stretched and revealed the clockwork mechanisms beneath.

Dear God, he was no longer human.

He laughed, a cold, cruel sound with a grinding undertone. Then he lunged forward and grabbed me by the throat.

CHAPTER TWENTY-NINE

HONORÉ'S MERCILESS GRIP CHOKED ME. I COULDN'T swallow or breathe. He dragged me to him. All the while the gears around his red eye twisted and turned as his gaze swept over my face.

"Should I kill you now?" he asked, squeezing harder. White pinpoints of light dotted my eyes. I scratched at his hand and kicked as hard as I could at his legs. I felt so weak as my toes bounced ineffectively off his shins. "I was given an order."

"You were ordered to put me into the maze," I choked out. I didn't know to what extent the mechanical parts of the man could take over his reasoning. His last orders had been to keep me alive.

He dropped me, and I fell to the ground coughing. I still felt as if I couldn't swallow. My jaw ached and my head throbbed, but my vision began to clear.

"Move the cart," he barked at me. He didn't have to say anything more. "Or you die" was clearly implied. He inspected the point of the pike and lifted it from the ground.

He wouldn't kill me yet. They needed me alive. If he murdered me, Papa would die before bending to any threat. They had held him for years, and they hadn't been able to break him before now. But now he was weak, on the verge of collapse. If they tortured him, he would die.

As long as I was still breathing, I had to keep my head. It was the only way I could discover a means to escape.

But "alive" and "unharmed" were two very different things.

I used the handle of the cart to pull myself to standing, then struggled to push it forward. The rusting metal dug into my palms, pulling the tender flesh there until it burned. I threw my weight forward, but the cart weighed more than I did, and it took throwing my hip forward against the cart before it would move over the uneven stone floor.

The tip of the pike dug into my back like a bee sting-ing below my shoulder. Though it was only the point, one false move, and the blade could cut into my flesh. It was like standing on the trapdoor of the gallows. Gritting my teeth, I struggled to maintain the momentum of the fuel-laden cart as I pushed it into the elephant graveyard.

My back ached, and the muscles of my arms burned and shook. Pain seared through my legs with each step. The enormous mechanical creations stared down on me, and I felt the heavy judgment in their lifeless gazes, as if I should be fighting. The handle of the cart and the pike at my back boxed me in.

I didn't know if I could fight anymore. I didn't know if I was strong enough. I had been struggling against my captivity, and at every turn Boucher managed to get the better of me.

I should have waited for Honoré to pass, then crept down the tunnel. I should have never tried to play the hero.

But it could have cost Papa his life.

I didn't know what to do. I was trapped and friendless, close enough to home that the stench of the Thames clung to the air, and yet I could see no way out.

The wheel of the cart bumped up against an uneven stone and stopped so suddenly, my own momentum threw me forward into the handle, knocking the wind out of me. My chest fell against the coal.

The pike jabbed into my back, stabbing into my flesh, and I cried out.

Honoré yanked the pike back, but the pain continued as my body shook. The cold air of the dark chamber felt like ice against my sweating skin. I could feel the sticky blood seeping into my corset. Every muscle trembled as I struggled to pull myself up. A cramp seized my leg, and I fell to one knee.

"Enough!" Boucher snapped at Honoré. "Take that cart and tend the firebox. Then bring the old man to me."

I didn't bother to look up as the hem of Boucher's fine dress swung into my view. She reached out with a black-gloved hand and tipped my chin up. She gripped my jaw, forced me to look into her withered face and fierce cold eyes.

"You are as slippery as an eel. Get up." She shoved my face to the side. I didn't move. "I said, get up."

I let all my hatred radiate outward until it felt like an aura of fire surrounding me. In it I found my strength. My entire body hurt, but I knew the cause of the pain, and so I could let it flow through me without succumbing to it. So long as I felt it, I knew I was alive. I rose.

"Dear me, whatever happened to your dress?" Boucher asked as she circled me.

"I improved it." I couldn't run. Honoré would catch me

too quickly, and I couldn't afford another gouge in my back.

Boucher clucked in disapproval. "Frankly, my dear, it's an affront to decency." Her voice bounced off the walls.

"It's such a shame that we are at odds, you and I," she said. "I would have loved to have a granddaughter like you—clever, resourceful, strong."

"You have a granddaughter," I said as she came back around to my front.

She slapped me hard. My ear rang, my teeth clattered, and my skin caught fire. I raised my head, lifting my posture until I could look down at the smaller woman.

She looked as if she could have been playing cards over tea. Not a strand of her snowy hair was out of place, while damp tendrils of mine clung to my forehead and touched my nose and eyes. "As I was saying, it's a pity you hold such loyalty to your dear grandfather. A girl with such potential should have the guidance of someone worthy of her." Boucher cocked her head to the side.

"Like you? A profiteer and murderer?"

She raised her bony hand again, but I didn't flinch. Instead I stared her down. She pursed her lips, then smiled again, the cold expression falling dead in the calculating look in her eyes.

"I have done remarkable things," she said. "I brought my son back from the brink of death. I built my own fortune. I survived, and now I will save the world from war. If I should profit from it, so be it." She circled again. "It was unfair to lay the burdens of my father's shame upon me. I was not to blame."

At one point I might have felt sorry for her, alone and expecting a child. "You're quite right. You should not have paid for the sins of your father. You made your own account long ago."

Just then Honoré arrived, prodding my grandfather forward with the pike. Papa saw me and struggled against his chains. "What did they do to you?"

"Move, or I'll stab her again," Honoré growled.

Boucher pushed me toward the back chamber, and I walked, feeling kinship with those who had faced the guillotine. Papa shifted, placing himself between me and the sharp end of the pike.

"Where is that worthless whelp of yours?" Boucher complained. Honoré didn't answer, but Papa stiffened at the mention of Josephine.

We came beneath the blades at the mouth of the horrible machine. I could see my reflection in the blades, softened by the layer of dust and the rust dotting the sharpened edges. Cobwebs hung between the twisting scythes. The webs waved ominously as we passed by.

I pulled myself up the spokes of the heavy studded wheel, then continued up a rung ladder to reach the top. The rungs felt cold and rough in my hands, and my legs and grip still felt weak. I kept myself focused on the top of the turret. I had never seen such heavy metal plating. It covered the innards of the machine, save several small holes at intervals, ports for more weapons. Every rivet in this machine seemed to radiate death.

And here we were with no escape from it.

At the top we crawled onto a wide platform.

I took in everything as quickly as I could. A short rail surrounded the platform, rising higher in the front, where a panel of controls stood behind a guarded shield. At the back of the juggernaut a sinister-looking device had been attached to the edge of the rail and stood as tall as the towering vent stacks of the juggernaut's boiler. Two large gear wheels disappeared into the turret on either side of the device's base. It reminded me a bit of an enormous bird, like a great stork or a crane, folded over and sleeping as it clung to the back of the juggernaut.

"Shackle the girl to the rail. She's caused enough trouble."

Boucher turned a wheel as my bastard uncle locked a heavy manacle around my wrist and latched the other end to a pipe railing, leaving the long heavy chain pooling at my feet. "And lock Henry over there." She pointed across the platform to the rail on the other side.

Boucher took Papa's key from around her neck and walked to a panel near the controls. She removed the plate, and beneath I caught a glimpse of a less refined version of the locking mechanism Papa had invented.

"Now then," Boucher began. "Who is willing to unlock this machine for me?" She turned to me. "How about you?"

"Never." I glared at her.

Honoré climbed up into the bird-like structure at the back of the juggernaut and took a set of controls in hand. The giant crane came to life, rising up and twisting to the side. The gears at the base spun as it moved and pointed directly at Papa. The head of the evil crane-like device began to glow with a hot white light. Papa rose to his full height and stared it down.

"Never is a long time," Boucher said, staying close to the controls of the juggernaut at the front, "especially when you are watching your dear grandfather die a slow and painful death as his flesh melts from his bones." She ran her hand over Papa's back, and he violently pulled his shoulder from her clutches.

"What demon has possessed you, Cressida?" Papa demanded. "You used to have a shred of humanity once."

"And what did it do for me? I was a naïve and silly girl. Now I know how the world works. It is driven by fear. Control fear, and you control man." She stroked the controls of the juggernaut lovingly. All the innocence and sweetness was still there in every wrinkle and soft wisp of white hair on her head. "Now, tell me, my darling love. Are you afraid?"

I couldn't fathom how someone who looked so harmless could be so corrupted inside. She turned to me, and it was then that I truly saw the depths of the darkness that had consumed her. She smiled, her dimples appearing in her weathered cheeks. "How about you, Miss Whitlock? Are you afraid? Don't doubt the power of the death ray. It focuses both heat and light to godlike effect. At this range your grandfather could be dead in a matter of excruciating seconds. But that would ruin the pleasure of watching him die slowly, with the intensity of the beam set to a lingering, torturous heat. I gave the order for your mother and father to burn. Don't think I'd hesitate."

A wave of terror threw my heart into my throat and twisted my innards into such knots, I desperately wished I could sink to the floor and heave until I couldn't breathe.

I couldn't watch my Papa die. Not now, not after everything we'd done. We were so close to freedom. But the whole of the world weighed on our shoulders. If this horrible machine were ever unleashed, war would turn into a more untenable nightmare than it already was, soldiers burned, sliced to pieces and shot. The blood would flow in rivers, and it would be on my soul.

I locked gazes with Papa. His face was stoic, but I saw the nearly imperceptible nod. There was peace in his eyes. He was ready to meet the next world.

Surely I would follow soon after.

A tear slipped over my cheek. I'd never see Will again. I'd never live the life I had sacrificed so much for. I didn't want to die. In spite of all I believed, I was afraid this would be the end and there would be nothing left of me.

I would never get to hold Oliver and Lucinda's baby.

I'd never get to see Peter or the rest of my friends again, or David, whom I hoped to still count as a friend. They wouldn't even know what had happened to me. I would become nothing more than dried-out bones in a dark hole where beautiful things were thrown into the dark and forgotten.

I looked at Papa. I never would have him back, not truly.

There was so much I wanted to say to him, so much of his knowledge I wished to know and pass on to my own children.

But there would be no children. No legacy. Nothing.

I would be no more significant than the dust, and my name would fully die.

I swallowed the lump in my throat, and though I was shaking, I fisted my hands and stood my ground. I had a million reasons to wish to live, but they were all personal reasons. I was still only one person, and I held the fate of hundreds of thousands—if not millions—of people in my hands. I couldn't fail them. Mine was one life. If I lamented my loss, I would have to rightly lament a thousandfold the loss of those I did not save. If I had to die, I'd die for them and all the potential they carried.

"I will not unlock this machine," I said, my voice echoing against the tall mirrors that stood sentinel to this atrocity. "I'm sorry, Papa. I love you. I love you so much."

"I love you too, my brave girl," he said, then closed his eyes.

"Well, damn it all," Boucher commented. I turned to her, and even though my thoughts and feelings left me overcome with fear and horror, I stood defiant. She stepped closer to me. "I had hoped to keep you. You have potential. I could have fitted you with modifications like Honoré, and finally given myself the granddaughter I deserve."

She snapped her fingers twice, and the head of the death ray swung to the left, then tilted down to point directly at me. I watched the light and the sparks swirling around in the crystal lens of the machine, a ring of gears constricted the lens, focusing it like a glowing eye. I felt a wave of heat come over me, so intense that the hair on my arms curled and withered. My skin burned, and sweat poured down my neck as Papa threw himself against his chains.

"Cressida," he screamed. "No!"

Honoré pushed a lever forward, and the machine glowed more brightly. Suddenly I felt as if I were standing on the face of the sun. I cried out and struggled to the side to escape the vicious heat. For as much as I was prepared to die, the pain had turned me into an animal who only wished to escape.

"The choice is up to you, my darling Henry," Boucher said as she reached out and touched his face. She placed the key in his hand. "Does she live, or does she die?"

CHAPTER THIRTY

I WANTED TO TELL HIM TO NOT GIVE IN, BUT THE WORDS stopped in my throat. I had to escape the burning.

I pulled toward him, and a loop from the chain that bound my wrist unwound, giving me more slack, but there was nowhere I could go to escape the ray. I felt the heat in my blood rushing through my veins so that it roared in my ears. I stepped closer to the machine, hoping I could find safety beneath it.

"To think." Boucher's voice sounded like treacle pouring from her throat. "She'll burn exactly the way her mother and father did. How very tragic. Only, this time you'll get to watch."

"Enough," Papa said, his shoulders sagging. "I'll do anything you want. Just don't harm her."

"Papa, don't. Please," I begged, knowing I was begging for my own death. I didn't want to die, but at least when I met the Maker, I would be able to hold my head proudly. That was what it meant to sacrifice. Pain was temporary. The grief of thousands torn apart by this abomination, would not be.

Papa looked at me, and for the first time I saw a broken man. "I cannot watch her die."

Boucher unlocked the shackle at his wrist, and he stepped up to the controls. I watched in horror as he opened the key. The killing heat ceased.

I had to stop this. Somehow there had to be a way. Honoré loomed over me with the death ray, holding me in its sights. The gear wheels turned at the base. What did I have that I could use? I had no weapons, my clothing was in tatters, and I couldn't escape the machine. I was chained to the rail.

By a ring. A ring that could slide. I scanned the length of chain and did a quick mental calculation. It could work, if my timing were perfect.

Papa hunched by the controls. The vent stacks for the enormous boiler rose up behind the death ray. I could feel the heat from the fire, but the engine had not been engaged yet. I listened as Papa played a sequence of notes that triggered resonant clicks. He let out a breath, and then his fingers faltered. He hit a wrong note, which slid into the key next to it, giving the song he had so carefully taught me a hiccup.

Boucher's gaze turned to ice. "Hurry, or you can say good-bye to your precious granddaughter forever." The floor beneath us vibrated, and then I heard a hiss and a loud squeal. The chamber under the controls opened as the power from the boiler reached the engines. Like a beast waking from hibernation, the machine shook itself awake. The blades in the front began to turn.

I had one chance, and only one moment when the old witch would be distracted. Boucher grabbed the plans, lifted them out, and held them before her like a precious treasure.

Now.

I dove across the platform, letting my feet slide forward and stretching my arms out so that the slack in the chain caught in the gear wheels at the base of the death ray.

Honoré shouted as the teeth of the wheels compressed on the chain. The gears strained, and the death ray whipped around on its jointed armature, the bird shaking its terrible head. Honoré lost his balance and fell away from the controls.

The manacles pulled tight against my wrist as Boucher dove toward me. Honoré tried to right himself but pulled down on the lever that controlled the ray's intensity.

A blinding light erupted from the machine, cutting through the steam and smoke now belching from the boiler. It hit the mirrors surrounding us and reflected at wild angles, nearly catching Boucher in its beam. She leapt away from the killer light, dropping the plans as she did so.

I pulled at the chain attached to my wrist. The teeth of the death ray's gears crushed the chain's link and snapped it in half. I rose and whipped the length of chain attached to my wrist at Boucher. It caught her across the face.

"Papa! Run!" I screamed as the beam shifted again, slicing across the platform and radiating heat as it drew closer to the vents of the boiler. It glowed with a thousand times the intensity of what I had endured. My skin still burned, but I had no doubt the ray could now melt flesh in a manner of moments.

Papa grabbed my hand and pulled me toward him, and we both swung over the side of the juggernaut. As we slid down the machine, rivets bruised my hip, and I crashed against a panel jutting outward over the spiked wheels.

Papa caught a ladder rung above me and clung to it as one

of the blades sliced by my head, so close that I felt the push of air in the tendrils of hair around my ears.

Dear Lord, we'd never survive this.

The machine hissed, then whistled. I didn't like the sound of it one bit. The juggernaut shook. I jumped down and landed on the stone platform, then threw myself to the ground, foregoing the ramp and the spinning blades at the front of the terrible machine.

I landed hard and let myself crumple and roll out of the way. The enormous spiked wheels began to turn. They strained as they gripped the stone platform.

Papa ran down the steps with agility at odds with his age, but panic did strange things to a person. Together we raced toward the entrance to the elephant graveyard. We had to reach the Academy before it was too late.

I worked my arms through the air, using my entire body to propel me forward as fast as it would take me. I ran toward sanctuary like a panicked horse in a fire, uncaring that my muscles screamed in protest and I could barely breathe.

The whistling turned into a strident scream as it echoed against the stone walls of the cavern.

Boom.

I fell forward, scraping my cheek against the stone as a rush of air pushed over the top of me. My ears felt like they were bleeding as I heard the tinkling of glass mirrors breaking against stone.

A wall of smoke and steam obscured my vision.

"Papa?" I pulled myself back to my feet and gave him a hand. He too stared at the billowing smoke curling against the ceiling.

He shouted something at me, but it sounded as if we were underwater. I couldn't understand him through the ringing in my ears. Whatever he had said, only one thing mattered. We had to escape. We ran from the juggernaut as quickly as we could. I hoped the death ray had managed to destroy the juggernaut, like a snake that swallowed its own tail.

My aching body screamed in protest, but I ran toward the archway and into the shadowy chamber beyond. We raced through the entire length of the chamber, stumbling, unable to catch our breaths. I could still hear the hiss of steam behind us, and the groan of metal.

Blood lingered on my tongue, and my lungs burned. Finally we reached the tunnel that led to the Academy.

"Meg!" My name sounded strange through my injured ears. It gave me a jolt of shock. I looked up to see Will running toward me through the shadows. He looked haggard and ill with worry, his cheeks sunken in as he ran as fast as I had ever seen a man run. He was glorious.

I couldn't speak. My legs gave out as he reached me. He caught me and held me, and I shook in his arms.

"I've got you," he said against my hair. He wrapped his arms around me like a man desperate to hold me to him forever. One arm wound around my body, supporting me, as the other found my hair and pressed my head into the warm strength of his shoulder. Both of us panted as we fought for our breath. "I thought I'd lost you."

"Help us." The ringing in my ears turned to a high irritating buzz. "Boucher has the juggernaut."

Will looked me in the eye, once again my rock. "Help is coming."

"How did you find me?" I choked out.

Just then a light bobbed out of the shadows, carried by a girl with short, thickly curling black hair.

Josephine.

"Thank God my father didn't kill you," she said.

"He nearly did," I said. "You brought them here?" I pulled away from Will enough to find my feet and face my cousin.

She shrugged. "I'm tired of death."

"Several of the Amusementists had already begun to gather for the Oath. I rallied those I could," Will explained.

I took Josephine's hand. "Bless you."

"This is Josephine?" Papa came up beside me.

Josephine took a step back, but I grabbed her hand again and nodded. Papa reached out and quickly pulled her into an encompassing hug, wrapping his arms around her and burying his face in her curling hair. Her arms wound around him, and the tension she always held in her shoulders eased, if only for a moment.

Suddenly I realized the tunnel was filled with hurried footsteps and bobbing lights.

"Damn it all, I hate running." David emerged from the blackness and bent over so he could brace his hands against his knees. "Whatever trouble you've gotten into this time, it had better be spectacular," he complained as Michael, Noah, and Peter joined him. To my surprise, Samuel joined the group of boys, followed by Manoj and Oliver.

"David?" I held a hand out to him and helped him stand straight.

His hand squeezed mine tightly. "For the Order."

I nodded.

John Frank led a party of Amusementists and Guildsmen,

all jogging down the tunnel. Gabrielle kept pace beside him, holding her lantern aloft.

Suddenly there was a loud crash that felt as if it shook the whole of the hill above us.

The crowd stilled and looked back at the eerie glowing smoke in the deep chamber. Two balls of fire erupted out of the haze. They billowed upward until they hit the stone ceiling. Another roar echoed through the chamber and the juggernaut emerged through the smoke and steam.

The blades at the front of the deadly contraption flashed. They sliced through the smoke, twisting and turning as the monstrosity sought to reap a harvest of souls.

"Dear God, what is that thing?" Oliver asked, stepping forward.

I could see now how powerful a weapon of intimidation it was. All I wanted to do was run. "It's Haddock's juggernaut."

I felt poised on the head of a pin. The Amusementists watched the juggernaut rolling through the far chamber, the blades whirling through the air as it belched flame and smoke. It was as though they all had been blinded by the Amusementist motto about science and beauty and had never considered that something truly ugly could come from the mind of one of their own.

Papa turned around to face it, and became the undaunted captain once more.

"To the Amusements! We must destroy this monstrosity at all cost," he shouted, still holding Josephine's hand.

As if in answer, the juggernaut released another ball of flame, and the light caught on the spinning blades. The death machine reached the archway supporting the chamber's ceiling, then suddenly veered to the right.

The juggernaut smashed into the side of the archway, sending bricks flying and crashing against the stone floor. If the juggernaut ran into enough pillars, the chamber could collapse, bringing the Royal Observatory down on top of us.

If we didn't stop it, none of us would leave this chamber alive.

CHAPTER THIRTY-ONE

MY FRIENDS SCRAMBLED TOWARD THE MACHINES SCAT-
tered around the room while the juggernaut worked to back
out of the ruins of the damaged wall. I headed for the elephant,
with Will and Papa at my heels. It was the only Amusement
that could match the size of the juggernaut, but it lacked any
weapons.

Somehow we had to stop Boucher, which meant we
had to get her away from the controls. A beam of light cut
through the chamber above our heads. We also had to stop
that death ray.

Papa came up and opened a hatch in the belly of the elephant. "Quick, get in."

Will linked his fingers together, and I stepped into his palms, balancing against his shoulders as he lifted me up through the hole. I had to duck to keep from hitting my head on a large pendulum in the stomach of the beast. It was shadowy inside, and I felt as if spiders were crawling all over my skin.

I moved toward the beast's flank, the chain on my wrist rattling against the metal interior of the elephant. Papa appeared through the hatch with a lantern. It was no wonder I thought spiders were crawling on me. Thick cobwebs draped over the gears and cogs, surrounding us like death shrouds. Papa and I reached down and pulled Will up.

He closed the hatch, and Papa nudged me toward a ladder leading up through a second hatch above us.

Papa tested the pendulum, frowned, and then said, "It isn't locked but it needs to be wound." He jumped up and pulled on a loop of chain, raising a large weight to the top of the elephant. Then he repeated the process for another weight. "We have to get that pendulum swinging. The motion of the swinging arm will wind that spring above us like a ratchet, and then we'll have power."

Papa banged his fist on a gear, adjusting the angle where the teeth interlocked with another. "Our only hope of stopping the juggernaut is to ram it head-on and destroy those blades."

"This has to be the most inefficient, terrible design I've ever seen. It's fatally flawed." I commented. Honestly, who put a pendulum in a moving vehicle?

"That's why it's down here in the graveyard," Papa said as he climbed toward the roof. "Don't complain to me. It's not one of mine. It only needs to go far enough to ram that thing."

Papa disappeared above us, and I could hear his footsteps clanging against the back of the beast.

I climbed atop the pendulum's weight and grasped the long arm attached to the pivot point above, then held my hand out for Will. The juggernaut moved slowly and was caught in the rubble from the wall, but I felt as if the beast of a machine were bearing down on us like a charging bull. We had to hurry. It was only a matter of time before the juggernaut shook itself loose from the brick.

Will climbed up opposite me and nodded. Standing on the weight and holding on to the pole, I threw my hips back and held on as the pendulum shifted forward by inches. That was it? I had expected it to swing more freely. This would take all our force, and we didn't have the luxury to wait for physics and poor design to catch up to us.

As I pulled myself straight, Will threw his weight back, and the pendulum swung with agonizing slowness in the other direction. I felt as if we were on a Russian swing, working in tandem to move the heavy weight.

"The gears are stiff. Throw all you have into it," Will said as he pulled himself up. I adjusted my grip, lowering my hands on the rod so I could thrust my hips farther behind me and intensify the shift in my center of gravity.

We found a rhythm, ticking off each swing like a clock counting down the moments until the juggernaut caught us and ripped through the elephant's side, but there was no possible way to increase the frequency of the pendulum. My shoulder burned with pain and my hands felt slick against the pole holding the swinging weight. My skin still felt the lingering effects of the burn, and fresh blood was seeping through the bandage on my arm again. As I leaned back, my grip gave way. Will caught the chain at my wrist before I fell into the gear-works turning behind me.

As we swung up, he changed his grip so he held me hand to hand. The two of us became a machine ourselves, moving together without a thought, driving the heart of the machine.

The pendulum swung with more freedom and momentum. My stomach rose and dropped with each swoop of the weight. At the crest of the swing, I found myself nearly parallel to the bottom of the elephant's belly, and at the opposite point I felt like I would fall backward into the turning gears.

We had suddenly become acrobats in a dire performance.

"Will," I called. "There's no way off this thing!" If we jumped, we'd fall into the gears.

"When we crest, grab that ladder," Will said, pointing behind me.

My heart plunged as we swung up, passing the ladder by inches. We swung down again, and I only had precious seconds before we reached the crest again. With my throat tight and time slowing to a crawl as my mind raced, I let go of Will and the rod, and reached out behind me.

I could hear each slow thump of my heart as I floated in the air and the pendulum dropped away from the soles of my feet.

My fingers reached the ladder, and I clung to it. Time came rushing back. My body dropped, but my hands held fast and I crashed against the ladder, hitting my cheek against one of the rungs. I found a lower rung with my feet and scooted over as the pendulum swung back. Will gracefully reached out and stepped over onto the ladder with the natural agility of a trapeze artist.

He wrapped an arm over my shoulder, and we clung to the ladder. "Are you hurt?"

I shook my head, then clambered up the ladder without much more thought, the chain at my wrist slapping against each rung. I no longer had the luxury to indulge in fear, so I did not.

I emerged into the howdah and into chaos.

Just as I looked up, an enormous phoenix erupted in a ball of fire, screaming in the center of the room. The wings touched the ceiling before the flames burned out, and a golden egg dropped back down to the ground. Crashing *booms* and grinding metal filled the chamber, along with the roar and whine of the battling machines.

Fireworks exploded from the back of the Chinese dragon. The serpent-like creature with the round lion face twisted and snapped as it dodged the light from the death ray.

The floor beneath me shifted, and the elephant flapped its ears. The articulated trunk rose high in the air, and our mechanical steed squealed. It rumbled forward, swinging its large mass as it marched.

Papa manned the controls, and I ran to be next to him, and held on to the edges of the howdah as Will joined us.

We heard a loud *boom*, and Will ducked as a cannonball

hit the roof of the howdah, bending the metal and snapping one of the supports.

"That thing has cannons?" I shouted.

"That's when I knew it wasn't meant to clear land," Papa shouted back, pulling hard on a wheel and turning the elephant. It swung its trunk and almost knocked it into the manticore. Oliver turned the more agile, lionlike creature to the left and spread its wings with a salute back to us.

"Get as close as you can. We can use the trunk to destroy the ray," I called, then held on while the elephant lurched along.

A rocket shot out from the mouth of the Chinese dragon, smashed into the juggernaut, and exploded in a million bright blue sparks.

"Use the levers to the left," Papa said. "They control the head and the trunk."

I grasped the levers and tested them. As I pushed and pulled, the trunk of the beast rose and twisted. I experimented with the motion as much as I could while the elephant marched toward the spinning blades at the front of the juggernaut.

Swallowing my fear, I hoped that the chest of the elephant could withstand the blades. Otherwise, the blades would cut straight into us.

I pulled the lever and swung the trunk. I nearly knocked over a mechanical bear running near the elephant's feet. It turned and looked up, and I saw Michael perched in its chest.

"Careful, Meg!" he shouted, then used the bear's mechanical arm to scoop up a piece of debris. He threw it toward the juggernaut with his machine-enhanced strength.

The debris disappeared into the blades. They stuttered and shook as they devoured the piece of metal and threw shrapnel back out.

A wave of heat passed over us, and I grabbed Papa and pulled him down moments before the death ray fired through the howdah.

"Here, get behind this," Will said. He fixed a large plate he had taken from the broken roof of the howdah as a shield for us.

Another cannonball fired, knocking into the manticore, which crumpled in a heap of metal wings. Its scorpion tail smashed into the wall.

Oliver.

I prayed he was unharmed, that he would live to see his child born and Lucinda wouldn't have to suffer the loss of another love. It would destroy her.

The manticore whined and died, but there was no sign of the duke.

I shouted for Oliver, but Will grabbed my shoulder. "Stay focused. There's nothing we can do for him now."

Papa pushed the controls forward, and the elephant let out a pealing trumpet before charging. "Take hold of something!"

I grabbed the levers and lifted the head and trunk of the elephant high into the air as Papa pushed the machine forward. It thundered toward the juggernaut. I ducked behind the shield. We had to charge blind.

The death ray had focused on our shield, and I could feel the heat through the metal plate in front of us. It began to glow, turning a burning red. Cannons fired. One hit the elephant, and it shuddered. The steps faltered, and the elephant stumbled forward in the throes of death.

I clung to the levers as the beast rammed the juggernaut. Each forceful shake of the impact yanked my arms, hurting my shoulders as I clung to the levers. We were thrown forward, and my momentum sent me crashing into the controls. I pushed the levers forward, and the head and trunk came smashing down on top of the juggernaut.

The elephant leaned to the side, and Papa began to slide

from the howdah. Will grabbed me and shoved me up. Finding footing on the controls, we climbed up over the beast's head. I grasped the large plate of the ear, then ducked behind it as the death ray nearly caught us.

I peeked around the ear to see the juggernaut struggling against the mass of the elephant.

The ray veered toward me. There was no way to escape.

"Meg! Go now!" David called as he rode in the back of an enormous charging rhinoceros with Samuel at his side.

They leapt off the beast in time to see it crash into the wheels of the juggernaut. The horn and head smashed into the spiked wheels and stopped two of them from turning.

The juggernaut twisted, pulling against the elephant as the wheels on one side of the juggernaut spun but the others did not.

The impact knocked the ray askew, and Will and I made a run for it. We charged over the elephant's cheek, using the tusk to balance as we climbed over the trunk and onto the control platform for the juggernaut.

Boucher was bent at the controls. Honoré clung to the back of the death ray.

A hatch opened up in the side of the machine, and a cannon emerged.

"David, look out!" I shouted.

Just then Michael in the mechanical bear galloped to the fallen rhinoceros. The bear rose up and roared. Beneath the sound, I heard the victorious shout of my friend.

The cannon fired straight into the heart of the bear.

"Michael!" I screamed.

I watched in horror as the bear fell backward, directly on top of David and Samuel.

I couldn't tell if they were alive or dead. I didn't want to believe they could have died.

But how could anyone survive what I had witnessed?

"Meg, watch out!" Will screamed as he knocked me away from the rail. The death ray passed dangerously close to where I had been standing.

I said a prayer for my fallen friends, then faced Boucher.

She would pay for this.

CHAPTER THIRTY-TWO

I LUNGED AT BOUCHER AND KNOCKED HER FROM THE controls.

She bore a cut across her cheek from where I had struck her with the chain. Her white hair flew around her face, and her dress was scorched and stained with black ash and coal. With her sunken, wrinkled cheeks and eyes, she looked like a standing corpse.

"Honoré, kill her," she ordered.

I turned around.

Honoré pulled on the levers of the death ray, but not before Will leapt onto the ray's supports. He climbed like a cat and threw himself onto Honoré's back. Will grabbed my bastard uncle around the neck, nearly taking the two of them backward over the rail.

"Will, watch out!" I shouted.

Boucher's footsteps clanged against the platform. I turned back to her, but she was reaching for the controls to the juggernaut.

Will continued to cling to Honoré as they struggled on the small platform of the death ray.

Honoré threw a punch, and Will's head snapped back.

"Throw him onto the vents," Madame Boucher called out.

For a moment I froze, not knowing what would save him—reaching him, or stopping Boucher.

I chose him.

Honoré grabbed Will and hoisted him. I slammed up against the rail and threw my arm forward, the chain whipping up toward Will's chest.

Will clung to Honoré, and twisted. Just then something hit the juggernaut and it lurched.

Will caught the chain and let go of Honoré. I dropped all my weight to the floor and braced against the rail as both men fell off the platform.

A heavy weight pulled on the chain. Pain seared through my wrist, and I feared it had broken, but I didn't care. I clung to the chain, knowing I held Will's life in my hands. I watched the chain swing against the rail. Then the weight suddenly released.

"Honoré!" Boucher screamed as the vents blew an enormous plume of fire. The inferno towered to the ceiling.

My heart splintered into a million pieces as I struggled to my knees and peered over the rail.

A man engulfed in flame fell off the back of the juggernaut, then bolted, waving his arms as he ran blindly into the maze of mirrors. He impaled himself on one of the shattered frames. The mirrors shifted and crushed him.

"Will?" I screeched. It couldn't have been him. He had to be alive.

My stomach clenched, and I felt my mouth water as if I were about to be ill. I wondered at the quality of my soul, because I was hoping I had witnessed the death of my uncle, and deep down I felt he deserved so gruesome an end.

Boucher grabbed my arm and spun me around. The chain slid back over the rail, the end empty.

"What did you do? You killed him!" she screamed at me.

"No, you did," I answered, gripping the chain as I pushed

to my feet. "This is your doing. All of it. So reap what you have sown."

Her face contorted as if some inner demon possessed it. "My doing? Was it my fault that my father was executed?" She stepped toward me, and I backed up until I pressed against the rail. Boucher stalked forward into the shadow of the death ray. I watched out of the corner of my eye as the beam generator for the ray sunk under its own weight, without anyone at the controls to hold the beam steady. The head of the machine still burned brightly, pulling the lethal beam of light closer and closer to us.

I had to keep Boucher distracted.

"Your father was punished for creating this," I said, motioning to the machine beneath me as she stepped forward onto the embedded Haddock seal on the top of the machine. "And yes, he deserved to be executed for this monstrosity. Now you wish to replicate it and sell it to armies so it can increase its destruction a thousandfold."

"No one would stand against it!" she insisted.

"I stood against it!" I shouted at her. "My friends stood against it. Stop this madness. Save yourself."

Her eyes narrowed to slits. "To what end? I have nothing." She balled her hand into a fist. "Your grandfather abandoned me." Her voice cracked, and her eyes shone in the flickering light from lingering fires.

Something moved behind Boucher. I tried not to react as the trunk from the fallen elephant rose like a cobra beckoned from the basket by a snake charmer.

Her pleas didn't fall on deaf ears, but she was not acknowledging her part in her own downfall. "Did you ever write to him? Did you tell him of his child? Did you even give him the chance to make things right?" I caught a glimpse of Papa, clinging to the controls in the fallen howdah. The rising trunk wavered and shook as the beam of light inched closer behind Boucher.

Boucher looked as if she had feasted upon rotting meat. "He should have come for me, no matter the circumstance. Instead he ruined me and then went on with his life while I suffered." Boucher's face grew red, and I hoped her sudden flush would hide the heat from the ray behind her. The edges of the Haddock seal began to glow. "And he will suffer too." She stalked toward me with a mad look in her eye.

Keep her focused on me. Keep her focused on me.

"So it was a test. You held back knowledge of your child from my grandfather so you could gauge his affections." The elephant trunk wavered. "You were a fool."

I took a step closer to her, and she shifted her weight back.

She raised her head. "Judge me if you like." She lifted a revolver. "It won't save you."

She aimed for my heart.

At that moment the trunk of the elephant came crashing down only inches from Boucher. The gun went off, and the ball pinged against the metal trunk. Boucher leapt back in shock, directly into the path of the death ray.

She screamed as her dress caught fire, the flames licking up her body. She tried to stumble out of the circle of death, but the elephant trunk had trapped her.

I fell backward against the rail, curling against it as if it could protect me from the death all around me. The metal grew warm as I wrapped my head in my arms in spite of the pain in my wrist.

Balling up on instinct, I pressed harder into the security of the metal behind me. Closing my eyes tight, I tried to block out the sound of her wail. And at every moment I anticipated an attack, but I was frozen in horror, too terrified to move.

The silence that followed was worse than the screams as the air filled with the most awful-smelling smoke, tinged with the scent of burned hair and flesh.

When I opened my eyes, all that remained of Boucher

was a charred skeleton with a necklace hanging on the grisly neck bones. In the center of the black stone, Haddock's mark glowed fiery red.

I let out a gasp, then huffed through my nose and clenched my teeth tight. I cradled my wounded wrist as I stumbled toward the controls and released the valves to the boiler. Steam rushed out of the dying juggernaut, and at last the lingering glow of the death ray faded, leaving smoke and ash rising from the top of the terrible machine.

It's over.

Whatever fear and desperation had kept me alive through the battle, it had suddenly abandoned me, leaving me weak and shaking, my entire body racked with pain.

I cradled my injured wrist to my chest, wrapping up the chain in my other hand.

Feeling lost, I looked around. From behind the rail I only had a clear view of the pillars throughout the chamber and the smoky ceiling. With the smoke and flickering fires, I felt as if I had entered a cathedral of hell.

I didn't know what had happened to Will. I didn't know if he was alive or dead. David, Oliver, Peter . . . Michael.

I let out another heavy breath and felt the stinging in my nose.

"Meg?" Papa crawled over the debris of the ruined elephant and the smashed blades of the juggernaut. "Meg, my darling girl."

Blood streamed down the side of his head from a nasty cut on his bare scalp. He limped as he approached, but then he wrapped me in the strongest embrace I had ever felt.

I felt the shaking in his chest, and I couldn't hold it in any longer. The tears began to flow. I let his arms surround me. He kissed the top of my head the way he had when I was a small child. "You did it. You saved us."

Holding my emotions back was too difficult to bear. I was exhausted, injured, and still terrified. But now I had him again. I felt as if I had stepped into the warmth of home after a long and cold winter alone and in the dark. He was here with me. I had someone to share in my triumphs and to comfort my sorrows. I had a family again. "I love you, Papa."

"I love you, too." He stroked my hair, and for a moment I felt safe and whole again.

But I couldn't savor the victory. I struggled to my feet. "We have to help the others." My stomach still ached with worry for Will. I had to find him.

"Will?" I called as I descended the rungs on the outside of the juggernaut. I couldn't grip or hold anything with my hand, so I tucked it close to my chest and climbed down as best I could one-handed. "Will? Where are you?"

I jumped down from the wreck and took in the carnage as I stepped around pieces of metal and broken Amusements. As I ran around the back of the machine near where I'd felt him drop, I noticed a boot lying, motionless, beneath the wheel.

CHAPTER THIRTY-THREE

"WILL!" I RAN TO HIM, THE WHOLE WHILE PRAYING A
thousand times in a matter of seconds that the Lord had
spared him. At least he was here. My uncle was the one who
had caught on fire. It was little comfort as I reached him.

Blood poured over his face from a gash on his cheek, and
he lay without moving.

I stopped breathing and brought my hand to my face.
The tears fell of their own accord, stinging against my burned
skin. "Will?" It came out as a plea.

He didn't move.

I heard footsteps behind me. "Please," I begged. "Don't
be gone."

Stepping forward, I knelt at his side. I reached out to brush his hair away from his softly closed eyes.

"Please don't leave me," I whispered.

I laid my head on his chest, because I could do nothing else. I desperately wished I could hear the beat of his heart, but I couldn't hear anything past the rushing in my ears. Holding his body to mine, I cried against him. What would I do if his arms never surrounded me again? It would be my fault. I'd drawn him into this. He'd done it for me.

"I love you," I whispered. And I did, truly. I had only once ever felt a pain as great as this, on the night my parents had died.

I felt a soft touch at the back of my head. Pulling myself up, I looked hopefully at Will's face.

His eyes blinked open.

"That's good." He coughed. "Because I wouldn't do this for just anyone. I love you, too."

My tears fell freely as I gathered his hand and pressed it to my face. I trembled with overwhelming emotion—love, grief, elation, and shock. "We did it, Will. We did it."

"I knew we would." He grinned, like the first warm light of sun after a dark winter.

I smiled back and sighed. "Then you are more clever than I."

"Was that ever in doubt?" He shifted, pulling himself up so he could sit. His motion tugged on the chain at my wrist, and I cried out.

"You're hurt." His entire tone changed as he lifted my wounded wrist.

Papa crouched next to me and helped him up. "Can you move, son?"

"I think my leg is broken." Will used his hands to support his knee, and grimaced. Then he wrapped an arm around his waist. "And a rib as well."

Papa glanced up. "That was quite a fall."

Will gazed at me, and I had no doubt of the depth of his love, but there was something else too. "I would have died if you hadn't thrown the chain. I was able to swing free of the vents before I fell."

Another moment, and he would have fallen into the fire. The fraction of time between life and death had been so slim. If I had tried to stop Boucher instead of reaching for him, he would have died.

Papa got to his feet and wandered off, searching for material for a splint. I stayed at Will's side.

He touched my wrist, and I flinched. "You injured it when I fell, didn't you?"

"Don't. If a broken wrist means you're alive, I'll gladly break my other one." I leaned forward and gave him a quick kiss. He reached up and caught the back of my head. I didn't resist as he pulled me back to him. His lips teased mine, lingering playfully as if all the pain racking both of us didn't matter in the face of that simple pleasure. I succumbed to it, and the kiss turned passionate. I could no longer tell what was him and what was me. It didn't matter. A million feelings and sensations flowed through me, and for a moment it felt as if I had died, only a little.

He broke the kiss reluctantly, keeping our faces close.

I allowed the warmth of his touch to comfort me even as I felt my exhaustion and pain in every bone in my body. Will brushed a bit of hair from my forehead. "The shadow is gone."

I kissed him again before weaving my fingers with his. "I thought when Boucher took us from Paris, I'd never see you again. How did you know they had taken me to London?"

Will smiled sheepishly. "I figured that if Haddock's daughter needed you to unlock the machine, she'd have to take you to it. The most likely place for it to be was England, not France. So Gustave and I came here to search the archives to see where the machine might have been hidden. We were still looking when a girl came in claiming that you and your grandfather were here and alive. We gathered as many people as would come."

Will was always resourceful, and I'd never take it for granted. "Thank you," I said. "Thank you for not giving up on me."

"Never." He leaned forward to kiss me again, but Papa had returned.

Papa cleared his throat. "I found some bars we can use as a splint, and I retrieved the key for the manacle." He took my wrist gingerly and unlocked the shackle.

I tucked my wrist against my stomach, then got to my feet as Papa knelt next to Will and placed the rods next to his leg. Will shrugged off his shirt and ripped strips of cloth.

I felt suddenly warm as I looked at him half-undressed. "I'll go see to the others." I could feel the heat stealing into my cheeks as I turned away. Papa and Will were safe, but there were so many more friends I cared about.

I swallowed a lump in my throat as I climbed out from behind the juggernaut.

War had been incomprehensible to me—the wanton destruction, the death—until that very moment.

What had once been glorious machines born of the creative

intellect of the finest minds in the world lay crumpled and broken in heaps around the cavernous chamber. Glorious beasts and magical creatures had become nothing more than dented and twisted plates covering broken gear trains and shattered axles.

Tendrils of smoke rose to join the clouds of steam swirling on the ceiling. It made the chamber smell like ash and death.

Men crawled like ants over the rubble. The whole of the Order, the Foundry, and the Guild streamed in through the archway that led to the tunnel.

I couldn't swallow. My throat felt tight, and tears gathered in my eyes. My gaze swept over the scene. Groups of men were dragging the injured out of the rubble.

My head felt in a fog as everything that had happened washed back through me. My heart raced, and I felt a stabbing pain behind my eyes when I looked up at the fallen elephant lying on its side. The twisted and broken blades of the juggernaut had sliced through its armor and cut through to the gears.

My mind flashed back to the cannon fire blasting into the heart of the bear Michael had commandeered.

Holding my wrist to my ribs, I ran around the elephant

and circled the juggernaut, searching for Michael, Samuel, and David.

A million flashes of memory came rushing back, small moments that had meant the world to me. Michael had always looked so awkward with his long limbs and toothy smile, but he didn't have a cruel bone in his body. We so often teased one another that he truly felt like a brother to me.

Poor Samuel. He had borne the resentment of his father his entire life, and while he may have reflected that resentment onto the world, David counted him as a loyal friend, and David wouldn't have held such an opinion lightly.

David.

A part of me was sorry I didn't love him the way he wished I would. If he were gone, I would feel the guilt of it for all time. I cared for him. I wanted all the best things for him. I wished I could be as close to him as I felt to his sister, Lucinda, and hold him as a brother of the heart.

I found the wrecked bear first and saw a shock of ginger hair as three of my instructors lifted a limp body out of the machine. My heart turned to a ball of thick lead, dropping heavily through my body as I struggled forward over debris and shattered bricks and mortar. His arms and legs were twisted, hanging lifelessly, like a lamb that had succumbed to the slaughter.

Dear Lord, no. "Michael?" I came up next to my instructors. They laid him down on the hard stone floor. I reached up and brushed his hair from his cold forehead. His once laughing eyes stared lifelessly at me. "Oh, Michael."

Tears slipped over my cheeks. I gently closed his eyes and continued to stroke his hair. He had given me a world of playful grief, followed by laughter. He'd never been malicious in nature. He'd never been that sort. He'd been good.

My tear fell upon his cold cheek and slid over his pale skin. "I'm so sorry," I whispered. "I'm so very sorry."

"Michael?" a man's voice shouted in panic. "Michael, lad?"

I backed away as Michael's father ran up with a howl that echoed through the stillness of the chamber. "Sweet Mary, tell me it's not so," he choked as he gathered his son in his arms and cradled him against his heart. Michael's father fell forward in sobs over his son.

As I let the tears fall, I heard another voice behind me. A cluster of men had gathered to my right.

David, please no.

I ran and pushed through the crowd. David was kneeling over Samuel. The dark-haired boy's lower body was crushed beneath the wreckage. "Damn it, Sam. Keep breathing. Don't you dare fail me."

A trail of blood came from Samuel's lip as he lay on the ground. "I can't feel my legs," he whispered.

David let out a strangled noise as he stood and attempted to lift the wreckage off his friend. I came up beside him and pushed my shoulder into it, but I couldn't grip anything with my injured wrist.

Josephine appeared and took my place. I dropped to Samuel's side. A trio of Guildsmen helped them lift the rubble.

"Don't worry, Sam. Things are going to be fine," I assured. He gave me a hopeless laugh.

"You look terrible," he whispered. "Really, you should do something with yourself."

I let out a disbelieving cough. "It's been a difficult day."

David and Josephine lifted the last piece of wreckage, and Samuel grasped my injured hand, squeezing it tight. I wanted to cry out in pain but didn't. His face was contorted with pain, and in that moment it was one thing we could share.

I glanced down at his crushed legs, and gasped. He would never walk again, if he could keep his legs at all. Oh, God.

David took my place. "Don't worry. We're going to get you well."

"It's bad, isn't it?" Samuel said. He didn't bother trying to lift his head.

"Not so bad," David lied. "You'll be walking again soon. I promise."

Josephine appeared with one of the fuel carts and two of the Guildsmen. "We have to find a surgeon, and quickly." They loaded Samuel onto the cart. He screamed in pain, and I felt it like a shot to my heart. I staggered to my feet and watched as they pushed Sam away.

David tried to follow, but he was limping terribly. Josephine took him by the hand and looped his arm over her shoulder.

"Thank you," he murmured, then looked over at me. "Where is Michael?"

"Michael is lost." And how many others? I didn't know.

David bowed his head, and his shoulders slumped as his bravado faded. A man ran toward us with a loose-limbed gait, his wild hair flying in all directions, the side of his face smeared with blood.

"Oliver!" I cried.

A terrible gash sliced through his eyebrow, but other than that he seemed unharmed. He folded both of us into his embrace. "Thank heaven," he said as he squeezed us so tight that I lost my breath. "Lucinda would never have forgiven me. What of the others? What do you know?"

"Michael is dead," I said. "Samuel's gravely injured. Will has a broken leg and rib. Papa is tending to him on the other side of the juggernaut." Oliver nodded, his mouth set in a grim line.

"And what of the Haddocks?" he asked. Josephine stiffened, then slipped away back into the shadows.

I felt for her, but now was not the time to reveal her heritage. I returned my attention to Oliver. "Haddock's daughter and her son, the man in the mask, are both dead. It's finally over. There is no one left who is a threat to us."

Oliver crossed himself and raised his eyes to the ceiling, then gathered himself and took command. "I'll help Henry and Will. Peter, Noah, and Manoj are making carts and sleds from broken Amusements so we can move the wounded. Go and help them. We must evacuate the chamber until we can determine the structural integrity. Everyone is to gather back at the Academy."

David and I found the rest of my friends near the tunnel. They were helping to lift John Frank onto a cart. John was one of the most vibrant men I had ever met, and yet he seemed listless as they placed him gingerly on the platform.

That's when I saw a flash of red and noticed that the lower half of his arm was missing. The bloody stump was covered over with cloth and a tightly strapped belt.

"John!" I ran to his side.

He grimaced weakly at me, but his flashing teeth still looked bright in his dark face. "I didn't think I'd see you again." He coughed. "I'd shake your hand, but I seem to be missing mine."

A tall Russian Amusementist whom I hadn't spoken to called another man over and wheeled John down through the tunnel.

I turned back to my friends, so terribly glad that they were unharmed. Peter took my good hand. He gave it a squeeze without saying any words. All of us looked stricken, and words eluded me as well. "Here," he said, leading me to another cart. "You look like death."

I shook my head at him as Manoj came to my side to aid me. "Is it true? Is Michael dead?" he asked.

I swallowed, then nodded. "Samuel's injuries are severe."

Manoj went quiet, his dark eyes downcast. He seemed to have difficulty piecing together all that had happened. We all did. Noah put his arm around David's shoulders, and the two walked away together. "That's at least nine dead. I don't know how many have been wounded," Manoj said quietly.

Just then Oliver returned with my grandfather, supporting Will between them. Josephine followed after them.

They placed Will on the cart. Papa had used Will's shirt to tie his leg to the splints and wrap around his ribs. Will had pulled his coat back on, but he was still a long way from decent.

It didn't matter. With my ruined dress I was hardly decent either.

I tucked myself into Will's side as Peter and Manoj wheeled us down the long dark tunnel.

Josephine carried a torch and walked beside us.

"So much is destroyed," she said. "So much is lost."

"It will be rebuilt," I promised. I took Will's hand. Some things were gone forever, and we would have to grieve them, but in time those wounds would heal.

"I don't know what to do now," Josephine said. "I don't belong to anyone anymore."

"I could always use some help in my toy shop," I offered. "Boarding is free for family."

Josephine glanced sideways at me, but the barest of smiles graced her lips. Papa came up beside her and placed his hand on her shoulder.

Yes, we would begin anew.

The rest of that night blurred by in my mind. As we passed out of the catacombs and into the courtyard of the Academy,

I stared up at the stars, and for the briefest moment, my heart felt both light and free.

I whispered a soft good-bye to my parents, feeling at last that they were at rest. Then I succumbed to the flurry of questions and chaos that seemed to surround me at all times.

Will, in spite of his injuries, remained my steady rock, and his calm presence bolstered my spirits as my exhaustion set in.

The Academy became a hive of activity, especially for the few members of the Guild and the Order who happened to be surgeons or bonesetters. I stayed with Will in the infirmary, as men from the Foundry surrounded us, peppering Will with questions about all that had transpired. Time passed in a blur as I slept for what felt like weeks and grieved.

Papa was hailed as a conquering hero returned like Odysseus from hardship and toil. I enjoyed seeing the faces of those who had made a habit of doubting me. It was amusing in the moment, but in the end I paid it little mind. It no longer mattered.

On December 31, as midnight settled over the Academy, a stillness fell over the mass of people filling the building. A bell pealed in the tower.

According to tradition, we were supposed to assemble

in the hall, but circumstances being what they were, those of us still in the infirmary linked hands with those closest to us and affirmed our commitment to each other. Simple words, a simple promise to protect and serve the Order. To place one another above the call of fame or fortune. To uphold bonds of fealty that extend beyond nations, and above all to keep the arcane fire of inspiration burning for as long as the Order stands.

It was our prayer. As our words, spoken in a multitude of languages, drifted up to the canopy of stars above us, I knew a new day, a new year was dawning.

The fate of the war that raged across the sea would now be decided by those who fought for what they believed. The juggernaut would never see the light of day. I felt a surge of hope that 1863 would be a year marked with the promise of freedom.

As I sat in a chair next to Will in the Academy's infirmary, I knew there was finally truly hope for us.

CHAPTER THIRTY-FOUR

Spring 1867

I SMOOTHED MY DARK RED SKIRTS AS I ASCENDED THE ramp into the courtyard of the Academy. It would be the last time I did so as an apprentice. My fellow classmates lingered about the courtyard, speaking to one another in hushed but excited voices as the birds in the gilded aviary sang "Ode to Joy" in greeting.

I held my head high, smiling as Peter greeted me from the corner where he had stood so long ago on the day I had first met him. As I'd predicted, he still hadn't entirely grown out of the roundness in his cheeks.

"Apprentice Margaret." He gave me a courtly bow.

I smiled and curtsied in response. "Apprentice Peter."

Noah shook his head as he joined us. It struck me how my friends—my brothers—had grown into such fine young men.

Manoj strolled over from the aviary, looking quite impressive with his neat beard. It had grown thick in the last few years. He wore a different turban. Instead of the small knot on the top of his head, his new turban was a bold dark red affair that he wore like a crown. A jewel with the seal of the Order hung on the front of it.

"Manoj, you look quite regal in red," I mentioned.

He smiled at me, his dark eyes glowing with warmth. "As do you."

Someone cleared his throat behind me, and I turned. David stood there with his lopsided grin. There was a new humility in him that served him well. "How far we've come," he said. I was glad I could finally count him as a true and trusted friend.

"Indeed." I was lucky.

He bowed and offered his arm. "Shall we?"

We entered the hall for the Gathering, nodding to John Frank, who stood at the door, holding it open with his mechanical arm. He winked at me, and I smiled.

The seats of the hall were filled with Amusementists, each robed in dark red with a hood covering his head. They held torches aloft. Those who had passed their apprenticeship filed down the steps and collected on the floor of the hall.

I remembered feeling alone during the night of my initiation, but no longer.

I was surrounded by friends, and I had family here to welcome me.

I cast my eyes to the ceiling as my grandfather, dressed in the ceremonial black robes and adorned with a gold chain around his neck, descended from on high. The platform lowered from the ceiling, surrounded by pillars of fire curling up brass armatures at all four corners.

As my grandfather stepped forward from the embrace of the arcane fire, he lowered his hood and smiled at all of us.

"As head of the Secret Order of Modern Amusementists, I greet you, the newest members of our noble fellowship."

One by one he called my fellow apprentices to him. As he did so, Oliver and Nigel adorned them with their own red robes. Grandfather then laid a chain around each of their necks, as pictures formed of light projected upon the back wall. The pictures proudly displayed the personal insignia of each new member.

He honored David especially as head of the class. It had been a very close race, but in the end David had deserved credit for the amazing things he had accomplished, and I was proud of his achievement. I was also proud that for the most part I'd matched him wit for wit. We'd often been set against one another in competition, and the record tipped only slightly in his favor, but the tipping point had been worth it.

We all turned as Samuel entered at the back of the hall, wheeling himself forward in his chair. Manoj and Peter reached him and offered a hand. He placed one golden foot forward, planting it solidly on the stone floor, and he rose.

The hall erupted in cheers as Samuel walked forward on his mechanical legs as easily as he had ever done before the amputations. I didn't fight the tears that stung my eyes. For as terribly as our relationship had started, I now called Samuel my friend. "Well done, David," I whispered. It was his finest invention.

After all others had been called, I alone stood on the floor, with the whole of the Order watching me.

"And finally, Apprentice Margaret Anne Whitlock." Papa's voice cracked.

Behind him, in bright white light, an image appeared on the wall.

A beautiful bird with wings outstretched looked to the sky, ready to take wing. Her feet rested on a perfect half circle, a rock beneath her feet. I walked forward, trying to remain stoic even though my heart felt full to bursting.

"Fine work, Meg," Oliver whispered as I held my arms out and he and Nigel wrapped the heavy robe over my shoulders. I could feel the weight of it as they lifted the hood, cocooning me in the pride of all that I had accomplished.

I stepped forward and ducked my head. Papa placed the chain around my neck. In the center a gold medallion had been inscribed with my mark.

Lifting my head, I looked into Papa's eyes. They shone in the glittering light. "I am so proud of you," he said and clasped my hand. Something cold pressed into my palm.

I looked down. In my hand rested the clockwork key.

"It's yours now." Papa pressed a kiss to my forehead, then reached behind him and took a torch from a stand there. He lit it from the pillars of fire and addressed the gathering.

"May the light of the fire spread in you," he declared, "As true Amusementists. *Ex scientia pulchritudo!*"

Our former instructors handed us each a torch. From

Papa's light the fire spread as we passed it from person to person. We held the torches aloft, and let them shine brightly.

It was the fire of a new dawn, and a new life for us all.

That evening I laughed as I entered the parlor of the Strompton townhome. The house was filled with friends and families as we celebrated our graduation.

"Come here, you little scamp. That doesn't belong to you!" I called as I chased after a knobby-kneed boy with wild brown curls. He had absconded with the doll I had brought as a gift for his newborn baby sister.

I caught him and lifted him as he squealed in delight, his bright green eyes alight with mischief. "Auntie Margaret, put me down!"

"Simon!" Lucinda entered the parlor, and I placed the boy on his feet. I'm not sure which one of us looked more chagrined. "You are a gentleman," she reminded him. She gave me a sly smile.

He dutifully handed the doll over to his mother, and she rewarded him with a kiss on the head. "Now off to the nursery with you."

I tucked my hand into the pocket I had sewn into my

dress and palmed a small figure of a knight on a horse, then held it out as the boy passed.

He took it, giggled in delight, and ran out of the parlor.

Lucinda gave me a scolding look. "You spoil him."

"It's a calling." I shrugged.

Lucinda grinned, then folded me in a warm embrace. She held me at arm's length and sniffled. "You did it, Meg. Truly I am in awe."

I leaned forward and hugged her again. She was my sister in every way that mattered. "I couldn't have done it without you. I owe you too much."

"You owe me nothing." She left to find her son, and I turned to admire a large bouquet of roses that had been set out as a gift in my honor. The deep red blooms smelled heavenly, and the one bright purple thistle—

A thistle?

Scotland.

Will.

My heart flew into my throat. I pushed past a crowd of people speaking with Josephine and Manoj, and finally escaped out the garden door.

The cool evening air brushed my skin and I glanced

around the terraced garden. Standing by a fountain was a strong young man dressed in his finest kilt.

I ran into his arms, and he held me tight. I felt at once that I was both aloft, flying through the air, and yet had my feet solid and steady beneath me.

"I've missed you so," I whispered against his warm neck as I inhaled the scent of far-off Scottish glens and the smoke of the fires of the Foundry.

During the whole of my apprenticeship, we had lived apart, visiting when we could, writing a flurry of letters until it had felt as if there should be no more to say, and yet every moment felt alive when I was with him.

"I've missed you, too," he said, giving me a soft kiss full of longing. He touched his forehead to mine. "I never doubted you, you know. I knew you could do it."

"It wasn't easy," I confessed.

"Good things never are." And with that he dropped down to kneel at my feet.

My heart suddenly hammered to life, and all thoughts fled completely from my head. I took a step backward, shocked, but Will caught my hand and held it to his heart.

"For the love of all things holy, Meg, *now* will you marry me?" He waited there, calm and steady, for my answer.

I snorted inelegantly, and Will did his best not to smile. I was in a right state. My head was rushing with a million thoughts, but not a single one objected.

"Of course I will. I love you," I said. "My beautiful rock."

He bowed his head and laughed, then pushed to his feet and swept me up. He swung me around until I felt I was flying. I clung to his neck, and he finally stopped spinning. Feeling dizzy, I cupped his rough cheek in my hand and kissed him with all the love in my heart.

"What am I going to do with you, my wild bird?" he whispered against my lips, then kissed me again.

"Live an amazing life?" I suggested.

He laughed again, holding me close.

And I knew it would be true.

ACKNOWLEDGMENTS

Writing this trilogy has been a remarkable experience, and I'd like to deeply thank everyone at Simon & Schuster for all your hard work, your dedication, and your stunning vision for this series. I'd especially like to thank my editors, Michael Strother and Liesa Abrams, for your keen eyes and all your support, especially Michael for his valiant efforts in helping me give a copy to my beloved high school English teacher, in spite of all the mishaps that happened along the way. I'd also like to give my deepest thanks and admiration to everyone in the art department for developing and creating such stunning covers for the entire series. They are true works of art, and I am proud to have them on my shelves.

I couldn't do this without the help and support of my family. I'd like to thank Mom for helping to brainstorm some of the Amusements for me, and also my engineer husband for pointing out that putting a pendulum in a moving object is a really bad idea. Thank you to my children for your patience while Mommy was working, and for your pride at what I have created.

This is the first book I have dedicated to my friend and critique partner, Angie Gwinner, but it is certainly not the first time she has deserved the honor. In a way, all of my books are dedicated to her, because it is true—I couldn't do this without her. We have been working together for many years, and I hope we continue to work so well together for many years to come.

And finally, I'd like to thank the fans of the series, who have loved these books and occasionally taken the time to let me know. You are the best. I don't write for me, I write for you. Thank you all.

ABOUT THE AUTHOR

Kristin Bailey grew up in the middle of the San Joaquin Valley in California. In the course of her adventures, she has worked as a zookeeper, a balloon artist, and a substitute teacher. Now she is a military wife and the mother of two children and several very spoiled pets. Find out more at kristinbailey.com.